THE BIRDS DON'T CARE IF YOU'RE PRETTY

AVA CALDWELL

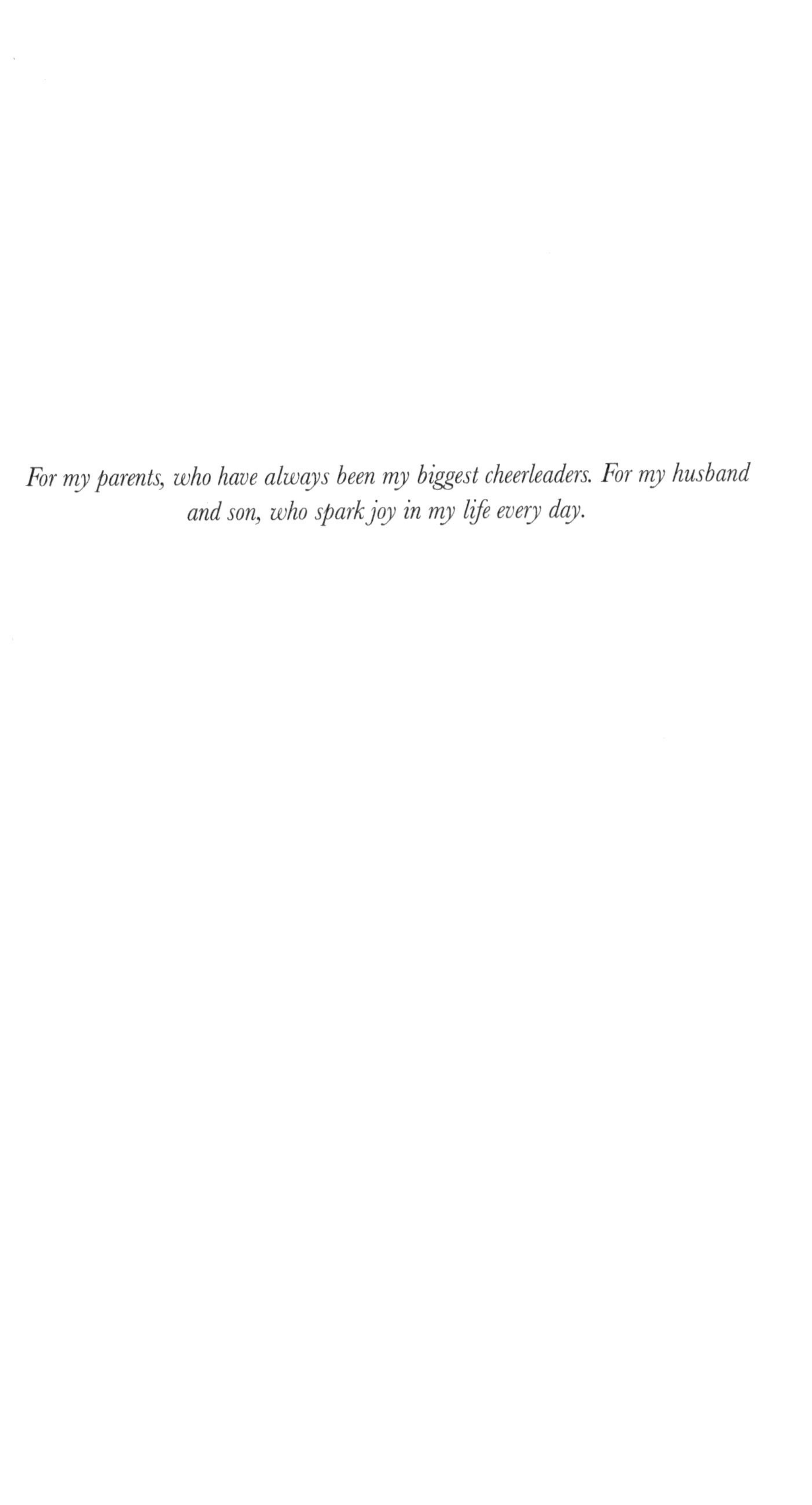

For my parents, who have always been my biggest cheerleaders. For my husband and son, who spark joy in my life every day.

While in the wild wood I did lie,
A child—with a most knowing eye.
—"Romance" by Edgar Allan Poe

CHAPTER ONE

VALERIA

The day before the trees died, I wasn't thinking about magic. I was thinking about a boy.

In my defense, the boy was Luke Nichols. Luke smelled like pine and beat-up leather. He had one of those Roman noses with a perfect little bump on the bridge. When I began my senior year at Dorado High, Luke felt like a single star in the otherwise dark sky that was my life. And he'd just texted: we need to talk.

I stood in the girls' bathroom, phone in hand, my eyes fixed on the ominous words. The fact that he'd sent a text at all felt wrong. Though we'd been together a year, he rarely contacted me by phone. He was more of a float-pebbles-at-your-bedroom-window kind of guy. Even now, a thrill tickled its way up my spine as I thought of the gentle tap of stone on glass, the sight of him standing below on the dewy lawn, the night dark around him. It was as easy to recall these things as it was to feel his hands around my waist, the rough bark on my back as we kissed against an ancient evergreen. The memories were welcome. Still, thinking of him now, I couldn't help but see the distant look that had clouded his eyes lately.

Before responding, I rummaged through my purse and retrieved my favorite shade of lipstick, Reckless Red. I ran it over my lips, then blotted the excess color with a brown paper towel from the dispenser.

Sure, see you at the palms. 10 minutes. I hit SEND, hoping my reply conveyed none of the panic that buzzed in my chest.

Before turning to leave, I scrutinized my image in the mirror. I wasn't naïve; I knew I was blessed with the kind of natural beauty that made people stare, that made people go quiet when I spoke. Still, I scrunched up my nose at my reflection, changing the part in my hair from left to right and back again. From my right bra cup, I withdrew a tiny vial of rose oil.

"Rose, lend me your beauty," I whispered, holding the vial to my lips. "Let none be fairer."

I dabbed a few drops on each cheek. Instantly, it was like a light had ignited somewhere within me, bathing my features in a gentle glow. I smiled.

That's when I heard the screams.

A boy on the quad was howling like he'd just lost a limb. When I hurried outside, I saw Benjamin Lewis standing on the grass, a cascade of smoldering liquid running from his mouth and dripping onto his black Adidas. His chin was bright red and starting to blister. He still gripped a paper coffee cup in one hand, little plumes of steam rising from the caustic liquid within.

So Celeste had decided to try that extra-complicated love spell she'd been eyeing in our Book of Shadows. If properly executed, the potion would prompt Benjamin to reveal any hidden crushes he might be harboring. It was intended to bring hidden feelings bubbling to the surface. The only thing bubbling now was Benjamin's first layer of skin. This would require damage control.

Celeste stood a few feet away from him in a short white sundress, her blond hair braided around her head like a halo. The youngest member of our coven, she looked as innocent as an angel plucked off the top of somebody's Christmas tree. But as she watched him struggle, there was no fear in her eyes. From across the crowd of onlookers, she shot me a sheepish look that seemed to say, *Oops.* A knot formed in my stomach.

Since we were kids, our parents had drilled two sacred rules into our heads. The first was to hide our magic from non-witches, aptly referred to as Mundanes. The second was to take full advantage of the forces of the universe.

Our parents were the kind of witches who used their power almost exclusively for personal gain. At coven gatherings, we recited the phrase *success and abundance* so often, they felt like our unofficial slogan. It had never struck me as unusual for us to practice magic this way. The pursuit of wealth was woven into our coven's history like a golden thread.

In the early days of the Gold Rush, our coven's founder, Delfina Garcia, had heard there were riches waiting to be discovered in California. Who better to find them than those with a certain magical advantage? Her fledgling coven had packed up their lucky jasper stones and green money candles and traveled here, to the place where the redwoods meet the winding river. It wasn't long before they struck it rich, settled here, and named this town Dorado, an enduring tribute to the pursuit of fortune.

So our ancestors cared as much about wealth as they did moon cycles. It sounded a little icky, even to me, yet I couldn't deny how special things were here. Witches were rare and getting rarer; those who remained were scattered, lonely dots on the map of the world, far from others of their kind. Most of the American covens dissolved long ago, driven apart by hardship or suspicious Mundanes. Yet ours has held fast for almost two hundred years, generation after generation continuing the pursuit of money and prominence. Perhaps that was the glue that held us together, kept us strong.

None of us coven kids were a stranger to luxury. When the coven founded Dorado, they forged a road winding deep into the redwoods. Each member built a home along it, far from the eyes of Mundane villagers. We still live in those houses today—towering Victorian structures with grand, echoing rooms and high, proud archways. Our own private opulence among the trees.

The lunch bell rang. Luke's talk would have to wait.

I pulled out my phone and texted meet at the palms, now to the coven. I headed toward our regular spot, bidding Celeste to follow with an impatient flick of my wrist. As teachers flocked to the screaming boy, we made our way through the quad, the crowd parting for us as we went.

The old art building sat at the top of a grassy slope. Towering palms stood on either side of the building's entrance, providing shade and a certain degree of ambiance. The building itself now housed a bunch of old gym mats and some obsolete science equipment, so there was never any foot traffic. Besides, the rest of the kids seemed to have an unspoken understanding: the Palms belonged to the strange rich kids from Cascabel Road.

When we reached our destination, Celeste and I paused, gazing at the tiny figures on the quad below.

"Was this about homecoming? 'Cause you know plenty of boys would happily go with you, no magic required," I said to her.

"Unless they thought they had a chance to go with *you*, Valeria. And besides, I wanted *that* boy." She added woefully, "Your mom's gonna kill me."

My mom was our coven's high priestess, and though she'd stop short of killing Celeste, she was capable of maiming a young ego with little more than a well-timed glare and a raise of one perfectly groomed brow. The knot in my stomach tightened.

The position of high priestess had always been held by a woman from the Garcia family, and I was next in line. My mom expected me to look after our new generation, to keep them out of trouble. These duties were all part of her ongoing quest to transform me into the kind of leader she thought I should be—the way an oyster creates something shiny and hard and perfect through constant pressure. A solitary pearl inside her jaws.

Anger welled within me. My mom would see this as my fault. I wanted to shake Celeste, scream at her that she'd been a careless idiot. I watched as she settled herself on the grass, smoothing her skirt neatly over her knees. She looked younger than her fifteen years.

I took a long breath, then released it. "Let's wait until everyone gets here. Then we'll figure out how we spin this."

I checked the group text.

On my way! Max had replied within seconds. Max was Celeste's older brother and a general coven enthusiast, so his quick response was expected. An eye roll emoji from Petra. Jayden had sent a meme with a reference I didn't get. And Luke…hadn't replied.

I scrolled idly through Instagram, letting Celeste sit in uncomfortable silence. My fingers danced past photos of Mundanes and their small triumphs—sports victories, shopping hauls, a group of girls laughing with their arms around each other, eager to boast their friendship to the world.

At last, I stopped on the image I'd been searching for: the last photo I'd posted of Luke and me. In it, we stood in front of Luke's cherished old convertible, a black 1963 Ford Falcon. I smiled at him as he gazed into the distance, looking handsome but a little uneasy. The Falcon's hood gleamed in the sun. A slew of positive comments from our Mundane classmates followed the post.

Adorbs! :)

<3 <3 <3

Damn, hottest couple ever!

Fire!

The compliments felt good, though I could practically feel the jealousy behind them. In truth, perhaps the jealousy felt even better.

I'd made Jayden take about twenty pictures of us before I'd been able to get a usable one. Luke was a horrible model, despite his looks. He found the whole process uncomfortably vain. I liked that about him. Luke never seemed to get hung up on the trivial things most people his age did. Maybe he really didn't care what others thought of him—or maybe he just had heavier stuff to worry about.

Luke and I had grown up together, but I hadn't thought much about him until an ill-fated class field trip when we were thirteen. Our class had visited Bodie, California, an abandoned Gold Rush town a sweaty three-hour bus ride from Dorado. I guessed our teachers wanted us to gain a better sense of Dorado's own gold-digging history, but I was less than intrigued. Our coven knew more about that than they ever would.

We'd spent the day strolling through the empty streets, gazing through windows at the relics former residents had left behind—an ancient player piano missing half its keys, a rusting wire bed frame, a roulette table covered in an inch of dust. Our class had been listening to a park ranger drone on about mining equipment when the adults noticed Luke was missing. Panicked teachers sent us out in groups to wander the dirt roads, calling his name.

No one bothered to search the houses, which were all padlocked. But I knew better. For Luke and me, springing a lock was simple elemental magic. Just a question of willing the metal to do what you wanted.

I split off from my designated group and began peering into windows, searching the shadows of homes left untouched for a hundred years. Before long, I found him sitting in the dark corner of what used to be somebody's living room. The room was empty, except for a broken bookshelf against the wall and a few old toys strewn across the floor as if some Victorian ghost child had abandoned them there.

He looked up at me when I nudged the door open. I'd known Luke forever. Our parents were both in the coven and his house was next to mine on Cascabel, making him literally the boy next door. Things had never been complicated between us. But as his eyes met mine in that empty room, I suddenly found myself unsure of what to say.

Luke had always been outgoing, vibrant, but a few months prior, his mom had packed up and left town after some big argument with Luke's dad. Irreconcilable differences could happen between witches just as easily as with the Mundanes. Ever since, Luke had been distant. He spoke rarely and smiled even less.

"Just leave me, Valeria," he'd said in a low voice. "Turn around and say you never saw me."

"I can't just leave you," I'd reasoned.

"Sure you can," he'd replied bitterly. "It's easy."

I'd pretended not to hear the sharpness in his tone. "Why are you hiding in here, anyway?"

"I think I belong here," he said.

I looked at Luke. He'd crossed his legs on the hard floor as if trying to make himself at home. I imagined him sitting there after all the tourists left, the only living creature in a world of dust. His dark hair was shaggy, and his limbs had that preteen gangly thing going on, but even then, something made me want to move closer to him.

For a long time, a cruel loneliness had been settling in my heart. Of course, it didn't look that way on the outside. The Mundane girls always smiled at me in the halls at school, and I seemed to be getting more attention from the boys every day. Still, it was there: an emptiness where something warm should be. I was beginning to realize Luke Nichols felt that emptiness too.

I'd gone and sat beside him on the floor. There were a dozen rangers and chaperones searching for us, but for a moment, it felt like he and I were the only two people in the world. It was hard to make out his expression in the shadows. I'd let a gentle flame gather at my fingertips, bathing his face in light. There were tears in his eyes.

"I think I'm going to die alone," he'd said without looking at me.

"Stop it," I'd scolded. "You'll always have the coven."

He shook his head. "That's not what I mean."

At thirteen, this was the heaviest conversation I'd ever had, but I was pretty sure I understood. Anyone who knew Luke's parents knew Luke's father had been wildly in love with his mom. And now she was just…*gone*. How could Luke not see love as fickle? As something that crumbled the moment you rested your weight on it?

"So, what—you're just gonna stay in this creepy old house by yourself for the rest of your life?"

He nodded. "Might as well. No one else can leave me if I never…" he trailed off. Eyeing an ancient wooden toy discarded on the floor, he added, "At least I'll get really good at landing a ball in a cup."

I laughed, and that was when the realization had hit me: I loved this strange, sad boy.

I was suddenly embarrassed. The flame at my fingertips began to flutter, and I hoped he didn't notice. We sat together like that for a long time, listening to the adults outside call our names. Then I'd taken his hand and led him out of that dark hiding place and into the warmth of the setting sun.

After the Bodie incident, Luke and I had gone back to our usual routines. At home, my mom was putting me through the gauntlet that was her version of magical training. At school, I found myself vying for approval from the Mundanes while never letting any get too close. And as I obsessed over popularity or coven responsibilities, Luke had kept to himself, apparently not very interested in either. Still, at night, I'd gaze out my window at the house next door. Sometimes I'd see a single light on in Luke's bedroom and I'd imagine calling out to him through the darkness.

Then, one night about a year ago, I'd heard a tap on my bedroom window, followed by another. I looked outside to see Luke floating pebbles gingerly at the glass.

"What the hell?" I'd hissed at him, trying not to wake my parents.

He'd gestured silently for me to come down.

When I met him in my driveway, my heart racing, he'd smiled and said, "Wanna go for a drive?"

I'd dated plenty of guys by that point, all Mundanes. Boys had always been drawn to me—or rather, drawn to the parts of me that interested them. My body, my money, the way the other guys looked on with jealousy when they saw us together. My relationships with them were like cotton candy, sickly sweet but never nourishing. They dissolved into nothing between my fingers.

This night with Luke was different. He took the westbound highway with the top down, the wind making my hair fly. We drove for two hours before he wordlessly put his hand on top of mine. We got to the ocean just as the hint of a sunrise was appearing on the horizon.

We walked together in the sand, the sound of the wind mixing with the waves, the blood rushing in my ears until it was one beautiful white noise. I'd bent and picked up a piece of red sea glass, brushing the sand from its smooth surface. When I stood up, he wrapped his arms around me and kissed me. I knew he was still that lost boy I'd seen in the ghost town. Only now, instead of hiding away, I wondered if he was ready to seek solace in another person. Perhaps I was too.

When we drew apart, my hair was a mess and my makeup was watering from the salt air. Normally, I'd be mortified if anyone saw me like that; I tended to cling to perfection with a white-knuckle grip. But as the sun hovered low in the morning sky, I just laughed.

When I'd seen him at school on Monday, I'd been gripped with a sudden panic, unsure if he would even acknowledge our strange midnight voyage. He hadn't. Instead, he went right up to me and casually took my hand. We'd walked down the hall together and stayed that way ever since.

It wasn't a relaxed, easy sort of love, but it was real, and that was something worth holding onto.

"Hey, femme fatale!"

A familiar voice shook me from my memories. Celeste and I turned to see Jayden walking toward us. He wore a black, eighties-inspired blazer, which felt like an intentional nod to the whole Grace Jones hi-top fade thing he had going on with his hair. His cheekbones were dusted with something luminescent that high-lighted the deep brown color of his skin, though I suspected he'd touched up with some rose oil of his own. He was shaking his head at Celeste in disapproval, but a bemused smile tugged at his lips.

"What the hell did you put in that poor kid's coffee?"

"Exactly what the spell called for," she replied, avoiding his gaze. "Cinnamon, cloves, a little chili oil, then I said the incantation—"

"What about lavender?" Jayden asked with genuine patience. "Lavender is the stabilizing agent in any love spell."

"Okay, it might have called for lavender," she admitted. "But the lavender is all the way in the back of my greenhouse and there were, like, a lot of spiders back there. Besides, I felt the spell might be better if it was more...*improvised*, you know?"

"Well, you almost improvised his face off," Jayden replied. "Next time, just ask me."

Most witches had a propensity for a certain skill. Jayden was definitely the herbalist among us, while Celeste was more of a crystal gal. And while crystals were great for drawing energy from the universe, their love spell capabilities were severely limited.

"Heard you put napalm in Benjamin Lewis's coffee." Petra kicked a pebble in Celeste's direction before plopping down beside me.

She flicked a stray lock of hair off her eyes only for it to settle right back where it had been. Her hair was blue right now—at least, the ghostly remains of blue still clung to her ends, while several inches of dark roots grew from her scalp. She wore a heavy ring of black eyeliner, and her posture was a permanent slouch. The overall effect made it impossible to truly look her in the eye, which I was pretty sure was her intention.

"What are they saying?" Celeste asked, cringing.

"That you gave Benjamin a coffee and it was, like, caustic or something. He's gonna be fine, by the way, if anyone cares. I saw the school nurse check him out. First-degree burns. He'll heal up eventually."

"Not in time for homecoming," Celeste muttered.

"Okay, big picture," Jayden said. "The boy's gonna live, and there are plenty more eligible young men you haven't maimed yet."

"Speaking of eligible young men," Petra said to Jayden, her eyes traveling meaningfully toward Max, who was making his way up the steps.

Jayden shot her an irritated look, but before he could say anything, Max sat down beside him. Max was handsome enough, with a square jaw and sensitive green eyes. Still, it made sense that Jayden was wary of Max's not-so-secret crush on him. They had about zero in common, Jayden with his cooler-than-you it-boy vibes and Max with his broad shoulders, an actual high school quarterback, sincere to a fault and painfully mainstream.

Max smiled at Jayden before turning to Celeste.

"Okay, sis, how are we gonna get you out of this one?"

That was the question. Below us, I could hear the shouts and giggles of the other students on their lunch break. I glanced hopefully at the steps, but there was no sign of Luke.

"The coffee was scalding," I said. "That's our story."

"Right," Jayden said. "Shame on the school for endangering a student like that."

Celeste seemed to brighten a little at what sounded like a pretty good cover-up.

"Okay, I want each of you to go back down there and tell at least three people about Benjamin's boiling latte," I instructed. "Let's get the rumor mill going."

Petra raised a hand. "What if we hate talking to people?"

I groaned. Petra always seemed to delight in shirking her coven responsibilities.

"Maybe you can write it on a button and pin it to your backpack," Jayden said, giving Petra's heavily adorned bag a playful shove. "That's your primary means of self-expression, isn't it?"

If anyone else had said it, she would have countered with something snarky, but he got a pass. Petra and Jayden were like bonded feral cats—cute, sharp-clawed, and a little distrusting of anyone but each other.

One last pitiful moan sounded from the quad below. I glanced down to see the nurse gingerly guiding Benjamin in the direction of her office.

"Jayden, can you think of anything that might help Benjamin?" Max said. "You know, healing herbs for the pain?"

Jayden looked as if the question had caught him off guard. He dropped his gaze in embarrassment. "The only healing magic I know involves acne removal," he replied. "I guess—I guess I hadn't thought about that."

Silence settled over the rest of us as we realized with vague shame that we hadn't considered Benjamin's pain either.

"Valeria."

I turned instinctively at the sound of Luke's voice. He stood at the top of the stairs, the sun silhouetting his lean frame. Luke was probably the only person I knew who could wear a leather jacket without looking ridiculous. On the contrary, the well-worn leather looked like it belonged on him, as natural as a second skin. He wore his dark waves combed back a little messily. The effect was vaguely James Dean with a dash of something darker, less all-American.

Maybe it was the way pain seemed to linger behind the cobalt of his eyes, a shadow of that little boy who'd hidden himself away all those years ago. It did nothing to detract from his looks, though—in fact, I wondered if it enhanced them. I was no aura reader, but even I knew there was an intensity to Luke that drew your gaze and held it. My heart quickened a little.

"Hey! Where were you?" I said before quickly adding, "Never mind, we got it all sorted out."

Luke eyed me seriously, "Listen, Valeria, can we go somewhere to talk?"

I kept my voice steady. If he was going to do this, I wasn't about to make it easy for him.

"We're all family here. Anything you have to say, you can say in front of them."

"You're sure?" he replied. They were all staring at him now, but he didn't take his eyes off me.

I felt my back stiffen. "Let's hear it."

"You know I care about you, Val," he began. "But I've been thinking lately about how different we are. Maybe we're just not right for each other."

Of course we were right for each other. We had to be. Rebuttals raced through my head, desperate words to make him understand. But his expression told me his mind was made up. Perhaps it had been for a while.

"Some things aren't meant to be," he went on. "It's nothing personal, okay?"

I let out a bitter little laugh. The loneliest boy in the ghost town had chosen to be alone rather than with me. Of course it was personal. I'd always kept my self-doubts so well-hidden that anyone who looked at me would swear I had none, but now I felt them rise like a lump in my throat. I swallowed and blinked back tears. I would not let him break my heart gently and walk away.

"Wow," I said, my voice flat. "I can't tell you how relieved I am. I've been meaning to do this for a while. Guess you beat me to it."

Luke nodded silently. He wasn't buying my little show, but he let me do it anyway. Damn him for taking the high road.

"And you're right," I added. "We *are* different. I'm not a loser."

He shrugged, and I saw my words slide off him harmlessly.

"Later, Val," he said. He turned and walked away.

It was done. The breakup was remarkable in its brevity. I exhaled. It took me a moment to realize the others were still sitting there, frozen, like a bunch of deer caught in the headlights of my pain. I took a deep breath in and turned to them.

"Shut your mouth. You look ridiculous," I snapped at Petra, who was staring—literally agape—at what had just happened.

She must have had some idea of how destroyed I was because she didn't sass me back.

"Meeting's over!" I said, louder than intended. "I don't know why you're all still sitting around. Get down there and spread that rumor."

With that, I descended the stairs and headed back into the throng of Mundanes. I fished a glittering compact from my purse and examined myself. My eyes were glassy with tears, but perhaps by sheer will, none had fallen. I let the faces on the quad blur before me as the hurt inside welled up. It had been so easy for Luke. A few words and it was over. But it wasn't. I still loved him. I was pretty sure I always would.

Idiot. I hurled the insult at myself as I dabbed at the wetness on my lower lashes.

"Hey," Celeste said, walking up beside me. "If you're worried about homecoming, we could perfect that love spell and—"

I cut her off with an icy glare.

Jayden hung behind her as if searching for some elusive word that might heal my heart. He settled on silence. Jayden was kind in a stealthy sort of way, but he was about as comfortable with human emotions as Celeste was with spiders.

I spotted Gwen Foster on the grass below. As usual, Gwen's thin frame was hidden under baggy clothes that fell short of "vintage" and landed on "moth-eaten." She was making her way across the crowded quad, balancing a truly ridiculous number of books. With her gaze squarely on the ground and her shoulders perpetually hunched, Gwen carried herself like someone who hoped to avoid being noticed at all costs—and it seemed to work. I watched as she dodged a group of roughhousing juniors who seemed totally unaware they'd almost toppled her. Gwen was the most mundane of the Mundanes, the weakest and easiest prey. The tiniest hint of a smile tugged at my lips. She'd make for a brief diversion, at least.

"What do you guys think?" I said, my eyes narrowing on Gwen. "Wanna have a little fun?"

"Yes!" Celeste hissed with conspiratorial glee.

Jayden sighed uneasily. "Come on. Didn't you used to be, like, friends with her?"

I paused a long moment before replying. "No...ew."

I set my sights on Gwen Foster and let the magic within me rise.

CHAPTER TWO

GWEN

The day before the trees died, I was thinking about survival. The long-term kind of survival was always on my mind: groceries, bills, keeping my dad out of trouble. But as I crossed the busy quad to the school library, my arms piled with books, I was immediately concerned with not getting bulldozed. Kids laughed and jostled each other, various guys tossed various balls. I'd always liked to stay invisible in a crowd, the only downside being that nobody bothered to get out of my way.

The collection of books I was returning was an ode to my love of Gothic literature: *The Turn of the Screw*, *Rebecca*, and, of course, several favorites by Edgar Allan Poe. I'd read everything by Poe a dozen times. I felt strangely at home in his world of echoing hallways and high-ceilinged rooms and walls adorned with portraits of some long-lost love. The lives in those books were very different from my own, but the loneliness was the same.

I spent lunch in the library almost every day. Sometimes the place felt too good to be true. It was quiet and they let you read books for free—plus, if I picked an obscure-enough table, the librarians didn't seem to mind if I ate my squished Wonder Bread sandwich there.

I stopped short to avoid colliding with Thomas Fitzgerald, a burly senior who was busy handing photocopied flyers to anyone he passed.

"Watch it!" he exclaimed.

I looked at the flyer in his hand, which declared FITZGERALD'S ECLIPSE BLOWOUT: NOVEMBER 6TH in aggressive font. The eclipse was over a month away, and he was already making sure most of the student body would be drunk for it.

"Sorry, Foster," he said, looking at the flyer, then looking at me. "I'm only inviting, like, sevens and above. You understand, right?"

For as long as I could remember, I'd loved the serenity of night, the comfortable blanket of dark sky, the brilliant moon overhead. There was something exciting about the idea of the night overtaking the day. And when it happened, the last place I wanted to be was Thomas Fitzgerald's "blowout."

Maybe a different girl would have told him that. Or maybe a different girl would have slapped him across the face and encouraged him to go screw himself. I just stood there, silently willing our conversation to end. I felt my jaw go tight.

Thomas examined me before adding, "You know, you'd be prettier if you smiled. I mean, not a *lot* prettier, but—"

"Excuse me," I muttered at last. The corners of my mouth tugged even further earthward as I shuffled out of his way.

I was preparing to reflect on what an ass Thomas was when I realized Valeria Garcia was watching me from across the quad like I'd just become her target in *The Most Dangerous Game*. I had bigger problems than Thomas. I wasn't surprised Valeria had set her sights on me. She seemed to love playing with me the way a cat unravels its favorite toy, tearing at the stuffing with indifference.

Valeria was wearing a strapless yellow dress that probably cost more than my dad's '99 Chevy Caprice. She was always in bright colors—reds, yellows, the occasional hot pink—and all her outfits included a healthy amount of bare skin. While all my clothing choices were a vain attempt to disappear, Valeria existed to be seen.

Her blood-red lips curved into a playful smile as her eyes flashed in my direction. The wind caught her long, dark hair, making her look like something out of a shampoo commercial from hell, her features at once perfect and unsettling.

I felt a chill travel down my spine. I was scared of girls like Valeria, girls whose looks demanded attention even before they opened their glittering mouths to speak. People were eager to follow beautiful girls, eager to laugh at their jokes, even the cruel ones. Perhaps especially the cruel ones.

I did what I always did when Valeria was around: I kept my head down and avoided her gaze. Whatever she was up to, she could find another victim.

I was a few feet from the library steps when something tripped me—only that was impossible because there was nothing there. No branch, no curb, just the green grass beneath my feet.

It hadn't *felt* like a branch either. It felt…*hot*, an invisible, fiery coil around my ankle. It pulled my legs out from under me and I tumbled forward, the contents of my bag flying everywhere. Before I could catch myself, I'd landed facedown, tampons and loose change strewn around me like humiliating confetti.

I lay there, pain shooting up my knees. Tripped by invisible fire? Mental stability had never been a strong suit in the Foster family. Perhaps it was finally my turn to lose my mind.

The laughter of every kid in the quad erupted around me. Come on, how funny was it to watch somebody fall? But I knew why they laughed. Each of them was overjoyed that it was me and not them lying in the dirt.

Then I heard Valeria's voice. Of course she would have a front-row seat to my degradation. That was just the natural law of the universe. So why did I have the insane feeling she'd planned it?

"Wow, Gwen, you just created some great content!"

I looked up to see Valeria triumphantly holding out her phone. Perfect. Whoever hadn't seen my fall firsthand would now be able to watch it over and over on the internet. The loose crowd of onlookers parted as she stepped closer. I watched her eyes travel over me, taking in the shapeless fit and fraying hems of my thrift-store clothes, the rubber separating from the sole of my right sneaker.

"Oh no, Gwen," she said, her voice dripping with sarcasm. "You got grass stains on your already unacceptable outfit."

Laughter erupted from the kids around us. Celeste, who had come to stand proudly by her side, was practically peeing her pants. But Valeria wasn't paying attention to anyone but me. She was studying me intently, as if searching for the hurt her words had caused.

I did hurt. Memories rushed and receded like waves in my mind: Two little girls barefoot in the woods. Hollow logs and black feathers. The crawling things revealed beneath a flat stone.

I wished I could stare back at her and make her feel as ugly as she was inside. Instead, I got on my hands and knees and began stuffing tampons and crumpled dollar bills into my bag as she quite literally looked down on me. The library books were scattered in a haphazard radius around me, and it looked like the whole crowd was just going to watch as I picked each one up.

My eyes froze on a small leatherbound notebook in the dirt beside my copy of "The Tell-Tale Heart." My journal must have flown from my bag when I fell. Instinctively, my hands shot out to grasp it, but Valeria read the desperation in my movement, and she pinned it to the ground with one designer heel.

"What's this?" she smirked. "Your secret diary?"

"Give it to me!" I cried in a tone that sounded far more pleading than threatening.

That told Valeria all she needed to know. She picked it up and began flipping through it as casually as if it were her own. To my horror, she began to read aloud.

"I am solitary as the moon, which only shows its face in the dark. Will I always be the lesser sister to the sun's blazing day? Oh, to be a meteor whose power lies not in light but in destruction. Oh, to combust with you until we are embers, innumerable and free."

Giggles erupted around me, Valeria's laughter louder than the rest. My face burned. I'd written that poem one night as I sat alone in my bedroom. I liked to listen to the night outside—the wind in the leaves, the sounds of living things—as I sat beside my open window and wrote whatever felt true.

That part about the meteor, I wasn't even sure what it meant. All I knew was, for as long as I could remember, I'd had the sense that I was destined for some sort of destruction. I just wasn't sure whether I'd be the one hurtling toward Earth or the one flattened under burning rubble.

"Okay, that was *steamy*!" Valeria gushed like we were two girlfriends at a sleepover. "Sooo, who's it about? Who do you want to *combust* with?"

She began thumbing through the pages excitedly, searching for a clue.

Celeste was grabbing at the book now, too, crying, "Lemme see!" like a little kid who didn't want to be left out.

Valeria elbowed her away and kept on flipping, her red fingernails shining like daggers in the sun. This couldn't be happening. Panic flooded my senses. I didn't know exactly what the poem meant, but I *did* know who it was about. She'd find his name if she kept looking.

"Enough, Valeria."

A gruff male voice spoke over the chorus of laughter. We turned in unison to see Luke Nichols standing on the edge of the circle that had formed around me. Luke wasn't the biggest guy in school—he was more lean muscle than brawn—but he was tall, and right now, something about his presence felt imposing. The crowd began to hush.

I thought a hint of nervous color rushed to Valeria's cheeks when she saw him, but it was so brief I could have imagined it.

"You on a charity mission now, Luke?" she said.

"Give her the book."

"Why should I?" she replied, flipping through a few more pages. "It's just about to get juicy."

He shook his head, and when he spoke, there was genuine pity in his voice. "Val, you think you're embarrassing her, but you're only embarrassing yourself."

The kids around us were completely silent now. All eyes were on Valeria. Her Miss America smile seemed to flicker like a candle in danger of blowing out.

"Screw you, Luke," she replied. She tossed the book at my feet and walked away.

I snatched up the journal and held it protectively to my chest as the group of onlookers began to disperse, heads down. After a moment, Luke and I were standing alone on the quad. I'd never been this close to him, face-to-face. His blue eyes were darker than I thought. Less like the ocean, more like the night sky.

I pulled my gaze away from his. I didn't trust any of the rich kids who lived on Cascabel Road, their towering mansions obscured among the towering evergreens. Some of them didn't seem so bad, but they were strangely close-knit, and Valeria was the sun at the center of their weird little galaxy. What was that de Cervantes quote I'd read once? *Tell me what company you keep and I'll tell you what you are.* I was aware of the company Luke kept. He was Valeria's boyfriend. For all I knew, he was playing his part in an elaborate prank.

But he was wordlessly gathering my scattered books, brushing the dirt off the worn covers. When he'd collected them all, he handed them to me. I accepted them, dumbfounded. *Thank you* didn't seem appropriate, but I felt the need to say something.

"I didn't need you to rescue me like that," I blurted. As soon as I spoke, I felt my face go red. I couldn't remember the last time I'd been this blunt with anyone.

He shot me an unbothered grin.

"I know," he replied. "See you around, Gwen."

He walked away, leaving me alone on the quad, my arms full of books.

In eighth grade, Thomas Fitzgerald—yes, prettier-if-you-smiled Thomas Fitzgerald—asked me out. I didn't even like Thomas, and I knew there was a good chance it was some sort of joke at my expense. But something inside my naïve heart had been thrilled. *Maybe,* I'd thought, *I'm the kind of person who gets asked on dates now.*

We'd arranged to meet in front of Diggin's, our local fast-food spot, after school. I'd waited outside for him, the damp winter air making my hair frizzier by the minute. Then, suddenly, he was walking toward me. My heart pounded. It had been real after all.

That was when I'd heard the laughter. Valeria and a few of her minions had stepped out from behind the line of shops across the street. She'd put him up to it, of course. Thomas had never thought twice about me.

I worked at Diggin's after school now. Every time I walked through those doors, I couldn't help but see the ghost of my thirteen-year-old self standing outside in faded jeans, waiting for Thomas Fitzgerald.

After Luke made his mysterious exit, I spent the rest of the school day half expecting him and Valeria to jump out at me from behind a pillar, tears of laughter in their eyes. Strangely, it almost made me angrier to imagine Luke's intentions had been genuine. Did he think he was some kind of saint because he'd picked up a few books? Valeria had implied he was on a charity mission. Well, I didn't need his charity. And I wasn't going to let him use me to make himself feel better about a lifetime of associating with horrible people.

I took my usual route home after school: down Main Street, past the fancy shops and cafes, then left over the iron bridge. There were no boutiques or five-star restaurants on my side of the river, just apple orchards and decaying farmhouses and, beyond that, the yawning mouths of defunct gold mines. I walked the dirt road along the water until I reached my gravel driveway. Across the river stood the lush evergreens that bordered Cascabel Road. Valeria's house stood somewhere within those woods—Luke's, too, though I didn't know for sure which rambling Victorian structure was his. The trees were so thick, the forest floor was dark beneath them, casting its surface into permanent dusk despite the afternoon sun. I longed to wander through those woods, to lose myself among the pines and brambles like I had as a child.

At the end of my overgrown property were the charred remains of an old wooden bridge. Railings still stood on either side of the water, nothing connecting them but empty space. My eyes lingered on the nonexistent bridge as old pain mixed with new in my heart.

I turned away from the beckoning forest and started up the driveway. My dad's car was in its spot, another newer car parked behind it. That wasn't good. I considered walking all the way back to town and killing time in the shops on Main Street until they closed or I was politely asked to leave, but the thought of wandering aimlessly through town made my heart weary. After the day I'd had, I longed for somewhere to land. Or, more accurately, I longed for somewhere to belong.

There's a journal entry, I thought wryly. *Dear diary, today I will dissect my literal and figurative desire for belonging. Cue the melodramatic music.* I would never put anything like that down in writing, of course. I told myself I preferred my emotions clouded in metaphor, or that I was content to live in a world of fantasy, reading about imaginary people's lives and loves. The truth was, there were some things that seemed so impossible, I had grown afraid to hope for them.

I took a deep breath and walked the gravel path to the front door. As I did, a man emerged from the house. He wore a cheap suit and his black hair was slicked back with what looked like a combination of gel and sweat. As he walked, he examined his knuckles, which were red. I felt my chest tighten. His eyes traveled over me in a way that was at once casual and intimate, as if he could see right through my clothes and it didn't make him uncomfortable at all.

"Hey, Pop-Tart," he said as we passed each other on the driveway.

My skin crawled and my steps quickened, but I replied, "Hey," like the fear of being impolite was somehow worse than whatever this man might do to me.

His left eye closed in what I think was supposed to be a seductive wink, but he kept walking. I heard his car start as I pushed open the screen door and stepped into our tiny living room. I was greeted by the familiar scent of smoke, the kind that clings to the walls when cigarettes are consumed in a small space with the windows shut. The living room was dark, but the TV was on, bathing my father in ever-changing shades of blue light. He sat on the living room floor, a thick red gash above one eyebrow, the skin around it already darkening to a bruise.

"Dad!"

I rushed to him and tried to get a good look at the cut above his eye, but he turned away from me.

"I'm okay, Gwen," he said, his speech slurred. An overturned bottle of Coors lay beside him, the remains of its contents dripping onto the faded carpet. "It's just a shiner."

"What did that man—" I took a deep breath. "How much do you owe him?"

"Don't worry about it," he replied, his tone more defensive than comforting. "I'll win what I owe him tomorrow night. And more."

The casino was about twenty miles east of town. My dad used to take me there all the time when I was little. My mom died when I was a baby, so it's always been just my dad and me. At first the casino felt like a fun house—neon lights and bright colors and cool video-game sounds buzzing out of the slot machines. But it got boring fast. He'd sit me down with a book as he played for hours at the craps table, pausing only to refill his drink. I can still see the pattern in the casino's multicolored carpet. He never came out of that place better off than when he'd walked in.

"Maybe I can take some extra shifts at Diggins for a while and—"

"Aw, honey, you're not going to earn that kind of money flipping burgers," he said. "Leave the grind to your old man and just be a kid for once, will you? Go hang out with your friends or something."

I didn't have any friends, but I smiled and nodded like the mythical normal teenager my father imagined me to be. "Okay, Dad."

"Now," he said, his tone brightening, "how was school?"

I sighed. *Well, Dad, a mean girl made fun of me. Then her boyfriend stood up for me for reasons that remain unclear. Oh, and I think I was attacked by invisible fire, so I might be losing my mind.*

"Weird," I said.

He gave my hand a little squeeze, then his eyes closed. His back had come to rest on the couch, his head lolling onto one of the cushions. I went into the kitchen and put some ice in a hand towel. When I pressed it to his eye, he barely flinched at the cold.

Somehow, he looked younger in sleep. Almost innocent. Without thinking, I ran a hand through my hair, feeling its even length. The memory of a dream floated back to me, one so distant and strange I hadn't thought about it since I was a kid.

A couple years after the wooden bridge burned down, I'd sat up in bed in the early morning. A flicker of movement drew my attention to the window. In the dim light of early sunrise, I made out two figures at the river's edge. One was my father; the other was a woman. I watched as he handed her something. Then, my dad lit a cigarette and the woman's face was illuminated momentarily by the light from his Zippo.

It was Lili Garcia, Valeria's mom. In her hand, she clasped what my father had given her, something long and wispy, alight on the breeze. A lock of dark hair.

I woke the next morning with the image of those hazy figures still hanging in my mind. I was no stranger to vivid dreams, probably a consequence of reading before bed and an overactive imagination. Still, all that day, my fingers worried through my hair as if searching for a lock that was shorter than the rest, a lock someone had snipped as I slept. But my hair, as usual, was tragically unkempt; all I found were knots.

In time, the dream faded like the others. I wondered why I was thinking of it now.

I draped a blanket over my dad's sleeping form and propped a pillow behind his head. I switched off the TV and the light in the hallway. I washed the dishes and rinsed out the ashtray that sat on our kitchen table.

This was my favorite time to be at home. My dad was safely sleeping, the world was shutting down for the night, and I was free. In my bedroom, I opened the window and breathed in the cool air. The trees stretched toward the dark sky like hands. I held my arm out the window, my fingers reaching for the half moon. Crickets and frogs sang their little songs to me, and I was at peace.

Leaning back inside, I retrieved my journal from my bag and placed it safely on my bedside table. No matter what else had happened today, I was grateful Valeria hadn't spotted the name scrolled idly between lines or tucked in the margins.

Luke Nichols.

That night, I dreamed I stood beneath the night sky. A blazing meteor hovered above me, crackling heat radiating from its surface.

It was larger and closer than the moon had ever been, so close I could almost touch it. I knew that if I did, something terrible or wonderful would happen. Hesitantly, I lifted my hand.

The smell of smoke filled my nostrils. My eyes opened and I blinked at the sight of my bedroom, now flooded with morning light. All the candles I kept on my dresser had burned down to stubs, and one of the flames had begun to ignite the wood itself.

Quickly, I snuffed out the fire with my pillow. After it was out, I stood for a long time, staring at the smoldering wood. I hadn't lit any candles before I went to bed.

CHAPTER THREE

VALERIA

The morning after I read Gwen's poem in the quad, I opened my eyes and gazed at the ceiling, motionless. The curtains were drawn and only a hint of gray light crept between them. Images flooded my mind: the look of panic on Gwen's face as I read her private words, her eyes shimmering with the tears she'd tried to hide. I pushed the memories away, but older ones came—a hollow in a fallen tree, crow feathers, words carved in ancient wood by small hands. I hadn't thought about these things in years, but now, as the darkness pressed in around me, I found my mind propelled backward in time, back to when it all began with Gwen.

When I was little, I loved to wander in the redwoods behind Cascabel Road. My house was vast and quiet, its treasures all meant for collecting dust, never to be touched by a child's hands. The forest wasn't like that. The forest was wild, imperfect. I was at ease there, one more living thing moving in the shadow of the trees.

To get there, all I had to do was walk out my back door and past my manicured garden. There was no fence, nothing to delineate where my property ended and the forest began. Why would there be? These were the coven's woods. The clearing where we held our gatherings was hidden away among the trees. Patches of medicinal herbs planted by our ancestors still grew beneath the brambles.

In those days, I didn't take the broad, easy paths cleared away by generations of witches. I followed the deer trail, picking my way over gnarled roots and shimmying beneath thick branches. Along the path, somewhere between Luke's house and mine, was an enormous fallen tree. It must have met its end a hundred years ago. Now it lay like a sleeping giant, ancient and covered in moss. I loved to walk its great length, my arms out like a gymnast on a balance beam. Toward its base was a child-sized hollow. The bottom was mossy and soft, its walls cool. I'd sit inside my secret chamber, watching the rabbits graze or listening to the warblers in the branches above me.

One day, when I was about eight, I sat in my hiding place and heard something moving toward me from the river. I rose quietly, expecting a fawn, maybe a doe. Before me stood a girl. She was skinny, dressed in clothes she'd outgrown a year ago. Her dark hair hung wild past her shoulders. I recognized her. Gwen Foster, a Mundane from school.

Our eyes met, and she froze like a startled animal. I could tell she knew this forest wasn't hers, that she'd just been caught doing something she shouldn't. In another second, she was gone. By the time I'd scrambled to my feet, all I could make out was her dark shape disappearing between the trees in the direction of the river.

I didn't go back to the hollow for a few days. When I did, there was a magnificent crow feather waiting for me inside. It had been laid with care in the center of the hollow's mossy floor. I picked it up, examining it like it was a precious artifact. I stroked the dark plume, holding it up to the filtered sunlight to watch the rainbow colors hidden in its black sheen. In the feather's place, I left a fallen jay's nest.

We continued like this for a long time, leaving one another our forest bounty. A cicada shell. The discarded skin of a rattlesnake, its scales as delicate as fine lace.

Life went on as usual. My parents bound gold coins with herbs, burned marjoram on Wednesdays for luck. The coven would gather in the forest at night, the others completely unaware of the hollow and the strange little exchange happening there. I loved watching my mom, the crown of the high priestess on her head, her eyes flashing in the candlelight. The slit in her long red robe would open to reveal the coven's ceremonial dagger strapped to her thigh. She was beautiful and powerful in equal measure, and somehow, as I watched her, I decided power and beauty must be the same thing.

One morning before my visit to the forest, I snuck into my mom's room, pulled on the robe she wore to our coven gatherings, and took the crown from its place in her wardrobe. It was solid gold. A brilliant sun was emblazoned in its center, with peaks radiating upward like golden rays of light. Just holding it, I could tell it was old, important. I put it on and let it settle unevenly on my too-small skull. I took the ceremonial dagger too. My thigh was far too skinny, even for the sheath's smallest loop, so I fastened it around my waist instead. I examined myself and decided I was as beautiful as a queen from a fairy tale. I did what any kid in her mom's clothes would do: I danced around in front of the mirror.

That's what I was doing when she and my dad walked in. My mother's mouth tightened into that familiar, lineless frown.

"Take those things off. You look ridiculous," she said.

I glanced in the mirror again, seeing myself through her eyes. My hair was plastered awkwardly to my brow beneath the crooked crown. My small frame was drowning in red fabric, the robe's extra length gathering sloppily at my feet. She was right. Humiliation washed over me, burning my cheeks. I turned to my dad, but he gave me an apologetic little shrug.

"Better do what she says, honey. That dagger's pretty sharp."

I didn't cry as I changed back into my T-shirt and jeans. But by the time I escaped to the hollow, shameful tears were stinging my eyes.

I discovered Gwen there, leaving a woodpecker's eggshell. She startled when she saw me, that same guilty look on her face. I thought she was going to bolt as she had before, but when she saw my tearful expression, she hesitated.

"What's wrong?" she said.

"My mom doesn't think I'm pretty," I replied, voicing my fear with a child's blunt honesty.

She gave me a funny look, but before I could say anything else, she'd disappeared back into the trees.

The next time I visited the hollow, I didn't find a feather or sprig of berries. On the hollow's back wall, in small, childlike letters, she'd carved THE BIRDS DON'T CARE IF YOU'RE PRETTY.

I stared at the inscription for a long time, a slow smile dawning on my face, a strange feeling washing over me. Like I'd just discovered the world was bigger than I thought it was.

A few weeks later, I saw her again at the hollow. This time, as she moved to run, I cried out, "Wait!"

We played in the forest every day after that, chasing each other over the pine-covered floor, following the birds that darted overhead. I loved the bright yellow finches that sang in the morning; Gwen loved the ravens and owls. This made sense to me. There was something nocturnal about her, her eyes as dark as theirs with the same quiet intelligence.

We went on like this for a year, our fragile bond only existing within the forest. Both of us seemed to understand our friendship was a secret without ever saying it aloud. At school, we breezed past each other like strangers. Our coven had always been carefully polite toward the Mundanes in town—nice enough to blend in, never close enough to arouse suspicion. Not only had I befriended a Mundane, I'd welcomed her into *our* forest. My mother would be furious if she found out.

Gwen kept her own mysteries. She never showed me the way to her bridge, never brought me to the water's edge, where her house would be visible on the other side of the river. I got the sense she was ashamed of it—or at least, she thought she ought to be.

One day, it was over as abruptly as it had begun. My mom went into the woods in search of Mayapple and discovered me in the clearing where our coven gathered. With a Mundane. Playing with worms.

It was as bad as I'd imagined. Gwen ran off into the woods, and my mom dragged me back home by the sleeve of my dirt-stained dress. She didn't yell or lecture, though I wished she would. I was used to that. Instead, a cold silence hung between us that was a hundred times worse, as if she were holding all the horrible things she wanted to say to me behind a wall of ice.

That night, as I lay in bed unable to sleep, I heard my mom slip down the stairs and out the back door. She came back after midnight, smelling of woodsmoke, her footsteps soft in the hall. The next morning at school, Gwen was silent, her shoulders slumped as if in defeat. At recess, I heard the teachers talking about the fire. It was the strangest thing, they said. The old wooden bridge near the apple orchards had burned down overnight like it'd been struck by lightning.

I thought of my mom slipping in the back door, the scent of smoke heavy on her clothes. So she hadn't just forbidden me from seeing Gwen. She'd found a permanent solution.

I could tell by the look of devastation on Gwen's face that she knew the bridge wasn't an accident. She probably thought my mom had doused it in gasoline, or that I had. I was sorry for what had happened, but for reasons I couldn't name, I was angry too. Angry that she'd come to the forest in the first place. Angry that I'd gotten in trouble. Angry that she stood there now, tears glistening in her raven eyes.

She tried to talk to me only once after that. She'd walked up to me as I sat with a few other girls on the playground. Her jeans were too short, revealing several inches of pale ankle. Her hair fell around her face in frizzy waves. She didn't look any different than she had in the forest. But out here, these little flaws were somehow irritating.

"Hey," she said. She stood there hopefully.

I looked at her, the cruel reality sinking in at last. We would never be friends. It would be better for her to go on with her Mundane life without me.

"Can I help you?" I said, doing my best impression of my mother's impatience.

The other girls giggled, and it felt good. Those girls were Mundanes, too, but they weren't like Gwen. It was easy to keep them at a distance. Gwen lingered awkwardly for a moment, then she turned and walked away.

"Did you see how skinny her ankles are?" I said to them as I watched her leave. "It looks like she's walking on stilts."

They giggled again, and I laughed loud enough for Gwen to hear as she disappeared across the playground.

I stopped taking the deer path after that, and I didn't visit the hollow anymore. I couldn't bear any of those secret places that had belonged to Gwen and me. I was too old to go running through the forest searching for snakeskins and eggshells, I decided. Whispers spread among the coven parents about the Mundane child who'd been discovered playing with me in the forest. But soon they faded, replaced by talk of next quarter's earnings. The kids never got the details, and the colder I was toward Gwen, the more they doubted what they'd heard. In time, the whole thing was forgotten.

A few months later, a wounded crow wandered onto the playground during recess. Thomas and some other boys began throwing rocks at it, laughing about targets and kill shots. I sat with my little throng of friends, watching the way the light danced off the bird's black feathers. I longed to cup its small body in my hands, to hold it to my chest and whisper soft, healing words. But I didn't move.

It was Gwen who stepped in front of the crow. She crouched before it, her body a shield, rocks flying at her as the boys jeered. She looked at me, and I was transported back to the forest with her, to a time when I was kinder. I turned my gaze away. That was the last time Gwen Foster looked me in the eye, until yesterday.

I ROLLED OVER IN BED, one hand reaching for my phone. The video I'd taken of Gwen's spill on the quad was saved in my camera roll. I had planned to post it today with a humorous yet derisive caption. I deleted the video and set the phone back down.

You think you're embarrassing her, but you're only embarrassing yourself. Luke's words echoed in my head. He was right, I *was* embarrassed. There was a sick feeling in my stomach that promised to linger all day. Luke had come to know me better than anyone. Maybe that's why he left, I thought bitterly. Perhaps he'd peeled back that shiny outer layer and decided he didn't like what he saw underneath.

Today I'd ditch the coven and ask Gwen to sit with me at lunch, I decided. I'd apologize to her in some cute, self-deprecating way. Soon we'd be laughing about the whole thing; maybe we'd even talk about our old adventures in the forest. Thinking about it felt like the start of something new. Maybe I was about to change in some momentous way. And maybe one night not too long from now, I'd awaken to the gentle sound of pebbles at my window again.

I got out of bed, energized by my new plan and intent on coffee. The first floor was silent, my parents still asleep. I stepped lightly down the grand staircase and into the tiled foyer. The dining room loomed to my right, its curtains drawn, its corners dark with shadows, yet even from here, I felt the painted eyes of Delfina Garcia on me. The portrait hung at the head of the dining room table. Our founder's gold-framed face stared at me, as it did during every meal my parents and I ate in that room.

I was Delfina's direct descendant on my mom's side. My family had always liked to flaunt our relation to our coven's founder. Going back generations, it was tradition for us Garcia women to keep our matrilineal name, which was why VALERIA GARCIA was proudly penned on my birth certificate. My father never even dreamed of objecting.

I eyed the portrait with a mixture of awe and anxiety. In it, Delfina stood before a rising sun, its rays surrounding her in fiery light. Her skin, like mine, was the rich color of terracotta, and her dark hair flowed to her waist in loose waves. On her face was a look of proud defiance. Her beauty and the power in her gaze were undeniable.

At seventeen, Delfina had barely escaped Mexico with a bunch of witch-hunting clerics on her trail. Ten years later, she'd gathered the most powerful witches on the West Coast and staked her claim. When she posed for that painting, her newly formed coven had just struck it rich in the California Gold Rush.

The gold mines had dried up long ago, but the money never did.

In the years after, our coven turned to modern financial endeavors: stocks, real estate. One way or another, our parents were all in the business of money. I supposed I would be, too, someday. Still, I couldn't shake the sense our coven was clinging to some long-gone glory. Our homes were like museums, proudly adorned with the gilded decor our ancestors had chosen. Delfina had been dead for more than a hundred years, but sometimes this house still felt like hers.

IN THE ECHOEY dining room of her newly constructed mansion, she had hung her own portrait like some sort of analog selfie, and it had stayed there ever since. I used to love to look at it as a little girl, imagining myself in the same pose. But lately, I detected a hint of disdain in those serious brown eyes, and I sensed the weight of her legacy on my shoulders.

From a corner of the dining room, the grandfather clock struck six. I jumped at the abrupt sound. There was something unsettling about this morning, I realized suddenly—something missing in the silence.

It hit me. I usually woke to the familiar tune of warblers and jays. But today, the birds were strangely absent. An uneasy feeling crept up my spine. Without knowing why, I strode to a window and drew the curtains wide.

A small, pained sound escaped my lips. The dense, green forest behind my house had been replaced by something jagged and color- less. Every tree was dead.

Last night, when I'd gone to sleep, they'd been the same lush redwoods I'd known all my life. Now their remains stood as tall as ever, but their branches were bare. Their skeletal arms reached this way and that, casting menacing shadows across the dirt.

I didn't think. I didn't call out to my parents. I pulled on the running shoes I kept by the back door and walked outside in my pajamas. My garden remained green and undisturbed, but even before I reached the tree line, an unshakable feeling of despair struck me. The air felt heavy against my skin, and it got worse the closer I drew to the forest.

Pine needles covered the forest floor in mountains as if they'd all fallen in a single moment. They crunched under my shoes as I approached one of the tree skeletons. It stood naked and obscene in the morning light, the bark dry but unblemished. There were no burn marks, no visible damage of any kind. But beneath its flaking bark, its surface was sickly black, as if it had rotted from the inside out.

The dead forest reached as far as I could see in any direction, vines and brambles turned to brittle sticks overnight. Every blade of grass was as dry as hay. Shivering in the morning air, I walked on, searching for a sign of life.

As I reached the fallen tree where Gwen and I used to leave our little offerings, something caught my eye.

Beside the tree's broad stump, a single, bright red flower grew— a hyacinth, its petals vibrant against the muted landscape. As far as I could see, that flower was the only living thing left in the forest.

The snapping of pine needles announced someone's arrival. My heart thudded in my chest, the oppressively bad vibes of my surroundings plunging me into an uncharacteristic panic. I whirled around, looking for the approaching stranger, but they were obscured behind the deathly trees.

A figure appeared in my periphery, and I didn't hesitate. With one arm outstretched, I summoned the fire inside me. I kept it invisible, just as I had when I'd wrapped it around Gwen's ankle in the quad, but this time, I struck hard enough to send the newcomer flying backward. I heard a dull thud, followed by the crunch of dead leaves.

"Watch it, dumbass!" an irritated voice echoed through the trees.

I took a few steps and Petra Sarich came into view. She was slumped against a dry trunk, looking pissed and more than a little scared. I exhaled, relaxing my death grip on the elements. Her house was half a mile down Cascabel Road. She must have come here with the same morbid curiosity I had.

"Sorry!" I exclaimed as she swept dead leaves off her clothes. "I didn't mean to—I'm just—"

Afraid. I wouldn't say it aloud, so I stood there, my sentence unfinished. She nodded, understanding on her face.

"I woke up and they were like this. All of them. I thought maybe if I walked this way, I'd find—I don't know. I wanted to find where it ends." Her voice shook in a rare betrayal of emotion. She rubbed the spot where my spell had struck her shoulder. "That superpower of yours is a bitch," she added.

That superpower of mine was called sunfire. All witches could summon fire to light a candle, start a campfire, that sort of thing. My power went beyond that. It was like there was a sacred flame always alight inside me, a piece of the sun itself. If I wanted to, I could push it out into the world. It was a rare ability passed down through blood, and it ran in the Garcia family.

My mother had trained me to control it with an energy similar to that of a particularly obsessive pageant mom. The power used to rush out of me like untamed wildfire. Once, as a child, I'd accidentally burned down the rickety garden shed in my backyard during a training session. To this day, I would catch my mom glancing at the place the shed used to be, her eyes narrowed with disapproval.

But in time, she taught me to hone my skills. I learned to control the hunger of the flames, to let them consume only when I wanted them to. I learned to make the fire so fine it couldn't be seen. My final test had been to loop a thin cord of invisible heat around the stem of just one flower and pick it. The day I passed, I think my mom almost smiled.

Sunfire was considered a defensive spell. The Garcias were considered warriors, capable of protecting our coven in the face of danger. That was why a member of the Garcia family had always been high priestess—only our coven had never needed defending, so my power went mostly unused, except for yesterday's moment of weakness on the quad. Still, that fire meant I would someday lead the coven. I wasn't ready for that. I didn't think I ever would be, but that was a secret I held as tightly as a closed fist.

"So, what the hell?" Petra said. "I did a little reconnaissance on my scooter before I ran into you. The trees in town are alive and well. Then you get to Cascabel Road, and boom, it's a graveyard."

"It's magic, obviously."

She nodded, tucking a faded blue lock behind her ear only for it to fall loose again. "Bad magic too. The aura of this place has me majorly depressed."

As opposed to your usual cheery disposition? I thought, but I held the words back. If I drew her into our usual catty banter, she might leave, and I didn't want to be alone out here.

"Pretty much," I replied grimly.

"Whoever did this didn't set out to just kill some trees," Petra said, closing her eyes as if trying to hear the magic around us. "The trees were…collateral damage or something."

I trusted Petra when it came to things like this. She'd always had a clairvoyance that went beyond mere intuition. All witches believed in a spirit world, an unseen realm where souls resided, where magic came from. Petra's connection to that world was stronger than the rest of ours.

I closed my eyes as she did and opened myself to the surrounding elements. The wind that brushed my face carried death and destruction with it. It terrified me, but I got a sense of the intention of the spell. She was right, of course. There was a malice behind it that wasn't directed at the trees.

"Did you see this?" I pointed at the single crimson flower near the old stump.

She reached out a hand and touched a satiny petal, her expression curious. As I stepped closer to it, I realized the flower didn't exude the same deathly energy as the rest of the forest. If anything, it felt like it was supposed to be there.

"This flower is here because of a spell too," she declared. "A different spell. This one wasn't about destruction—it was about restoration. Something put back into balance."

Silently, we walked on, scanning for anything other than death. In the distance, a newly fallen tree lay across our path, its great length stretched before us, dead branches crushed against the ground. Its stump was cleanly severed, and though it had turned the inky color of sickness, I thought I could make out a faint streak of red along its flat surface.

"This is where it happened," Petra said. "Some kind of ritual."

I pursed my lips. Even I could sense it; the air was heaviest here. The felling of this tree had been done with some dark magical intent.

The bare branches seemed to close in around me. Witches were scarce these days, especially witches strong enough to do magic like this. What if one of us—

"Who did this?" I demanded.

She shook her head. "Sorry, I just get an aura. I'm not, like, psychic Sherlock Holmes."

Her phone buzzed. She took it out of her pocket.

"Fifteen missed calls," she said, scrolling. "Jayden, my parents, Jayden again. Guess they've all noticed the forest."

I watched her type a message to her mother. Trees dead. I know. She hit SEND.

A moment later, her phone buzzed again. She studied the reply. Concern marked her impassive features for just a moment, then she turned the screen to me.

There's more. Meet at the Garcias NOW.

As we picked our way back to my house, my mind raced. *Meet at the Garcias* meant this would be a coven gathering, with my mom presiding. *There's more.* The words repeated in my mind, but I was helpless to guess what *more* might be. We climbed the steps to the back door in silence and headed inside.

The whole coven, young and old, was gathered in the grand living room. The curtains were open now, the enormous picture window displaying a mess of skeletal branches. Jayden sat on the couch with his mom, his expression stoic. Max was beside them, his eyes red with tears. As I walked in, Celeste looked to me as if hoping she'd find some kind of answer on my face, but I didn't even know the question.

Luke was near the window with his dad, his dark brows drawn. My hands instinctively went to my hair to check for pine needles. There were several. I was still wearing my pajamas, muddy running shoes on my feet. It was stupid to want to look perfect at a time like this, I knew. But the scarier things were, the more I yearned for the comfort of perfection.

As I took in my parents' faces, I realized they looked worse off than anybody from my generation. My dad sat beside my mom, his brown eyes boring a hole into a spot on the carpet. Lili Garcia had dressed in the long red robes she always wore for official gatherings. She wore the crown of the high priestess, but it perched off-kilter as if about to topple from her head. Her makeup wasn't done. For the first time in recorded history, she looked unsure of herself. This must be bad.

"Okay, what the hell is going on?" I said.

"Valeria," she began. "Something's happened. Maybe you two should sit down."

I didn't move. Neither did Petra.

"Tell me," I insisted.

"Yes, dear, I was about to," she said. At least her capacity for mild condescension had remained intact. "It seems our powers are gone."

"No they're not," I protested. "I practically gave Petra a concussion just now in the forest—"

"No, Valeria, *our* powers are gone." She gestured at the parents sitting dejectedly around her.

Our parents, unable to use magic? I couldn't fathom it. Defiantly, I took the cup of coffee Mr. Sarich had been drinking and thrust it into my mom's hands. I'd been very young the first time I could recall seeing my mom use magic; she'd poured cream in her morning coffee, then she'd idly twirled a long, delicate finger over the steaming cup. I'd watched as a mini whirlpool formed at the center of the cup, mixing the cream with the coffee until the liquid was a lovely caramel color. I'd stepped close to her, and we'd sat together, taking in the small beauty her power had created, both of us understanding that I had just become aware of something important.

"Try," I now said gently.

With a sigh, she extended a manicured finger and twirled it over the cup. The liquid within remained still and lifeless.

Tears stinging my eyes, I took the cup from her and passed my hand over it. The coffee stirred itself in a spiral as pretty as hers had been on that day, all those years ago.

"Why?" I demanded.

She shook her head, her eyes fixed on the lifeless trees outside.

"We don't know yet. All we know is, as of right now, you kids are the only witches left in Dorado."

With that, she took the golden crown from her head and handed it to me.

CHAPTER FOUR

VALERIA

I stood in my kitchen, listening to the sounds of my house: the low chime of the grandfather clock, the liquid hum of the dishwasher, the TV in my dad's den announcing the biggest Toyota sales event of the year. They combined to create a symphony of vague unease. Running beneath it all—like the world's most unsettling metronome—was the incessant sound of my mom's fingers tapping over her keyboard in the study.

It had been three days since our parents had lost their powers. My mom and dad had retreated to opposite ends on a strange spectrum of grief. My dad spent most of his time in the den, his eyes fixed indifferently on the TV as ESPN played across the enormous flat screen. This wasn't too far off from his usual behavior in his downtime, only now there was a lot more downtime and a lot more beer.

My mom took a more pragmatic approach to coping with devastating loss. My family had acquired our fortune with the help of green money candles and jade rituals for the health of our investment portfolio. Now, my mom had thrown herself full force into the task of maintaining our wealth sans magic. When she wasn't scrolling through Nasdaq reports, she was hurling demands at our investors with the same zeal she used to reserve for coven gatherings. I knew she had real concerns about our financial future. But I also suspected that, without a purpose, my mother would wither away like the trees. For now, her purpose would be this.

I couldn't blame my parents for their flawed coping strategies. Magic was our identity—what made us special, what connected us to the universe. I picked up a teaspoon from the kitchen counter, feeling its cool, smooth surface. I let it hover a few inches above my fingers. It didn't take much concentration. I felt the metal, I felt the air around it, and I just…let the air take it. It was as natural as swimming once you got the hang of it—no, it was more like when you used your feet to push off the side of the pool. You floated, propelled by your own momentum, your face to the sky, cool water rippling in your wake. Magic was that buoyant force surrounding all of us, holding us up. I couldn't imagine what it'd be like to lose that.

I floated the teaspoon down onto the silver tray I'd prepared. It landed neatly beside a china cup filled with steaming chamomile. Then I sliced an apple into wedges like I was preparing a snack for a child home sick from school, though I stopped short of topping them with peanut butter and raisins. I took a breath and climbed the stairs to the study.

I knocked, but there was no response. After a moment of hesitation, I turned the knob.

My mom was hunched over the glow of her laptop, numbers in red and black scrolling across the screen. Her fingernails were round and painted with light pink gel. She'd found the time for a midcrisis manicure.

"Thought you might want a little sustenance," I said in an artificially bright tone, setting the tray down on her desk. The tea sloshed a little, sprinkling the apple slices with amber-colored liquid.

She turned away from her computer and examined the sad spread I'd prepared for her. I took in the tiny red veins in the whites of her eyes, the worry lines around her mouth, no beauty spells to cover them now.

"A little sustenance isn't going to fix this, Valeria," she said. Still, she took a tiny, performative bite from an apple slice. At least I'd seen her eat *something* today.

I realized I had no idea what to say next, but she spoke again.

"You'll have your hands full tonight. You better start getting ready now. Remember your tendency to be late."

"I'm going to figure this out," I told her, my tone as certain as I could make it. "The trees, your powers, all of it."

"I'm sure you will," she replied, but she'd already turned her attention back to her screen, its ever-moving contents casting blue shadows across her face.

Upstairs in my bedroom, I dressed in the flowing red robe as little seeds of anxiety planted themselves in my gut. I strapped the ceremonial dagger to my thigh, and when I could delay no longer, I placed the crown on my head, the cold metal settling evenly on my temples. The robe smelled of my mother, of lavender and campfire smoke. I tugged at the hem of one dramatic bell sleeve, remembering how I'd danced around her bedroom in these clothes as a child. I felt like that child now. A silly girl in someone else's crown.

I didn't have a single clue how to restore our parents' powers. And, if there was someone out there waging attacks on our coven, I didn't know how to protect us. I grabbed the satchel of goodies my mom always used for gatherings, then marched downstairs and out the back door. The harsh magical aura of the forest had mostly dissipated, but seeing the expanse of dead trees still filled me with a sadness of the unmagical variety.

I made out silhouettes moving between the trees, just visible beneath the quickly darkening sky. The others were already there.

Late to lead my first gathering. My mom had been right.

When they heard me approach, they stopped talking, the way kids do when the teacher walks into the room. I absorbed the shock of seeing our coven reduced to its youngest members. Gatherings were only open to those who possessed magic, but even if that wasn't the case, I suspected our parents were too lost in grief to be of much use.

"Okay, guys," I said, my throat dry. "Shall we begin?"

I felt their eyes on me. It was remarkable how quiet the forest was in death. We took our places in a circle within the clearing. I passed candles to each of them and lit them in unison. I spoke the words I'd heard my mother use a hundred times to commence the gathering.

"May success and abundance forever grace this coven."

"Success and abundance," Petra echoed. "Have you guys ever reflected on what a crock of shit that incantation is?" She lit a cigarette off her candle's flame, exhaling smoke into the night air.

"How's everybody's parents holding up?" Max said, ignoring her disregard for tradition.

"Are they as catatonic as ours?" Celeste added.

"My dad barely leaves his office," Jayden said. "And my mom has spent the last three days wandering the house in her bathrobe, crying and drinking sherry from a monogrammed decanter set."

"You gotta respect her flair for the dramatic," Luke said dryly. He shot Jayden a grin, but the expression was more pained than amused.

"How's your dad, Luke?"

It was the first time I'd spoken to him directly since the breakup. That day beneath the Palms felt like ages ago, but the hurt was still fresh. His jaw tensed.

"Not good," he replied. Worry flashed in his eyes.

"Luke." I took a tentative step toward him but stopped, unsure of what to say.

"On the bright side, his obsessive baking has reached record levels," Luke added, that forced smile back on his face. "If anybody wants scones, you know where I live."

Alexis Nichols was known for his baking. His creations were always in high demand at our holiday celebrations—blackberry muffins for Midsummer, spiced ginger cookies at Yule. Mr. Nichols had a wholesome quality that didn't seem compatible with Luke's broodiness, but they loved each other fiercely. They'd had to rely on one another ever since Luke's mom left. Of course Luke was worried about his dad. I fought the desire to lean over and hug him.

"I figure our parents fall into two categories now," Jayden said.

"Those who've totally given up, like my mom, and those who've become obsessed with maintaining their previous levels of success."

"I think you nailed it," I replied, eyeing him. Sometimes Jayden reminded me of my mother, his perfectly moisturized face a mask of indifference, but I was beginning to suspect he was more intuitive about people than he let on.

"Guys, serious question. What does this mean for me? I mean—us?" Celeste corrected herself quickly. "Our parents have no magic, so do we all have to stay here after high school and keep the coven going?"

There was silence as we all considered this. Our ancestors had founded Dorado as a place for our coven to thrive, and it had. We were free to do our magic under the cover of the trees, undetected and undisturbed by the Mundanes. There was nowhere else like it in the Northern Hemisphere. Our parents had always made sure we understood how important it was to keep the coven alive, to keep the coven here in Dorado. We had an understanding: We kids could travel the world, attend prestigious colleges, and pursue our internet startups or influencer empires while our parents held down the fort. But we all agreed we'd someday return to Dorado to carry the magical torch for the next generation. Now we were all that was left of the coven.

"I'd stay," Max said.

"Of course *you* would," said Petra, examining her split ends with interest. "You're, like, the Wiccan Captain America. But I'd prefer a life after high school."

"We won't have to make that choice," I told them. "We're going to get our parents' magic back."

"Now that's the bold leadership I like to see," Jayden replied. "Who's got ideas?"

"What about you?" I said to him. "Do you know of any healing potions that might restore them?"

He kicked a patch of dead leaves with one toe. "Talk to me when they need a pimple popped. This is way beyond anything I can do. Besides, it's not like they're sick."

I felt the others deflate in disappointment.

"I think we have to find out what spell took our parents' powers, so we can…undo it," I said hesitantly.

"Do we know of any magic that can take another witch's power?" Luke asked.

No one did. As we stood there in awkward silence, I realized, for the first time, that there was very little I knew about magic. The universe held energy that we witches could affect, an energy that the Mundanes could not access. We had some control over the elements; we could bend the air to make objects move, summon weather, manipulate the dirt beneath our feet. And of course, fire was a major theme. Outside of that, most of the magic we knew was self-serving.

Our coven had a Book of Shadows, an ancient, leather-bound tome in hard-to-read cursive. I was pretty sure it was in my attic somewhere, covered in an inch or two of dust. Generations ago, our coven had compiled all the spells they considered essential—spells for prosperity, beauty, attraction—and bound them into a new book they'd aptly titled *The Golden Spells*. That was what we used today. My mom even had a PDF of it on her phone.

Those spells had served us well, kept us comfortable. But they were all we knew. Killing trees? Revoking the power from another witch? This went way beyond our comfort zone.

Another unpleasant thought struck me. All our lives, our parents had seemed wise and powerful—the omnipotent adults, able to handle any challenge. But what challenges had they faced, besides a few tax increases? When it came to magic like this, they were just as lost as we were. Without magic, they didn't even have a place to start. It was no wonder they'd retreated to their dens and sherry decanters.

The cold realization sank in at last. We were the coven's only hope.

"Somebody knows what happened," I said, remembering what Petra had said in the forest about the trees being collateral damage. "This wasn't just a magical fluke. Someone set out to take our parents' powers, and the forest was some kind of sacrifice. So we have to consider the possibility—"

"Right," Celeste said. "Which one of you witches did it?"

"No way!" Max shook his head vehemently. "This is some seriously dangerous magic. None of us even know *how* to do something like this. And if we did, we wouldn't. Ever."

"Then who was it?" Luke said. "An outside witch? Because those are pretty scarce."

He was right. Many witch bloodlines had died off. If there was no suitable partner within the coven, our predecessors had had to travel long distances using locator spells to find a magical spouse.

"A locator spell!" I said aloud.

I rummaged through my bag and withdrew a smooth, pale hunk of selenite. I placed it on the ground beneath us as my mother had shown me once during a training session.

"Think of this crystal as our position on a map," I told the others. "Now join hands and concentrate."

They did as I said and we stood in a ring, surrounding the stone.

"Spirit world, hear our plea. We seek any witch who be a stranger to this coven," I said, straining to recall my mother's words. "Let them be seen."

Far from the selenite, a few tiny embers began to burn on the dirt. They glittered like lonely stars, these other witches, far from the outskirts of our galaxy. I sighed in relief.

But as I watched, a flame ignited so close to the stone it threatened to char its cool surface. I heard the others gasp.

"Okay, what the hell?!" Jayden exclaimed.

"There's another witch in Dorado," Max said, his green eyes wide.

"So whoever did this is out here somewhere, watching us?" Celeste gasped. She stepped closer to her brother instinctively, as if ready to hide herself behind his broad shoulders.

"It's all right, Celeste. I'll protect us," I said, hearing how hollow my words sounded.

"Okay, but this witch has already done a superpowerful spell none of us have even heard of, and you can, like, light a bigger-than-average bonfire, so forgive me if I'm not comforted," Celeste said, bitterness mixing with the fear in her voice.

"That's enough!" I replied between clenched teeth.

I held my hands together to keep them from shaking. My first gathering as high priestess was unraveling beyond my control.

"Guys? I think I can help."

It was Petra who spoke. We all turned to look at her, our mouths falling open in unison.

"You know I pick up things from the spirit realm—vibes, whispers. They're annoyingly vague most of the time, but maybe if I listened harder, I could get some answers," she said.

The girl who usually scoffed at her coven responsibilities was stepping up. Perhaps she'd decided to play psychic Sherlock Holmes after all.

"You sure?" I said, hesitating. "Most of the time, your idea of getting spiritual is just you getting drunk in the woods—"

"I can do this." Petra met my gaze with surprising confidence.

"I know you can," Luke cut in, "and it's not like any of us have a better idea." Putting a hand on her shoulder, he added, "Thank you."

And just like that, we had a plan. It hinged on a clairvoyant black sheep with an attitude problem, but it was a plan.

"Welp, better head home and hit the talking board," said Petra, backing away stealthily. "Those spirits aren't gonna contact themselves."

"You mean you're not going to the dance?" said Celeste, appalled.

"Yeah, it's a shame I'll have to miss such a a time-honored high school tradition," she replied, "but duty calls."

"A legitimate excuse to ditch homecoming," said Jayden, eyeing Petra's disappearing form with affection. "It's my girl's lucky night."

"Thank you!" I called after her. Then I turned to the others. "Don't worry, guys. We'll get through this together."

My inspirational message sounded weak, even to me. What did I know about getting through something difficult? I was the witch who summoned a thunderstorm so I didn't have to run the mile in PE.

"Okay," I said, checking the time on my phone. "We better start getting ready. Jayden, Celeste—you guys coming back to my place for the beautification process?"

Jayden surveyed the contents of his vintage shoulder bag. "You best believe I am. I have an arsenal of herbs in here."

"And I brought the citrine," Celeste added, proudly producing a handful of orange crystals like a kid showing us her Halloween candy.

Normally, none of us were into school dances; they were cliché and reeked of Mundane desperation. But the homecoming dance had always coincided with our autumnal equinox festivities, so it had integrated itself into our seasonal traditions. We usually celebrated with a harvest feast, then we'd show up to homecoming fashionably late and enjoy being regular high school kids for a night. It was fun in a winky, ironic kind of way.

Only this year, there would be no harvest feast. No scent of apples roasting in the kitchen. No ceremonial wine spiced with ginger and cloves. But there would still be homecoming. I wasn't going to let the others miss out on that. After all that had happened, they needed something normal.

And if homecoming was a convenient opportunity for Luke to see me in the arms of a cute guy from the soccer team, that was just an added bonus.

The others began to disperse, too, leaving Jayden and Celeste by my side.

"Hey, Luke," I called as he walked away. "See you there?"

He turned back and gave me a half smile. "Sure."

I felt my heart rate quicken. For the first time since the trees died, I allowed myself to feel the full devastation of losing him. The last three days had been the most difficult of my life. I would have given anything for him to hold me just once. To let the grief and the dread melt away for five minutes and allow myself to exist in the comfort of his arms.

"Who's he taking to the dance?" Jayden whispered once he was out of earshot.

"Some boring Mundane, probably," I replied. "Or he's just gonna show up solo with Max."

"Nope, Max is taking Bryce Strawn," Celeste said.

"Bryce Strawn?" Jayden snorted in disgust. "Last year in history class, he thought Paris was in England."

"Well, he asked Max last week. But," she added hopefully, "I'm sure he'd have a lot more fun if he were going with you."

It was a valiant attempt on Celeste's part, but Jayden didn't reply. He'd suddenly become very interested in the satchel of lavender he was holding, It seemed Jayden's attention was always elsewhere when the topic of Max came up. Jayden preferred to date Mundane guys from school—artsy guys, guys in bands, cross-country runners, like the one he was taking to the dance tonight. The only thing they all had in common was the fact that Jayden didn't seem to like them very much.

"I don't get it," I said to him. "Max is kind, handsome, *and* he's a witch. Why won't you give him a chance?"

Jayden was quiet for a long time. "I refuse to date anyone who wears a letterman jacket unironically."

Something told me the letterman jacket had nothing to do with it, but it was clear this was the end of the discussion.

Two HOURS and one serious beauty spell later, Jayden and Celeste left to pick up their dates and I studied my reflection in the full-length mirror. My dress was perfect, a rose-gold nod to the flapper era with strings of glass beads dangling from the fabric like tiny chandeliers. Its hem trailed the floor, but a high slit revealed a significant amount of my bronzed thigh.

The windows were dark, and the house was still. Moments like these reminded me how much I disliked being alone with myself. Alone, there was nothing to distract from the things that scared me. Alone, my insecurities pricked like splinters lodged beneath my skin.

But in the mirror, my eyes sparkled under a fringe of dark lashes. My lips were painted with Reckless Red, my signature scarlet shade, and my hair fell in soft waves. I knew looking like this, I could walk into any room and heads would turn. I could speak and conversations would come to a halt because people would want to listen to me. Beauty is immediate, visceral. It commands a room in a way substance does not.

I still felt the splinters, but the glitter seemed to hide them for now.

Michael Boyd was waiting outside his house when I pulled up behind the wheel of a red 1929 Cadillac convertible. Limos were too conventional; besides, my dress was Art Deco. I might not have bothered for Michael, but I'd booked the car a month ago, back when I thought I'd be riding to the dance with Luke.

Michael got in and shut the passenger door. A huge, boyish smile spread across his face as I backed out of his driveway.

"Wow," he remarked, like the lead in a romance movie. "You look great."

"You too," I replied with a flirty grin. He blushed behind his freckles.

He was benignly handsome in a gray suit and rose-colored bow tie to match my gown. We'd look perfect together at the dance. In my fantasy, Michael and I dance together amidst a crowd of onlookers. Luke can't help but notice us, and something stirs inside his heart—something he thought he'd lost. He asks me if I'd spare a dance for him, for old times' sake, and I smile and tell him, *Just one.* I wouldn't want to be rude to my date. But as we begin to sway together, that reawakened feeling takes over. Luke pulls me close, and we kiss beneath the twirling lights of the disco ball.

The sound of pop beats shook me back to reality as I pulled into the school parking lot. The dance was always held in our gym. The idea of partying atop painted-on free-throw lines made the whole night feel extra cheesy, but again—tradition.

I parked the convertible along the loading zone and stepped out, the slit in my glittering dress riding up my outstretched leg. Several dozen kids were milling around outside the entrance, and a little hush fell over them as I exited the car. Michael came around the hood to take my hand. He even opened the door for me as we entered the booming gym.

The interior was as perfectly tacky, as I'd imagined. Shiny

helium balloons, streamers, and yes, a disco ball spinning overhead. Still, I loved the way the bass pounded in my chest like a heartbeat, filling me with a sense that something incredible was about to happen.

Jayden and Celeste were already on the dance floor with their dates. The beauty spell clung to them like a cloud of expensive perfume. Jayden wore a perfectly tailored burgundy suit and matching cape that made every other guy's Men's Wearhouse attire seem painfully boring. His always-striking cheekbones looked like they'd been carved by a renaissance master. Celeste was more angelic than ever, her waves of long blond hair floating around her face as she danced. I noted her date's smooth, decidedly un-scalded skin, and I was grateful she hadn't made a second attempt at that love spell.

I allowed Michael to guide me through the crowd of dancing couples to a spot in the center of the gym. He put his arms around my waist as a slow song came on. It was a cinematic moment, the part where we kiss as the music swells—but all I could do was scan the crowd for Luke. I danced Michael slowly in a circle until I could see the other side of the gym. My heart leapt with that sweet half panic only Luke could produce.

He was standing alone, beyond a group of laughing juniors. He'd ditched the leather jacket for a well-fitted suit, no tie. The top button of his shirt was undone, which would have looked silly on most guys, but on him it was surprisingly sexy.

Michael and I were right in Luke's line of sight. I leaned closer to Michael, lifting one hand to brush the stubble on his cheek. He grinned, adorable dimples appearing on his face. His arms tightened around my waist. My gaze traveled subtly back to Luke. He was looking at me, and for the first time since the trees died, I saw him really smile.

No, I realized. He was looking *past* me, his eyes locked on someone in the distance. I swiveled to see who it was, not caring if Michael noticed.

A girl in a black lace dress was making her way through the crowd toward Luke. She held her head proudly, her long black hair tumbling behind her as she walked. She was tall and thin, her skin so pale it seemed to glow in the dim light of the dance floor. I had always assumed her body was weak and unsubstantial beneath all those layers of baggy clothing, but now I could see the strength in her arms, the lean muscles in her calves as she negotiated the floor in a pair of black heels. Her dress was fitted to her narrow waist, the neckline plunging to reveal a deep V of white skin.

I'd stopped dancing by now. My feet frozen in place, I stared.

I was pretty sure she wasn't wearing an ounce of makeup. Her features were severe, all sharp angles with dark eyes and full brows. There was something otherworldly about her face that I wasn't sure I could interpret as beautiful, but it was certainly interesting. Her eyes flashed like obsidian under the lights. Her hair was longer than I'd expected. For years, she'd worn it tied in a messy bun or hidden beneath an old hoodie. Now, it fell almost to her waist, the way it had in the forest.

She'd spent so much time hiding, her eyes on the ground as she walked the halls at school or hidden behind a book's cover. She'd been willing the world not to notice her, but now here she was, striding confidently through a crowded room in delicate lace. This wasn't the cliché where the shy girl takes off her glasses and she's suddenly hot—it was like the shy girl had spent seven days alone in the desert and come back changed. Same body, different spirit. She wasn't hiding anymore.

Gwen Foster blew past me without so much as a glance in my direction. Luke kept his eyes on her as she drew closer. When she reached him, he embraced her before taking a step back to admire her dress. He leaned in and they spoke for a while, his lips moving next to her ear. He must have been saying the right things because her pale face lit up like the full moon on a dark night.

The slow song ended, replaced by a synth-pop beat. Luke offered his hand to Gwen, and they walked onto the dance floor.

Suddenly, I became aware that Michael was staring too. It seemed half the gym had stopped what they were doing to watch Luke Nichols and Gwen Foster. If the pair noticed, they didn't let on. Their eyes were on each other, locked with *Pulp Fiction*-like intensity.

Gwen didn't seem to know any typical dance moves, but she moved to the music with a peculiar grace, as if she might start floating a few inches above the floor at any moment. Luke twisted his body toward hers, one of her hands ran through his thick, dark hair.

"Ha!" I let out an audible cackle. It was an involuntary reaction, as if the absurdity of my life had just reached some new, unsustainable level.

But no one else was laughing. I watched as Luke pulled Gwen close and kissed her beneath the spinning lights of the disco ball.

CHAPTER FIVE

GWEN

For eighteen years, I stayed invisible. I told myself things were better that way; I thought I understood the universe and my position in it. Then a bunch of candles in my bedroom ignited by themselves, all the trees in the forest died, and I asked Luke Nichols to homecoming.

As I entered the busy gym, searching for Luke, I wasn't sure what was craziest—the candles, trees, or my current situation. Perhaps the candles had been the first sign of a psychotic break and now I was experiencing a full-blown hallucination. A few days earlier, that would have seemed like the most plausible explanation to me. But ever since I'd dreamed of that meteor, my existence had felt inexplicably and strikingly different. It was like an alien force had taken hold inside me.

No, it was more like something strange and powerful had come home to me at long last. Something I'd been missing all my life.

I spent a full day mourning the forest. I sat at the river's edge, staring at the dead trees on the other side, tears streaming down my cheeks. But even as I cried, I felt an unfamiliar strength inside me, making me bold, restless. I asked Luke to the dance the next day.

I found him outside the English building between classes, his hands in his pockets and a far-off look on his face. Before I could think, I heard myself speak.

"Hey, there's a dance on Saturday. I've never been to one of those, and I'd like to go with you."

His eyes went wide with surprise, but a hesitant, almost shy smile crept across his face.

"You know what? I'd be honored," he said.

"You would?"

"Yeah." He seemed amused by my disbelief, but his eyes grew distant. "You couldn't have asked at a better time. I've…had a really weird week."

I was silent a moment.

"Me too," I replied.

And that was that. Now here I was, walking across the dance floor toward Luke Nichols, my homecoming date.

Normally, crowds and loud music filled me with the kind of anxiety that made me want to retreat somewhere quiet with a well-loved book. But tonight, the pulsating bass and buzz of activity didn't bother me. In fact, it was kind of exciting. The gym looked beautiful at night, a dark sea of lights and moving bodies. I weaved between groups of dancing kids, Luke holding me in his gaze all the while.

As I drew closer, I noticed the other kids watching me, too, hundreds of eyes taking in my new look, scrutinizing me down to the freckles on my bare limbs. I wasn't afraid. Why wasn't I afraid? I lifted my face to the disco ball, imagining it as a twirling moon in a dark, peaceful sky. Then Luke was right in front of me.

He embraced me. I breathed in the scent of pine and leather.

"You look beautiful," he said.

Beautiful. The word echoed in my head in Luke's deep voice. Beauty was a prize other girls competed to claim, vying against each other like players on some vast, uneven field. I'd decided long ago I wouldn't even join the game. As a child, I'd never cared about those things, but as I grew older, I became aware of the flatness of my chest, the boney, inward turn of my knees, the way my hair refused to tame. And I became aware that those features were bad. They drew snide whispers from the other girls, jeers from boys on the playground. My solution had been to disappear, to shrink into nothing until I could be alone again at the end of the day.

Luke stepped away and held me at arm's length. "Great dress!"

A hint of shame tugged at my insides. After I had asked him to the dance, as the rush of adrenaline faded, I'd realized with a little jolt of panic that I didn't own any clothes appropriate for a night like this.

"Hope you're cool with me showing up in jeans and a T-shirt," I'd told him, throwing in an unconvincing laugh, like it was no big deal.

He hadn't laughed with me. Instead, his expression had grown serious. The next day, I'd found an envelope in my locker—it was gold, made of heavy paper. Inside was a money clip holding five crisp hundred-dollar bills. Luke's surprisingly neat penmanship decorated the card. It read: *In case jeans and a T-shirt weren't your first choice.*

I'd taken the money. If this had happened a week ago, I probably would have given it back to him, pressing it wordlessly into his palm. Then I would have slunk away, my cheeks burning in humiliation, and avoided him for the rest of my life. But whatever had awoken inside me didn't want to do any of that.

A little bell had jingled as I entered Larkspur Couture on Main Street. I'd killed time in there before on one of the lonely evenings when my dad's poker game had driven me from the house with clouds of smoke and drunken laughter. Only this time, I hadn't come here to escape. I was here to shop.

I'd circled the store, feeling the different materials between my fingers—smooth satin, heavy velvets, beaded lace. Lost in a sea of possibilities, I'd pulled something with blue sequins off the rack.

"Hey, can I try this on?" I'd asked the shop clerk.

She'd approached me cautiously, her rigid bun drawing her features tight. Her eyes had traveled down to my dirty sneakers, the frayed hem of my jeans.

"I'm sorry, um, miss," she'd said with forced congeniality. "I've seen you in here before. Our fitting rooms are for paying customers only. I'm sure you understand."

I understood perfectly. I could afford a dress now, and I had a date to homecoming, but for a moment, none of that mattered. This woman had seen who I really was, and it was her duty to remind me. I knew this could be my *Pretty Woman* moment. I could have waved Luke's money in her face as I walked out of her store, declaring, "Big mistake. Big. Huge!" but I didn't. I'd simply shuffled away, eager to put the whole exchange out of my mind.

At the next dress shop, I'd grabbed the first black dress I could find and marched into the dressing room. It was perfect. I loved the delicate pattern of the lace—the long, slender silhouette. I didn't look like a little girl trying on dress-up clothes. Instead, gazing in the mirror, I felt this was how I was *supposed* to look: serene and strong, wrapped in the color of the night sky.

I'd heard a knock on the dressing room door.

"I'll take it!" I'd cried before the woman on the other side had a chance to speak.

Now I watched as Luke admired the slender straps on my shoulders, the thin satin trim at my waist.

"You know"—he smiled—"I never got the chance to tell you I loved your poem. I only have one critique."

My heart threatened to beat out of my chest. The bass pounded and he leaned closer, putting one hand on my arm.

"Who says the moon is the sun's lesser sister? Some of us like the night."

The people and lights seemed to blur in my periphery until my whole world was his eyes, his touch on my bare arm.

"You wanna dance?" I asked.

He offered me his hand, and we began to step into the throng of gyrating bodies. For a terrifying moment, my breath caught in my throat. What did I think I was doing?

"Wait." I tugged at his arm. "I forgot. I don't know how to dance."

"So?"

"So people are gonna do that thing where they point at me and laugh. It's kind of the story of my life, in case you haven't noticed."

"Screw 'em," he replied, and his smile was contagious.

As he led me onto the floor, I scanned the rafters for the inevitable bucket of pigs' blood. But I found only streamers, suspended like vines in a disco jungle. *Screw 'em.*

I let the music fill my body. I felt it beat out of my pores, my skin vibrating in time with the speakers. And then I started to move. Luke fell in sync with me immediately, as if he knew how to anticipate my every step and shift. We danced closer.

It was amazing not to think. To be free of the relentless stream of worries that play in my mind like a grim news ticker—my dad passed out in front of the TV, the bills on the kitchen table, the empty feeling that tugged at me in the middle of the night, keeping me from sleep. All gone. Nothing was left but the music and darkness and flashes of Luke's blue eyes. Was it possible, I wondered, to live without those burdens? As the lights twirled around me, I had the sense that as long as I was with him, perhaps it was.

As if he'd read my mind, Luke pulled me to him, and his lips met mine.

In the middle of a crowded dance floor, Luke Nichols was kissing me. The music had been blaring, but I swear it went silent. All I heard was the rush of blood in my ears, the beating of my heart. Luke brought one hand to the back of my neck, his fingers entangled in my hair. My eyes were shut, but in the blackness, I saw the white-hot glow of a meteor burning in the distance—the image from my dream. There it was, behind my eyelids, that bright orb of destruction. Maybe I was having a mental breakdown after all. I didn't care. I didn't want it to end.

The song faded out, and somehow, we drew away from each other. That's when I realized everyone was staring at us. I tried to regain that I-don't-give-a-damn attitude I'd begun to master these past few days, but after such an intense moment, it was beyond my reach. A wave of embarrassment washed over me, and I wondered if they were asking themselves how much I'd paid Luke to go to this dance with me. Then I spotted Valeria Garcia.

I'd never seen a look of pure rage come to rest on such a pretty face. The result was frightening. Before I knew what was happening, she was marching over to us, her dress shimmering with every angry step she took. Her date—a tall, dumb guy from my physics class—stood motionless, unable to look away. In fact, it seemed everyone at the dance had become the audience to our little drama.

Her beauty was more intimidating than usual tonight. Looking at her was like undergoing a strange hypnosis, one that caused me to doubt myself. How silly I must've appeared next to her. I imagined she could hold a hand out to Luke right now, and he'd take it and follow her anywhere. I took a deep breath and tried to stand up a little straighter.

She didn't falter for a second. She raised one finger at me, and I wasn't sure if she was about to gesticulate or poke my eye out with her long red fingernail.

"You and I need to talk. In private," she said, her voice calm, barely above a whisper.

Of course. She wouldn't want there to be any witnesses to my murder. As scary as Valeria Garcia was, the new strength inside of me made me reckless.

"Okay," I replied with a halfway-convincing shrug. "Sure."

She seemed surprised at how easily I'd agreed. But she replied gruffly, "Come with me."

"Wait," Luke called to me. "You don't have to do this."

I turned to him. The flashing lights silhouetted his face, and suddenly, I didn't care about Valeria or the throngs of staring kids. I wanted to take him away from this place, deep into the forest as it used to be, and live with him there, alone and wild among the trees. I exhaled.

"It's all right," I told him over the sound of my pounding heart. "I'll be right back."

Why did those sound like famous last words? I followed Valeria out the gym's back exit and onto the quad. She led me over the path and up the steps to the old science building.

A brilliant waxing moon hung above our heads. Insects chirped and hummed, the sound bringing a peaceful rhythm back to my anxious breaths. Whenever things were at their worst, I'd tell myself, *I'll always have the night. No matter what else comes and goes in my chaotic life. No matter what gets taken away from me.* I thought of Luke, of his worried expression as I'd glanced at him over my shoulder. I didn't want him to be one of the things that came and went, that got taken away.

We stopped beneath a pair of palm trees at the top of the steps. Drops of dew clung to my ankles. My high heels squished into the damp earth.

"You and Luke broke up," I said to her. "It's all over school. So it's not like I—"

"Why him, Gwen?" Valeria said without looking at me. "You could have gone with anybody. Okay, maybe you couldn't have gone with *anybody*, but you probably could have found some weirdo who was willing to date you. So—why Luke? Is this your idea of revenge for all the times I picked on you when we were kids?"

"You picked on me last week," I corrected, "but no. For one second, consider the possibility that not everything's about you."

"Oh!" she cried, like she'd just solved a puzzle. Laughter escaped her lips. "That poem was about him, wasn't it? You've been harboring some secret crush on him!"

I didn't answer. I didn't need to.

She laughed some more, wiping at the corners of her eyes. "Wow," she said. "I've had a really weird week."

"Me too," I replied.

We stood in silence a minute, and I wondered if our talk was over, but of course it wasn't. Only a fool would believe Valeria Garcia could give up that easily.

In the distance, I made out figures moving across the quad toward us—Luke, followed by Celeste, Max, and Jayden. I supposed Luke had decided to make sure I was still alive, and the others had come to see the show. Valeria saw them, too, but she didn't seem to care. She smiled that terrifying smile at me. Now there was a fire behind her eyes that hadn't been there before. I took a step back without meaning to.

"Let me explain this to you," she said in a harsh whisper. "There are things you do not understand. You couldn't possibly. Just believe me when I say he will never love you. You're not his…type. Sooner or later, he will see that, and *he will leave you.*"

I thought I heard her voice waver on those last words, and I realized how much pain she still held in her heart for him.

"So," she went on, the control returning to her tone, "do yourself a favor and forget about this strange little romance."

Her eyes burned with self-righteous anger. I'd come out here convinced I was through being afraid of her. Now I wasn't so sure. The old me would have run all the way home by now. What would this new version do? I stared back at her defiantly, anger pulsing through my veins. I felt something else rise inside me, too—a cold heat from deep within. It seemed to hum through my limbs, pricking at my fingertips.

"And what happens if I don't?" I asked. "What happens if, for once in your life, Valeria, you don't get what you want?"

She took a step toward me. For a second, I thought she was going to hit me. Instead, she just stood there, but her eyes changed somehow. I could have sworn I saw a flame flicker behind them as the blackness of her pupils grew.

"Valeria!" I heard Luke call.

He and the others stood at the top of the stairs, watching us. She ignored them. Power radiated off her like heat from a bonfire. She didn't seem to realize I could sense it. Her eyes stayed locked on me in her best intimidating stare, but suddenly, I knew it was the same invisible heat that had wrapped itself around my ankle that day in the quad. With perfect clarity, I understood Valeria was doing this somehow.

No. Whatever this was, she would not use it against me again. The crackling sensation at my fingertips was stronger now, buzzing like a live wire. Her eyes bore into mine with pleasure.

"Get back!" I cried, and as I did, something impossible happened.

I felt the power that had been building inside me crash forward into the night. A silvery light exploded from my fingers, striking Valeria, knocking her to the ground. It glowed in the darkness, as pale and brilliant as the moon, before fading into black. I stood over her, my breaths ragged, my knees weak.

"What—the actual—" Jayden began.

"She's a witch!" Celeste cried.

"She's one of us," Max breathed in disbelief.

"Gwen?" Luke took a step toward me, then stopped as if at a loss for what to do next.

"She can't be!" Valeria's voice was hoarse as she struggled to her feet, grass clinging to the beads of her evening gown. "I would have known! She would have told me back when we—"

She didn't finish, but I knew what she was going to say. *Back when we were friends.*

"What? No! I didn't used to be able to do—whatever that was," I cried, my head spinning. I added, "I mean, I *can't* do whatever that was."

Luke withdrew a match from his pocket and handed it to me. Numbly, I took it. His eyes were wide. I noticed he stood at arm's length as he handed me the match, keeping a safe distance between us as if I were a coiled rattlesnake.

"Light it," he said.

I looked around for something to strike it on.

"No. Tell it to light."

I stared at the head of the match in my hand. The burst of light I'd created before had been involuntary, born out of some primal combination of fear and anger. This new task seemed impossible.

"I can't," I said, holding the match helplessly.

Luke raised an eyebrow. "You said you couldn't dance either."

My heart raced. My limbs felt alive with electricity. That white heat passed through me, less intense now. The tip of the match between my fingers ignited in a phosphorescent burst. The fire wasn't orange the way it usually appeared on the head of a match; instead, it burned silver. I stared into it, and it felt like a part of me, something I'd created. I heard the others talking, some shouting, but their chatter was background noise, like when you fall asleep with the TV on. The only thing that mattered was that silver flame.

For the first time, I understood the mysterious feeling that had been with me ever since I had that dream. It was as if something had come home to me. A strength. A power I had been missing before.

Celeste's declaration rang in my ears. *She's a witch!* It sounded truer by the second.

I pulled my gaze away from the match and looked at them. They were all staring, utter disbelief on their faces. Suddenly, I recalled Max's words. *She's one of us!*

I thought of the fiery strength that had pushed against me and the way it radiated with Valeria's anger. She was a witch too. They all were. Even Luke.

"Ow!"

The flame had burnt down the matchstick to my fingertips. I dropped it into the damp grass. There were too many eyes on me, eyes of people I did not trust. Luke looked from me to the others helplessly, but I backed away. I put one foot behind the other until, at last, I turned and ran.

I left them all behind me, my legs pumping, my high heels abandoned in the grass. I'd never run so far in my life, but I barely felt the pain. I didn't stop until I was halfway down the dirt road, my modest house silhouetted in the distance.

I stumbled into my kitchen exhausted but mercifully alone. I dug in the counter drawers until I found what I was looking for: a crumpled book of matches my dad had grabbed from the local dive bar.

I went to my bedroom and opened the window, inviting in the moonlight and the cool breeze. Not bothering to turn on the light, I sat on the edge of my bed and pulled a match from the book. Pressing its paper stem between my fingers, I willed it to light. For a moment, nothing happened. Then—

Whoosh. A silvery flame shot up into existence.

That night, I sat in the dark, lighting match after match, letting each one burn down to my fingertips until the book was empty and a smoldering pile of ashes lay at my feet.

CHAPTER SIX

VALERIA

Morning broke through my bedroom window, filling the room with pale light. Finally. I'd been up awaiting the sun for hours. My mind churned with a dozen competing thoughts like eddies in the river after a storm.

In the hazy, predawn hours, I'd almost convinced myself last night had been a vivid nightmare. But as I sat up in bed, gazing at the barren forest outside my window, I could feel the tender spot where Gwen's spell had hit my sternum. In the mirror on the wall, I made out the beginnings of a bruise that would be purple by midday.

Gwen Foster was a witch. Gwen Foster was that bright, flickering flame we'd seen in the locator spell, threatening to engulf our coven's little stone. It should've been impossible. Our power was in our blood, ancient and sacred, passed down through generations. Gwen's family had no magic. It was as if she'd just woken up with it. I couldn't wrap my mind around the how, the when, or the intense irony.

And I was baffled by the magic she'd used against me. As far as I knew, sunfire was the only spell that could strike someone down with a column of flames, but Gwen's fire wasn't bright orange like mine. It was silver—a pale, nocturnal brilliance.

I dragged myself out of bed and descended the great staircase. The grandfather clock struck seven as I passed the dining room. I paused to stare at it towering in its shadowy corner. The clock had belonged to Delfina Garcia herself. Like so many things in the Garcia house, its surface was inlaid with a smiling, gilded sun. Above the sun, little clusters of stars adorned the wood. Once, Luke had taught me the names for those stars and the constellations they made. I went to the clock and touched them with a gentle fingertip. Virgo, Libra, Cassiopeia. When Luke had shown me, his hands on top of mine as we'd traced the smooth wood, that sun's smile had seemed warm, inviting. Today, there was something smug about its laughing face, as if it understood perfectly well the poetic justice of last night's events.

I turned away from the clock indignantly and stumbled to the kitchen in pursuit of coffee. While the French press steeped, I opened Instagram. I'd posted a photo of me and Michael Boyd before the dance. My red lipstick shimmered; my hair lay perfectly over my beaded gown. How much simpler things had been a mere twelve hours ago. I scanned the comments. It seemed I wasn't the only member of the student body trying to process what happened at the dance.

Cute pic, but who saw Luke Nichols with Gwen Foster?

Strangest couple ever, but I'm kind of here for it. Does this mean beauty is out and weird is in?

Yes, please! Gwen had a #glowup

I put the phone down on the kitchen table with a bang, bitterness settling in my stomach. Luke and I understood each other's loneliness, if nothing else. When he dumped me, it had killed me to know he'd rather be alone than with me. Now, he'd rather be with *Gwen Foster.* This was a new ring of hell I was completely unprepared for.

I hated Gwen for everything that happened last night. For her fingers in Luke's hair. For her mouth on his. For the silver flash in her dark eyes as she lit that match with her power. But a secret part of me remembered Gwen as she'd been when the forest was ours: scabs on her bony knees, the two of us laughing as she boosted me up the trunk of a young evergreen. In those days, she was so wild and unafraid that it had made me believe I could be that way too. In all the years that followed, I'd never had another friend like her. Perhaps I'd never had another friend at all.

Footsteps on the stairs jolted me from the bleakness of my thoughts. My mom appeared in the kitchen.

"You're up early," she said. "Didn't you have a dance last night?"

"Yeah, I just…couldn't sleep." I poured a cup of coffee and retreated to the end of the kitchen table.

She would find out about Gwen's little magic show soon enough. Word traveled fast through our coven. But as she stood in the kitchen, silk robe cinched at her waist, dark circles beneath her eyes, I decided she wouldn't hear it from me. I couldn't deal with the barrage of questions that would follow, questions I didn't know how to answer. But maybe she could answer one for me.

"Mom?" I began as casually as I could. "Have you ever heard of a spell that makes silver flames?"

She turned to me curiously as she poured the remainder of the coffee into her favorite red mug.

"Moonfire," she said. "It's a defensive spell like ours and just as rare. The source of its power is the moon, rather than the sun."

"Our ancestors got pretty creative when they named these spells, didn't they?" I replied.

She shrugged weakly, uninterested in my sarcasm this early in the morning. Or ever, really.

"So," I went on, my pulse quickening just a little, "if you have moonfire, does that make you a protector like us?"

"It could. It's a powerful spell for a powerful witch. But we've never had any families with moonfire in our coven"—she paused a moment, her eyes on the trees outside the window—"as far as I know." I could see impatience gathering in her brow. "Valeria, I have to leave to meet an investor in"—she checked her Rolex—

"twenty-eight minutes. Is there a reason for this line of questioning?"

My phone buzzed. A message from Petra appeared on the screen. I have news from the great beyond. You can thank me in person.

I stood, practically tipping over my chair.

"No reason, Mom. Gotta go!"

I grabbed my shoes and headed to the door, leaving her standing there with a look of perplexed irritation on her face.

Petra's house wasn't a far walk through the forest. I went out the back door. My garden's short green grass and landscaped azalea bushes were as vibrant as ever, but the dead tree line loomed before me. I had the weird urge to hold my breath as I stepped into the crooked shadows of a hundred bare branches. I was pretty sure I'd never get used to seeing the forest like this. The silence seemed to press in around me. I kept my head down and walked west until Petra's house appeared through the trees.

Her garden was less contained than mine, a mess of rock and vines. In the center of that natural disarray sat Petra, eyes closed, an old wooden talking board in front of her. Her fingers, decorated with chipped blue polish, hovered above the planchette. She exhaled and the planchette began to glide over the ancient carved letters.

My toe caught on a loose stone, and I stumbled forward, twigs cracking beneath my feet. Her eyes fluttered open.

"You can't resist making an entrance, can you?" she said with a wry smile.

"Did I ruin your concentration?"

She shrugged. "They were getting sick of me anyway."

I pointed to the talking board. "Who are you communicating with?"

"Spiiiiirits from beyond the veil," she replied like the narrator in some low-budget horror movie. Then she grew serious. "I think they're our ancestors, like, the coven members who came before us. This bad stuff that's going down—it's old."

"Old?"

"Yeah, it's a whole feeling I'm getting. This thing goes way back to the coven's early days."

"So did you ask these spirits what the hell is going on?" I said impatiently.

She looked at me as if I'd just asked for a Top 40 album at her favorite indie record store.

"Specific questions are way too needy. It pisses them off. You just have to"—she closed her eyes again—"let them know you're here and you're open. It's like those damn spirits have all the knowledge, but all they'll give the living are crumbs. Vague, maddening crumbs."

"Oka-a-y," I said. "And what crumbs did you pick up?"

"Malevolent magic," she said. "That's the type of magic that took our parents' power."

"Malevolent magic," I repeated.

"It's bad. You know how we draw power from different natural elements, crystals, herbs, the *sun*?" She pointed at me like I was exhibit A. "Well, malevolent magic doesn't come from anything in nature. It comes from anger, hate, jealousy—all the harmful stuff we keep inside."

An old fountain stood in the center of Petra's garden, water cascading over its crumbling tiers. I raised a nervous hand and pulled a water droplet to my palm, letting it float above my fingers.

"Sounds lovely. What else?"

"That's all I got on malevolent magic and you should be grateful, 'cause it wasn't easy. Now, moving on to Gwen Foster—"

"So you've heard."

"Yeah, Jayden called me and relayed the whole story last night. I never thought I'd regret skipping a high school dance, but I stand corrected," she said. "Okay, brace yourself because I have a bombshell and I cannot wait to drop it. Last night, when I found out about Gwen's sudden powers, I jumped back on the talking board— you know, to put the WTF vibes out there. Well, over and over, the talking board kept spelling MIDSUMMER."

"What's Midsummer got to do with anything?"

"I couldn't figure it out either. Then I remembered there's this book, a Shakespeare play in my parents' study. *A Midsummer Night's Dream.* This thing is old—like, it's probably been sitting on that shelf since the dawn of time."

"Since the coven's early days," I said, flicking the water droplet into the grass at my feet.

"Yup. I opened it and I found a letter tucked into the pages. Some Victorian predecessor of mine must have used it as a bookmark."

From her back pocket, she withdrew a yellowed piece of paper and handed it to me. Deep creases ran across the page as if it had spent a century folded somewhere dark and quiet. I began to scan the flowery, ink-spotted script.

"It was written by my great-great-great-great grandmother, Mary Sarich, in 1880, twenty years after our coven founded Dorado. It's mostly about her boring trip to San Francisco. Probably took her like three weeks to get there via covered wagon. But look."

She rose to stand beside me and pointed to a faded paragraph. I took a breath and read.

I passed a woman in the street yesterday. She was destitute and mad. She made me think of poor Elizabeth Foster, whose power was revoked by our coven many years past. Elizabeth walks the streets in town like a mad woman, weeping and speaking aloud to no one. I can imagine no greater shame that could befall a witch. I fear all her children and her children's children will be destined to endure lives of equal misery, for it is truly against nature for those with witches' blood to live deprived of their powers.

I pulled my finger away from the page as if it had burned me.

"What—?" I began, but I had no words to finish the question.

"Get it? Gwen Foster is descended from Elizabeth Foster," Petra said. "She's descended from witches."

I gave her a cold stare. "I think I'm getting it."

"Our coven took Elizabeth's powers!" Petra announced, flinging the hair from her face triumphantly.

I'd seen Gwen's dad around town dozens of times. There was an emptiness in his wide, strung-out eyes. It was the same emptiness I could make out in my parents' eyes ever since they'd lost their powers. The Fosters had been tragic, miserable people for as long as anyone in town could remember.

"That's why her family's always had a few screws loose," I concluded aloud.

"Can you blame them?" she replied. "Ever since they lost their magic, it's like this piece of them has been missing. They forgot what it was generations ago, but they never stopped missing it."

My mind reeled. It was barely eight in the morning, and somehow, the mysteries surrounding Gwen had grown even more confounding.

"Why did the coven revoke Elizabeth's powers? There must have been a reason."

"It doesn't say. I've read the letter front to back. This is the only mention of the Fosters. But"—Petra's expression grew distant—"there's another letter we need to find. When I was on the talking board last night, this image kept appearing to me. Old yellowing paper covered in inky cursive. I think it's a love letter."

"A love letter?" I said skeptically.

"Yup. That's the energy I got from it. And I could sense its importance. I think it holds a lot of the answers we're after."

"Great," I said, leaning forward intently. "Where is it?"

She looked away, suddenly embarrassed. "I don't know. It might not even exist anymore. It might…have burned a long time ago."

"What?"

"When I saw it in my mind it was on fire, okay?"

"Oh," I replied, a hint of my mother's trademarked disapproval in my tone. "Isn't that helpful."

I wondered at this letter between lovers, its pages engulfed in flames. But there was already too much to puzzle over. My mind quickly jumped back to suspicion.

To Gwen.

"Our parents lose their powers and Gwen becomes a witch overnight? The timing is questionable." I pulled another drop from the fountain, letting it swirl uneasily above my palm. "She must have taken their magic. Some kind of spell or ritual to get powers for herself."

The thought had been rattling around in my head all morning, even before this new revelation. It felt good to say it out loud.

"Did you hear anything I said a minute ago?" Petra protested. "Malevolent magic took our parents' powers. So unless that silver flame thing she did last night is malevolent magic…"

"It's not," I replied, a little disappointed. "It's called moonfire."

"Cool," she said. "Like your thing, but with the moon."

I glared at her. "Yup, like my thing."

"Okay, so if Gwen didn't have magic to begin with, how'd she do a spell to get it?" Petra said, raising a brow beneath her shaggy bangs.

"I don't know! But it's the most logical possibility."

"The universe is full of possibilities," she replied. "Maybe she did it without even realizing it. Maybe she made a wish on a cursed dandelion or something."

I rolled my eyes. "Somebody chopped that tree down in the forest. You saw the leftovers of the ritual yourself. It had to be her."

Even as I said the words, I felt doubt tug at my insides. I'd seen the look of surprise on Gwen's face when those silver flames shot from her fingers.

"Fine," I admitted, irritation rising in my voice. "*Maybe* there's a chance she didn't know about her powers, but that doesn't make her any less dangerous."

"And this suspicion of yours has nothing to do with the fact that Gwen made out with your ex last night?"

Of course it did. As I'd lain in bed in that dark, predawn delirium, it wasn't the thought of Gwen's magic that kept me awake. It was the image of Luke as they danced, his face alight with a happiness I'd never seen before, his eyes on Gwen like he'd finally found something precious. Luke never looked at me that way.

"This has nothing to do with…who she chooses to date. I just don't trust her. She spends years moping around school, avoiding everyone in her path. She could have been planning this the whole time."

"So you think she had a two-part plan? Do some seriously evil magic, then throw on a pretty dress and go to a dance with your man?"

"The dress was not pretty," I corrected. "And her hair was a mess. Don't listen to the hype. Her makeover was unimpressive."

"From what I hear, Luke was impressed."

I shot the floating water drop right at Petra's forehead. She wiped it away with an unbothered grin.

"Luke hasn't been thinking clearly lately," I sneered. "He breaks up with the hottest girl in school, and now he's into a gangly, flat-chested weirdo?"

"Val—" Petra tried to interrupt.

"Who wears black to homecoming?" I went on, ignoring her. "She looked like she was going to a funeral."

"Val—"

"And who wears open-toe shoes with *no pedicure*?!" I hurled the question at her with righteous indignation.

"Valeria, shut up!" Petra threw her hands in the air as if she'd just flipped an invisible table. "I don't care about her hair, or her boobs, or her toes! Maybe if you spent less time on your petty rivalry and more time worrying about the coven—"

She looked away, unwilling to finish her thought.

I opened my mouth to speak, then closed it again. My cheeks were hot.

"Listen, all I'm saying is maybe Gwen isn't your enemy. There are far bigger foes in this world than the girl who stole your boyfriend."

"She didn't steal him." I swallowed, my throat squeezing tight around the sobs that wanted to come. I felt stupid and mean and alone.

"Aw, come on. I was only hard on you 'cause you deserved it. You wanna talk about it and braid each other's hair or something?" Petra said, patting the grass beside her.

"No."

"Thank god," she sighed.

The sky was getting bluer overhead. The fountain bubbled a

peaceful song. From her back pocket, she withdrew a crumpled pack of cigarettes and lit one with a silver Zippo.

I sat down next to her, my legs crossed.

"Why do you smoke those when you know they'll kill you?" I asked. There was no judgment in my question, only curiosity.

She gave me a strange little shrug. "Life is short," she replied. "Some lives are, anyway."

"What's that supposed to mean?"

"I don't know. Just more crumbs."

She leaned back on her elbows as she exhaled. Her hair fell away from her brow, and for once, I saw her eyes clearly. They were gray in the morning sunlight. She looked fragile like this, her vulnerability laid bare.

Despite myself, I recalled the vow I'd made the morning after I'd tormented Gwen on the quad. I'd sworn I would treat her better, show her compassion. Part of me still wanted to honor that promise. But everything was different now. Gwen wasn't my innocent victim any longer. Perhaps she never had been.

"What am I gonna do?"

The question wasn't directed at Petra, but she flicked some ash into the grass and said, "Try not being a dick."

The sound of crunching leaves broke the silence and Jayden emerged from the forest, a startled look on his face.

"Jayden?" I said in surprise. "What are you doing here?"

He held up a metallic thermos with one purple-nailed hand. "On Saturday mornings, me and Petra drink elderflower tea and gossip about everyone. What are you doing here?"

I rose to my feet suddenly. "I was just leaving."

"Hey, don't go. I thought we were having a moment!" Petra protested.

"There's another moment I need to have," I replied. "And believe me, I'm not looking forward to it."

A few minutes later, I was trudging back through the forest, hundreds of dry pine needles crunching beneath my feet. The tears that had threatened to fall in Petra's garden had retreated, but her words rang in my head, mingling with the myriad of conflicting thoughts already bouncing around in there. I couldn't bring myself to trust Gwen now, but I had to admit—the girl I'd known in the forest had been immensely kind. I walked on, my steps quickening until Luke's house appeared.

Luke's house was a rambling, white, ivy-covered structure. The ivy, like the rest of the house, seemed to wind itself around a central tower, topped with a dome-shaped observatory. Yes, an observatory. The Nichols family's particular magical talents lay in astrology. It wasn't the kind of astrology you'd find in the back of gossip magazines. Luke loved the stars; he recognized the constellations like old friends. And sometimes he saw things in the night sky—things that had yet to happen.

Last year, not long after our midnight trip to the coast, he strolled up to me at school and said, "Ever seen an aurora?"

"A what?" I replied.

He shot me a sly grin. "My place, midnight."

At 11:58 that night, I'd quietly lifted the latch to the iron gate that bordered Luke's property. By now, we had an understanding. If his dad found out Luke's girlfriend had stopped by for a midnight visit, he would melt down like ganache over a double boiler, so Luke had moved a tall ivy trellis, leaning it conveniently beneath his bedroom window. His light was on, its glow warming the surrounding darkness. He'd been waiting for me.

A little rebellious thrill had run through me as I ascended the trellis toward his windowsill and slid the pane up. Once inside, he'd led me silently by the hand up the winding stairs to the observatory, the hum of night insects drowning out the sounds of our hushed footsteps.

"Look." He stood behind me, his hands on my shoulders, positioning me beneath the observatory's glass ceiling.

"What am I looking for?"

"Just wait."

The sky had lit up with brilliant waves of color—red and yellow, crimson and rose. Stars speckled the horizon like glittering shards of a mirror. It was the most beautiful thing I'd ever seen, the kind of beauty that makes you feel small and unimportant.

"I didn't know this was supposed to happen tonight," I'd whispered.

"These things aren't easy to predict," he'd replied. But Luke had predicted it. Down to the minute.

He'd slid his arms around me, his lips on my neck as the lights danced above us. I'd leaned into his kiss, pressing myself against his beating heart as if trying to fold myself inside it.

The bittersweet memory faded, and suddenly I thought of the eclipse. It was still over a month away, but I knew that when the moment came, I would feel Luke's absence like a thorn in my heart. I had imagined he and I would watch the darkness fall from the observatory's stony deck, his arms around me and his low voice in my ear, speaking of celestial things. Now I wondered if I'd spend the day alone in my room as the shadows gathered in the dead forest below.

I lifted the latch on Luke's gate. There was no giddy anticipation today, only dread in the pit of my stomach. The ivy seemed thicker, as if its green expanse claimed a little more of the house's white walls with every passing day. I skipped the trellis and walked up the steps to Luke's heavy wooden door.

I knocked once. There was a sound from behind the door—furniture creaking, followed by heavy footsteps. Alexis Nichols opened the door.

Luke's father had always been dapper in a dorky sort of way, but today his hair hung in unruly waves, and he squinted as the daylight touched his face.

"Valeria," he said, an unfamiliar rasp in his voice. "It's always a pleasure. Come on in."

Mr. Nichols wore a bathrobe over silk pajamas. I had the sneaking suspicion he'd been in pajamas for days. Possibly these pajamas.

"Thanks," I said, stepping into the foyer. "Is Luke home? I need to talk to him."

"Luke! You have a visitor," Mr. Nichols called up the winding wooden staircase before turning back to me. "Do—do you have any news? About how to get our powers back, I mean." I detected a note of desperation in his voice. It made me cringe a little.

"Um, not exactly."

An enormous chandelier hung above us in the foyer. I'd always loved its sparkling layers of crystal, the way it cast tiny rainbows over the walls. I trained my eyes on it now so I didn't have to look at Mr. Nichols. His slumped shoulders and obvious lapse in self-care reminded me too much of my own parents.

"I understand, I understand. I'm sure you'll get it sorted out. You've always been a bright girl."

He closed the door behind me and returned to the kitchen, his slippers shuffling on the hardwood floor.

"Oh!" he called as if he'd just remembered. "I made croissants. I hope you'll take one. I've made too many, as usual." I heard the sound of silverware tumbling to the floor and his strained exhale as he bent to retrieve it. "And take some home to your mother!"

"Um, sure. Thanks, Mr. Nichols," I mumbled.

"Valeria?"

Luke stood at the top of the stairs, not bothering to hide the look of surprise on his face. He wore jeans and a black T-shirt that fit him superbly. I stood in the foyer, looking at him for what felt like an inappropriate amount of time.

"Can we talk?" I said at last.

"Sure. Come up to my room."

"Keep the door open a crack, you lovebirds!" Mr. Nichols called from the kitchen.

So Luke hadn't bothered to tell his dad about our breakup. We both stood there a moment, frozen with humiliation, and then I climbed the stairs to meet him.

It was strange to find myself in Luke's room again. The familiar scent of pine and clean linen greeted me; the same leather jacket was slung over the chair. Everything about the room was familiar except the way we stood now, alone in opposite corners. We watched each other, neither of us speaking, until at last, I couldn't hold back any longer.

"You certainly move on quickly," I said, keeping my tone as casual as if I was commenting on the weather.

His cheeks flushed a little, but he still looked me in the eye, waiting for me to continue.

"And you went from me to Gwen Foster. That's quite a switch." Idly, I unfastened my ponytail, shaking my glossy hair free and letting it cascade over my shoulders. "Some might say you're a man of diverse tastes. Personally, I think you've lost your mind."

I held my chin high, waiting to see what my words would do to him, but in my chest, my heart beat like a wounded bird. He didn't flinch. He'd been expecting this.

"With all due respect, Val, who I go to a dance with is none of your business. Besides, don't we have something more important to talk about? Gwen's a—"

"I know," I interrupted, unwilling to hear the word from his lips. "That's why I'm here. I need to speak to her. I don't think she'll see me right now unless I'm with you."

He eyed me like I was a cartoon villain who was about to announce my evil plan. "What are you going to do to her now?'

I took a deep breath and forced the words out. "I'm going to invite her to her initiation."

CHAPTER SEVEN

GWEN

The sun was setting as I stepped out my back door, clutching a rusty knife in one hand. There was an unsettling absence of a breeze. The river behind my house barely rippled, and beyond it, the dead trees stood as still as statues. My gaze paused for a second on the remnants of the old wooden bridge at the river's edge. I wondered if Valeria had burned it herself. Had her power been strong enough as a child? Or had her mother done it? I could still see the ire in Ms. Garcia's eyes the day she'd found us playing in the forest clearing. It occurred to me suddenly that tonight would be the first time I'd set foot in that clearing since.

Luke had avoided me since homecoming. And even when he met me at the Palms to go over the initiation, he'd kept things strictly business. He told me I should learn to float a dagger before the ritual, as if moving inanimate objects with magic was as easy as mastering a few notes on the recorder. He'd even demonstrated on a yellow number two pencil, never meeting my eyes as it hovered above his open palm.

I sat down and put the knife in front of me. He'd be here soon, but instead of practicing, I found myself idly tracing lines in the dirt. It'd been a week since Luke and Valeria showed up at my door, asking me to join their coven.

The logical part of my mind still couldn't believe any of this was real. But I'd felt the power inside me, the cool electricity at my fingertips. I could do things with that power. The bruise peeking out from Valeria's shirt as she stood in my doorway proved that.

If I'd read this tale in one of my novels, I would have fantasized about it for days. A lonely reject discovers she's a witch, and she's invited to join an elite circle of witches? It was something out of a dream. But as the light faded and the reality of my situation set in, I felt anxiety tighten its grip on my chest.

A crash sounded from inside the house as something made of glass tumbled off the kitchen table. My dad swore.

"Hey, Gwen!" he called. "Are we out of mustard?"

"I'll go shopping when I get paid on Thursday!" I shouted back.

"Thanks, hon. You keep this house running! What you want for dinner? We have bologna or…bologna."

"I ate at Diggins," I said, grimacing at the memory of the greasy burger I'd scarfed down after my shift. "I'm, uh…seeing a movie tonight. With some friends."

There was a confused silence, and I could practically see his brow furrow as he tried to decide if movie dates with friends had always been part of my routine. I'd certainly never mentioned them before, but for all he knew, I was hitting the town with my buddies every night while he was at the casino.

"Great," he said at last. "You have fun, sweetheart!"

"I will."

Guilt nagged at me, but I didn't dare tell him the truth. He needed me to be the steady one, the anchor in the chaotic sea that was his life. He would freak if I started ranting about magic and initiations. Still, I thought again of that long-ago scene—my dad and Valeria's mom at the river's edge, the lock of hair passing from his hand to hers. Now that I knew what the Garcias were—what I was—the recollection raised even more questions. Had it really happened? Or had it been another vivid dream with hidden meaning, like the one about the meteor?

Valeria had shown me the letter Petra found, the one that said Elizabeth Foster's powers had been revoked by the coven for some unknown reason. The discovery was disturbing, to say the least, but as I read, I understood why my magic felt like something had come back to me. The power my family had lost all those years ago was home.

Valeria also told me the coven's parents had mysteriously lost their magic right around the time I got mine back. The coincidence was strange. I knew at least half of them believed I was the cause of all this trouble. Perhaps I was, somehow. There was still so much I didn't know about my power. The possibilities were endless and frightening, and yet I had accepted Valeria's invitation. I had barely thought it over before blurting out my agreement.

I'd spent my life in unwelcome solitude, looking in on places I didn't belong. My power gave me a right to join the coven, so I was going to do just that. Even if its members didn't trust me. Even if I didn't trust some of them either.

Now, if I could just get this damn knife to float. I laid it in front of me again, its rust-specked blade reflecting the colors of the setting sun. I heard Luke's voice in my mind. *It's elemental magic. Floating an object is about controlling the air around it.* Easy for him to say.

I stared at the knife and the empty air above it, drawing what concentration I could from the sounds of nightfall around me. The blade shivered and rose. For one glorious second, the knife hovered a few inches from the ground. It shot up wildly before freefalling to rest tip-first in the earth.

I laid it flat to try again, but tires crunched on the driveway. Luke had arrived. Nervous energy shot through me as I walked around the house to meet him. He was leaning against the driver's side of his car, his jaw set. That strange stillness hung in the air, making it hard to breathe.

"Hey," I said.

"Hey," he replied. "Ready?"

"Not so much. You wanna blow this thing off and go bowling or something?"

I giggled nervously, but he didn't even crack a smile. He reached in the back seat of his car and retrieved a black garment bag.

"You should put this on before we go," he told me. "Ceremonial robes. You know, tradition."

"Oh."

Suddenly, I realized that I hadn't changed after work. I was still wearing my Diggin's uniform, khakis and an oil-stained button-up covered in pictures of cartoon chickens. Luke Nichols was here to take me to an ancient, magical ritual, and I was dressed in fast-food chic. I took the robe and hurried inside to change. The fabric was an earthy brown, and it draped heavily over parts of me while leaving others more exposed than I would have dared only weeks ago.

I rushed past my dad and back out the door before he noticed my strange costume. I climbed into Luke's car, doing my best to keep the fabric from gapping between my boobs. He drove us east to the wide iron bridge downtown. The radio wasn't on, and the seconds crawled in silence.

I searched for meaning in the minute line of tension at his brow, the subtle downward turn of his lips. I wished he would talk to me. I wished he would look at me the way he had when we danced together, his dark blue eyes on mine like I was the only person in the room. Over the past two weeks, I'd come to believe in so many crazy things. Perhaps my only delusion was the idea that Luke Nichols had been interested in anything more than a fling on the dance floor.

As we turned onto Cascabel Road, I pushed the painful thought from my mind and focused on nothing but the emerging moon.

A minute later, a pair of ornate iron gates swung open, and we pulled into a long driveway. The house before us was strawberry red with swirly white trim everywhere. It looked like an expensive cake I might be scolded for tasting.

Valeria Garcia's house. In my wildest nightmares, I never thought I'd find myself here.

We climbed the steps as Valeria opened the door, revealing a world of velvet wallpaper, antique fainting couches, and armchairs accented in gold. I was so distracted by the migraine-inducing opulence, it took me a second to look at Valeria.

She wore a long robe with the same flowing sleeves as mine, only hers was red. Of course it was. Her hair fell in loose waves around her face, wilder than how she wore it to school. A gold crown rested on her head, looking so perfectly placed it seemed it had always been there. A long slit traveled up the left side of her skirt, and I could see the handle of a dagger strapped to her thigh. The sight of the knife caused a fresh wave of anxiety to wash over me. Was I ready for this?

Valeria shot us a crimson smile. "Hey, witches."

She moved aside, and I stepped into the gilded fever dream of her living room. Jayden, Max, Celeste, and Petra were already there. The mysterious rich kids from Cascabel Road stood before me in hooded robes, looking more mysterious than ever.

Then Lili Garcia herself emerged from a shadowy hallway and headed straight toward me. I hadn't known it was possible to be more nervous than I already was. Her face was symmetrical perfection like Valeria's, but her eyes were tired and red-rimmed. I would have paid a large sum of money to know what she was thinking. To my utter shock, she smiled.

"Welcome, Gwen," she said. "Can I get you anything? We have some snacks in the kitchen."

"*Snacks?*" Valeria repeated, as if her mother had just begun speaking in tongues. "Since when do you serve snacks?"

"Um, no thanks, Ms. Garcia," I mumbled.

"Something to drink, then? We have sparkling water, orange juice—"

"Shouldn't you get back to work, Mom? Weren't you drafting a vital email to our accountant or something?" Valeria interrupted, ushering her mother out of the living room.

I wondered at Ms. Garcia as she disappeared down the dark hall. She'd seemed almost…nice.

"You'll have to excuse her. She's been a little loopy since she lost her powers," Valeria said. "You wouldn't know anything about that, would you?"

"No, I swear." I forced myself to ask at least *one* of the questions that had been keeping me up at night. "Valeria, why did you invite me to join the coven?"

"Give us a moment," she called to the others, grabbing me by a flowy sleeve and pulling me into the vast dining room. "I'm gonna be brutally honest," she informed me, as if this was somehow a deviation from the norm. "Some dark stuff went down here, and I think it's very possible you're at the bottom of it. But"—she lowered her voice—"I remember you as the girl who used to rescue spiders from rain puddles. So maybe you're not the type to mastermind an evil plot."

I felt my shoulders relax a little. It was the first time we'd ever spoken about our days in the forest. Maybe this wouldn't be so bad.

"Thanks?"

She smiled. "I'm not finished. What's that old saying? Keep your friends close, keep shady witches even closer? If I'm wrong and you're against us, then I damn well want you where I can see you. And hurt you."

I swallowed.

"Oh," she added, her eyes boring into mine. "And if you choose to keep dating Luke, just know that I won't make it easy for you."

"Hey, Gwen?" Jayden called from the living room.

"Yes?" I replied, alarmed at how shrill my voice sounded.

"Just making sure you're still alive," he called back. "She's alive, right, Val?"

"I was just giving Gwen a little pep talk," Valeria said, tugging me back to rejoin the others. "Does anyone have any burning questions for her before we begin?"

"What about your father?" Max said, his tone curious. "He's a Foster too. Is his magic back?"

Here in this strange, lavish home, it was hard to think about my dad. He hadn't acted any differently since the night the candles had ignited in my room. I still found him asleep on the couch in front of the TV most mornings, And I caught him leaving for the casino every night, as usual.

"No, he's…the same," I replied. The lavish decor seemed to press in around me.

"And you didn't know you were descended from a witch?" Petra inquired.

"No."

"Okay, but why should we believe you? I mean, what if you're a secret psychopath or something?" Celeste said, twirling a lock of long blond hair. "Should we really be jumping into this initiation? Maybe we could do, like, a trial membership."

They all stared at me—except for Luke, who seemed more interested in the darkening vista out the window. I longed to disappear the way I did at school, to retreat to a quiet corner until I could be alone again.

Instead, I pulled my robe tighter around me and said, "I know you all have a million questions about my magic and how I got it. Believe me, I do too. Until two weeks ago, I was just a girl with an abnormal interest in moon cycles. All I know is that this power feels like it belongs to me. And I want to learn to use it…for good."

"As high priestess, I've decided," Valeria said, her eyes narrowing on mine. "Gwen will join the coven. She'll learn to use her power. And I'll be watching her. Every step of the way."

"Let's just initiate her already," Petra groaned. "These robes are itchy."

With that, we shuffled out Valeria's back door and into the midst of those naked trees. Each coven member held a candle, the flames illuminating their solemn faces. At the clearing, the coven formed a circle facing me. In the fading light, I made out the fallen tree with the hollow where Valeria and I had left each other our little offerings. Even the moss over its mighty trunk was dead now.

"Who wishes to join our circle?" Valeria's voice rang clear and strong in the cold night air.

I responded the way Luke had instructed me to. "It is I, Gwen Foster, of witches' blood."

"Come forward."

I approached Valeria, regal in her crown and red robe. Here in the forest, she was more than a pretty schoolgirl. She was a force of nature, a wildfire burning before me.

"Prove yourself and become our sacred sister," she replied.

She reached for the garter at her thigh and withdrew the dagger. I'd figured the knife would be elaborately adorned like everything else in her house, but the wooden handle was surprisingly plain, its surface worn with time.

"This dagger has been in our coven since its inception," she said, holding it up for the circle to see. "It is an honor to be inducted with it."

She placed it on the ground at my feet. Cold metal glinted in the candlelight.

"Now let it hover at your breast and take your vows."

My legs shook. I thought back to the rusty knife from my kitchen, how it had darted wildly out of my control.

"Is there a problem?" Valeria said, still loud enough for everyone to hear.

"I—I can't do it," I told her. "I mean, I don't know how yet."

"I thought that might be the case," she said, smiling as if she'd anticipated this moment. "Most witches have years to practice before their initiation—normal witches, anyway. But don't worry. I'll do it for you."

Before I could speak, the knife rose threateningly and came to a stop with the blade pointed at my chest. It hovered there, suspended by Valeria's will, an inch from my heart. This was nothing new for her, I thought. She was always holding a metaphorical knife to some poor girl's heart.

Every muscle in my body tightened. She could kill me now with a glance, a passing thought. Perhaps she would.

"It would be better for you to fall upon this dagger than to enter this circle with fear in your heart," she said.

I forced myself to meet her gaze. The power inside me hummed. For one frightening moment, I imagined turning the blade in midair to point at her. Maybe I could send it flying in her direction with a flick of my wrist, with no more effort than it took to swat away a fly. The candlelight danced on the dagger's edge.

"How do you enter?" she demanded.

I spoke the words I'd rehearsed in my head for days. "With perfect love and perfect trust."

I knew what was coming next, but that didn't make it easier. The blade inched closer until its cool tip pierced my skin, right above the neckline of my robe. I managed not to scream as it cut a slow, painful figure above my heart. Blood spilled onto my bare skin, its wetness chilling me. After what seemed like forever, Valeria opened her palm, and the dagger floated mercifully back to her. She knelt and wiped it in the dirt as I took in the perfect red circle carved over my heart.

"Our union is etched in blood. Congratulations, Gwen Foster. You're one of us," Valeria declared.

A wave of euphoria washed over me, partly thanks to the pain, partly thanks to the strangeness of it all. I was a witch, damn it. And now I had a coven.

"All right!" Max applauded. His enthusiasm broke the tension, and we all felt the weight of the ritual leave us.

He bounded over and raised his hand to me. In the daze of blood loss, it took me a second to realize he expected me to high five him like I'd just scored a field goal. I slapped his palm, a silly smile spreading across my face.

Celeste greeted me with a curt double-cheek air kiss.

"Welcome," she said. "It's so great that our coven is accepting of, like, anybody."

"Congrats. Call me when you're ready to try some potions," said Jayden, wrapping me in a quick embrace.

"And call me if you wanna ditch class and summon the dead," Petra said.

Valeria finished fastening the knife to her thigh and gave me a chilly smile. "You did well."

"We did the thing. Now let's pop the ceremonial wine!" Petra announced.

They began to make their way back toward the glittering lights of Valeria's cake house. I didn't want any wine. My head was already swimming. I felt alive, powerful.

"Luke," I called as he started up the trail. "Wait!"

He stopped and turned to me as the others disappeared into the trees.

"I like you," I said over the sound of blood rushing in my ears. "When we kissed, I felt something real. Maybe you didn't, and that's okay. But—"

"Gwen," he began, his features tightening.

"No, hear me out. You at least owe me that. We're going to be seeing a lot more of each other now. You have to stop avoiding me like—like I'm going to burn you if we touch or something."

"Okay, now hear *me* out," he replied. "I've been alone a long time. So long I stopped hoping for anything different."

"No you weren't. You were with Valeria," I retorted, indignation edging my voice.

He shook his head, his eyes downcast. "I tried. In the end, I realized there's no lonelier place than in the arms of someone who doesn't understand you. I figured being alone was my fate, you know? I accepted it. Then you showed up with your wit, your quiet beauty, your magic. Now it's like for the first time in my life, everything I was afraid to hope for is right in front of me. And it scares me more than I'd like."

"Luke." I stepped toward him, and he didn't move away.

"But I don't want to be afraid anymore, Gwen." He put a hand on my waist, pulling me closer. "I want you."

For a moment, I forgot to breathe. I thought I felt the crackle of electricity in the still night air.

"Okay," I said.

There were no more words, just his lips on mine. We stayed in the forest a long time before rejoining the others, his arms around me, my head against his chest, the waxing moon rising in the dark sky.

CHAPTER EIGHT

VALERIA

I allowed myself three days to brood after Gwen's initiation. Three days of avoiding her before I forced myself to face the inevitable: Gwen was my responsibility. As high priestess, I knew I was supposed to do the Obi-Wan Kenobi thing and take her under my wing to teach her to use her new power. But every time I saw her in the halls at school, she was hand in hand with Luke. And all I felt was the empty space in my heart where he used to be, the air between my fingers where I used to cling to him. Now, alone in my bedroom, I examined myself in the mirror as if searching for something to grab ahold of.

Gwen's knock shook me from my reflection. My young Skywalker had arrived.

I went downstairs and opened the door to Gwen standing with her arms crossed, her shoulders hunched as if shielding herself from some inevitable blow. For an uncomfortable moment, neither of us spoke. The clouds were gray and the air was calm, like it had been at the initiation—not a reassuring kind of calm but the kind of calm that seems to warn of something catastrophic to come.

"Well, let's get to it," I said at last.

I turned and headed through the house toward my back door

and the forest beyond, letting Gwen follow without a glance in her direction. My mom was typing away in the study upstairs. Good. The last thing I needed was for her to spot Gwen and offer her a charcuterie plate or something. I still wasn't past the irony—of all the decisions I'd ever made, inviting Gwen to join the coven was the only one my mom seemed to approve of. I wondered if she felt guilty over the way she'd treated Gwen. When she'd burned the old wooden bridge to keep Gwen out of our forest, she'd been casting a witch from her rightful place. It was strange to imagine my mother regretful of anything, but everything about this was strange.

I'd asked my mom what she knew about the Fosters and their long-lost magic, but she'd told me what I suspected as she gazed blankly out the window: None of the parents had any knowledge of Elizabeth Foster or the reason her magic was revoked. Whatever had happened to Elizabeth back when the coven was founded was lost to time, forgotten beneath years of money jars and prosperity rituals. *The Golden Spells* had been our go-to spell book for generations. My mom rarely glanced at our original Book of Shadows, but she was sure it bore no mention of the Fosters.

I tried not to let the echo of Gwen's footsteps annoy me as we descended the back steps and passed through the garden. We were alone in the forest. We stepped effortlessly over roots and under branches. Both of us knew the landscape like the face of some familiar friend. It was strange, walking with her the way we used to as kids, like reliving a memory, only upside down. The laughing ease that used to float between us was gone, replaced by tense silence.

Gwen wasn't dressed in her usual hand-me-downs either. Today, she wore a flowy black slip dress over black tights and pointed ankle boots.

"I see you've kept up your makeover," I said into the stillness of the trees.

She nodded. "Celeste and Jayden took me shopping. They said they wanted to help me find my self-expression."

"Your self-expression is pretty funereal."

"Thanks," she replied, as if it was a compliment.

I was certain that Luke had funded their shopping spree. It

wasn't like Gwen had spare cash lying around for a new, expressive wardrobe. Beneath the gray sky, her pale skin clashed jarringly with the dark of her eyes. Her hair was untamed, her nails bare and chewed. As I studied her, I found myself irrationally bothered by her little flaws, each one a reminder that Luke preferred this imperfect girl over me.

We stopped when we reached the clearing where we'd held her initiation. The tall trees surrounded us like protectors, even in death. We were free to practice magic here unseen.

"So, what are we gonna do first?" she asked.

I flung a small burst of sunfire at her, striking her in the right shoulder.

"Ow!" She rubbed the spot where the spell had made contact.

"Defensive spells?" I suggested, one brow raised.

"Is this going to be a training session? Or just an excuse for you to hit me?" she said skeptically.

"Can't it be both?"

She extended both hands and I braced myself, remembering how she'd knocked me down on homecoming night. But she aimed away from me toward the line of bare trees. She stared at her hands as if waiting for her magic to appear. Nothing did. I wasn't surprised. Moonfire wasn't like turning a light switch on and off.

"I don't understand," she said. "Last time, it just happened."

"I'm guessing the last time you used it, you were angry at me. Magic flows like an extension of yourself—it can manifest in ways you don't expect. But your mind has to be focused if you want to control it."

Gwen's eyes narrowed in thought. "Where does it come from?"

I held back a sigh of exasperation. "We draw our power from the universe. You know—the air, the earth, the stars. All our magic, even the silliest love spell, pulls from the elements in one way or another. My sunfire is fueled by the sun, and that fireworks show you put on at the dance came from—"

"—the moon," Gwen finished.

At least she knew *something* about her newfound power.

"And one more thing before we start," I said. "Don't go practicing in front of the Mundanes, okay?"

"The who?"

"Unmagical people. You used to be one until a few weeks ago. We have to hide our power from them. Believe me, history hasn't exactly been kind to witches."

Gwen's heavy brows wrinkled in concern.

"Welcome to witching." I shrugged. "Don't worry, the better you get at magic, the better you get at hiding it."

"That's how you tripped me in the quad," she said suddenly.

I'm sorry. The words sounded in my head, but I didn't say them aloud. I kicked at a pile of pine needles.

"Yes. That's how. Now close your eyes."

She did as she was told.

"There's a piece of the moon inside you," I told her. "If you try, you can feel it burning, the flames clinging to your heart."

She went still, searching for the flames I spoke of. After a moment, she nodded.

"I feel it," she said. "The moonfire. It's like…the hum you hear when the night is alive with living things."

"Grab hold of it," I instructed.

A spark crackled at Gwen's fingertips, then another. Her hands trembled.

"See that tree over there?" I pointed. "Hit it."

Gwen aimed, and a torrent of silver flames flew from her hands, bouncing in every direction before fading into the still air. The tree stood untouched.

"Sorry, I'm a little nervous," she said.

"You think *you're* nervous? I had to learn this stuff from my mother. Believe me, you're getting off easy. Now breathe. Focus," I told her. "When your hands stop shaking, try again."

She obeyed, and this time, the fire flew from her hands, striking the dead tree. A branch tumbled to the ground with the impact.

"Wow!" she cried, running over to investigate the damage.

"See?" I said. "You need to be in control of the fire, not the other way around. If you're not in control, it can overtake you—

even hurt you. You end up like a fish in a fiery net. The more you struggle, the harder it holds you. It happened to me once, training with my mom."

"How do you get out of it?" Gwen asked.

"You better hope there's someone or something around to break your concentration. I believe a well-timed bucket of water to the face did it for me."

Gwen was quiet, her eyes wide. I bent to touch the place where her spell had charred the dead wood. It was still hot. I felt a tickle at my wrist and discovered a huge, fat-bodied spider crawling on my bare skin.

"Ah!" I let out an involuntary shriek and raised my other hand to swat it away violently.

"Wait!"

I stared at Gwen in momentary surprise. Of course. Gwen Foster, protector of nature's ugliest creatures. She placed a finger beneath its wriggling front legs and it climbed on as if it understood she was its savior. As she held it in her palm, it no longer seemed huge but tiny, fragile.

"What do you think it is? A false widow?" she asked me as if I was capable of identifying spiders on sight. Back when we were kids, perhaps I had been.

"Uh, sure." I shrugged.

Gwen stepped further into the forest, searching for a suitable place to set it down. The enormous fallen tree came into view. Our eyes landed on it at the same time.

Our hollow was partially covered with strings of dead moss, but I could still see the dark enclosure within. She smiled.

"Come on," she said. "For old time's sake."

I felt a smile tug at my lips too. She drew the moss back like a curtain and, as she did, I felt my eyes drawn to the words she'd carved there so many years ago.

THE BIRDS DON'T CARE IF——

I looked away before she caught me staring. She set the spider down on the hollow's floor and watched it crawl away with something like affection. I remembered suddenly what it was like to have

Gwen as a friend. She was the kind of person who loved all of you, even the ugly parts.

"Thanks," I said, "for not letting me kill it."

"It's the first living thing I've seen in the forest since the trees died," she replied. "Maybe it's a good omen."

She took another step and froze. At the base of the fallen tree was the lone red hyacinth I'd spotted with Petra.

"How?" she said.

"We don't know." I gazed at its green leaves and brilliant petals. "But there's definitely magic involved. Petra said it was supposed to be here, like it's restoring balance or something."

"It's beautiful." She turned to me as if she'd just remembered something important. "Hey, do you guys—I mean, you *witches*—ever have weird dreams?"

"Once I dreamed I was naked at my history final. Does that count?"

She laughed, the corners of her dark eyes crinkling. Then she grew serious again. "I mean, have you ever dreamed of stars or planets, or maybe a meteor?" When I gave her a blank look, she chewed her bottom lip. "Guess I'm just crazy."

I squinted at the flat sky, which hung overhead like paper. The sight of it put a sick, wary feeling in the pit of my stomach.

"So, what else can you—I mean, *we*—do?" Gwen said, filling the silence.

I thought a moment. "Watch this," I instructed. "Then you try."

I gazed at the clearing and let my mind go still. Beside me, I felt Gwen hold her breath. An isolated rain shower blanketed the clearing, forming little puddles in the dirt. After a moment, I raised a hand casually. The drops ceased.

"Wow, that's not intimidating or anything."

"We're witches. Nothing intimidates us," I lied. "Tell the universe what you want. See the rainfall, imagine you can feel the drops on your skin, like—"

"Like tears," she said.

I rolled my eyes at the girl clad in black beside me. "Sure, if you wanna be all broody about it."

She laughed again. I did, too, the sound tumbling lightly through the trees. For a second, we were the way we used to be, back when things were simple and the forest was green. Gwen closed her eyes, her lids flickering in concentration.

Wind picked up suddenly, tossing dead leaves around on the ground. The clouds above us darkened, but no rain came.

Gwen opened her eyes. "Well, I guess it's a start?"

It was more than a start. I hadn't gotten nearly as far on my first try. My arms pricked with gooseflesh in the sudden cold.

"Come on, let's get inside," I said.

Gwen had been to my house for her initiation, but she still acted like she was visiting a museum—like if she let herself get too comfortable, she might break something and have to pay for it. In my bedroom, she sat cautiously at the edge of my bed, taking in the elaborate canopy, the antique armoire, the tall, gilded mirror.

"What's next?" I said, rummaging through an old box of coven supplies. "Beauty spell?"

She glanced out the window. The sun was setting somewhere behind the clouds in that uneasy sky.

"It's getting late. I need to get downtown. I'm—" She lowered her eyes to the plush carpet beneath her feet. "I'm supposed to meet Luke tonight."

I was quiet a moment, my fingers idling over the contents of the box.

"Don't be ridiculous. Tell him to pick you up here," I said finally. "I mean, he's right next door."

She eyed me skeptically but withdrew her phone and began texting him.

"Seriously," I insisted. "It's fine. Look, I know I was hard on you at the dance. And the initiation. But maybe I was a little immature. You and I are going to be spending a lot more time together. We can't go on hating each other."

"I don't hate you," she said.

"Oh."

"I'm a little afraid of you, though," she added as if for my sake.

"Well, knock it off," I said, smiling. I took a silver necklace from the bottom of the box. On its chain hung a single white pearl carved in the shape of a flower. "Here—we use this charm for poise and confidence. You should wear it on your date tonight."

Hesitantly, she took the necklace and pulled it over her head. "Thanks."

A cruel resentment was burning inside me. I gasped as if I'd just thought of a terrific idea. "You should borrow an outfit for tonight too!"

"No!" she exclaimed. "I mean, no thanks. I'm good."

"You're not planning on going in that, are you? It has no shape." I watched as Gwen examined her outfit, wondering at its inadequacy. "I guess you were. Don't worry, there's still time to change."

Before she could answer, I began rummaging through my closet, pulling out a few of my staples, all bright colors and sexy cutouts. She stared at the garments piling up on my bed with increasing discomfort.

"This was Luke's favorite." I held up a plunging red cocktail dress. "It won't fit you, of course—it would be far too loose in the bust. But between you and me, the night I wore this, he couldn't keep his hands off me. He used to say I was just his type."

She bit her lip as she absorbed my words.

As if reading her mind, I added, "I guess one guy can have two completely different types. Like, *completely* different."

Gwen was fidgeting now, her hands smoothing over her unruly hair and tugging at the hem of her slip. They were the worried gestures of a girl who was doubting herself.

"Anyway," I said, putting the red dress aside. "There has to be *something* in here that'll work on you."

"No, I think I'll wait downstairs," she blurted, getting up.

She was shrinking, the way she did when she longed to hide behind something. I had meant to hurt her, of course. As she hurried down the stairs, I waited for the empty sugar rush I usually felt when I picked on her, but it didn't come. Outside, the storm clouds had turned a sickly green.

"Gwen, wait—" I called, but it was too late.

There was a knock at the door. Luke had arrived. She opened the door as I descended the stairs. I heard their hushed embrace.

"Hey, there's my girl!" Luke stood in the open doorway, one arm around Gwen's waist. "You look great." He paused when he saw the necklace around her neck. "Uh…why are you wearing that?"

Her hands flew to the necklace. Her face flushed and she began to realize she'd made some kind of mistake. "For poise and confidence?"

Luke's eyes narrowed as he understood what I'd done. "Not quite. It's—you know what? It doesn't matter. You ready to go?"

"Tell me." Her voice was high and tight.

"You sure?"

She nodded.

He glared at me from the doorway. "I gave it to Valeria last year. It…was supposed to symbolize my love and commitment."

No one moved. The grandfather clock ticked.

"Oh," she said softly.

She removed the chain from her neck and let it drop to the floor, her cheeks crimson. *I'm sorry.* My lips formed around the words, but I held them back. Her body went still like the gathered clouds. She shut her eyes against tears.

Then the rain came. It was as if the eerie calm in the air all day had been building to this downpour.

Sheets of water pummeled the house, the shutters rattling. Wind rushed through the open door. Lightning flashed across the dark scene, and the swaying trees were lit up in silver for one feverish second.

The bare redwoods shivered and swayed. Above us, the last bit of light vanished from the dimming sky and the unmistakable sound of thunder rumbled in the distance, low and menacing.

There was no question Gwen had done this. We all understood it. Tears streamed down her cheeks as the rain fell. Suddenly, I realized we were standing frozen in awe, the front door still wide open. Water splashed the hardwood floor of the foyer, forming a slick puddle at our feet. I rushed to the door and swung it shut. The howling of the wind diminished somewhat.

Gwen's eyes were wide. The look on her face was one of awe but not of disbelief. Luke turned to her in adoration.

"No point in getting worked up over a stupid necklace when you can do this. You're incredible, Gwen Foster," he told her.

I could barely make out his words over the sound of the storm. They weren't meant for me.

A sickening crack sounded from outside as a heavy branch tumbled to the ground beneath the merciless wind.

"Make it stop!" I shouted to Gwen.

"It'll rain itself out in time," my mom said, stepping into the living room.

I watched her take in Gwen's tear-streaked face and the torrent outside. Her eyes settled on me with disapproval, like I was a kid again and she'd just caught me scribbling on the wallpaper.

My phone vibrated in my back pocket, making me jump. I answered it. "Hey, Petra. What's up?"

"I had a breakthrough! The spirits didn't just give me crumbs this time. I think they gave me the whole damn cookie. The trees, our parents' powers, Gwen—"

My heart thumped. "Tell me everything."

"History is repeating itself. It's happening again, like it did when Dorado was founded. There's this prophecy—" she paused. "Are you alone?"

"No. Should I be?"

"Meet me in the clearing," she said. "Now. This weather's crazy, but I'll brave it."

She hung up.

"Sorry, gotta go!" I announced as I hurried toward the back door.

My mom shot me a confused glance, but Luke and Gwen were only looking at each other. I could have disappeared into thin air and they wouldn't have noticed. I didn't bother with a raincoat or boots or anything that might protect me from the elements. I was desperate to know what Petra had to say. Comfort could wait.

Outside, the wind pummeled my face. The rain fell so hard it hit my skin in tiny pinpricks, the torment of Gwen's magic.

I grabbed a flashlight from my porch and clicked it on as I hurried through my soggy backyard and into the darkness of the forest. Dead leaves flew at me in the wind, sticking to my soaked clothing. Soon I was at the clearing. The darkness was thick here, surrounding me in a cold curtain of black. The moon was hidden by storm clouds, and my flashlight shone a tunnel of light no wider than a dinner plate. Where was she?

I took out my phone, trying vainly to shield it from the sheets of rain, and called her. I waited, hearing the ring in my ear. The wind whirred past me, unrelenting white noise, but through it, I made out the familiar ring of Petra's phone in the distance.

"Hello?" I called, stepping forward into the dark. "Are you—"

I stopped midsentence. A rectangle of light popped into view as if materializing from the night itself. Petra's phone lay faceup in the mud a little distance away, unanswered. Fear pricked at the back of my neck.

"Petra?"

I TURNED my flashlight in the direction of the phone's glow and froze. The light revealed a pale, delicate hand, palm-up in the mud.

Why was that hand so still?

I took a step closer, and an overwhelming melancholy hit me, the way it had the day I'd discovered the dead trees. The unmistakable trace of malevolent magic.

The hand—Petra's hand—didn't move. With a shuddering breath, I stepped closer.

She lay gazing skyward, her wet hair sticking to her brow, her gray eyes open and unblinking in the rain. I ran to her.

It couldn't be true. I would wake her, and she would be all right.

"No!" I cried as I reached her side. I shook her, tilting her lifeless face to mine. "Come on!"

My words disappeared into the wind. I rose to my feet beneath the freezing rain. I should have been afraid; Petra was still warm. Whoever killed her had not gotten far. I should have thought of escape, home, safety. But that was not what I wanted. I wanted to find the witch who did this, to make them pay.

My fingers tightened around the flashlight. An animal blend of panic and rage hummed inside me. The flashlight's beam grew as wide and intense as a spotlight, cutting through the darkness of the forest.

There. Beyond the clearing, I spotted the unmistakable shape of someone retreating. The trees scattered my beam into a hundred crooked shadows, obscuring the figure in shards of light and dark. Man or woman, young or old, I couldn't tell.

My heart raced and tears stung my eyes. I fixed my gaze on the fleeing witch and let the sunfire fly, a coil of fire searching for something to seize. I felt it close around the witch's ankle. But my hands were shaking, the magic pulsing with every panicked beat of my heart. The spell was turning on me; I felt the fire creep up my arm toward my throat.

No! I couldn't stop now, couldn't let Petra's killer get away. I held on as the heat wrapped itself around my neck. There was no one to save me this time—no one to snap me out of it like my mom had all those years ago.

Suddenly, the earth gave way beneath my feet. I tumbled to the ground, the impact freeing my mind from the spell's grip. The sunfire dissolved into darkness. The witch's ankle slipped away, my fingers closing around nothing. I tried to get up to fire again, but the mud held my legs, pulling me down with relentless force. The witch was manipulating the earth beneath me, making it swallow me whole.

I writhed vainly like an animal in a trap. Dirt covered me up to my chest now, roots scraping my sides as I sank. I was going to die, I realized—buried, just as Petra would be when they found her. My eyes fluttered shut. Petra and I would be together forever beneath the earth. The thought was not horrifying but strangely peaceful. Neither of us would be alone.

It took a moment for me to understand I was no longer sinking. The ground was wet and cold but solid beneath me. I gasped and air filled my lungs. I clawed at the dirt around me, dragging myself free. At last, I rose to my feet, shaking.

I knew the witch was gone by now. I'd been spared, and Petra was dead.

My flashlight lay near her unmoving body. I took it numbly, then turned toward the lights of my house, no longer feeling the cold or the pain of what I'd been through. I was propelled by anger, my body moving out of sheer determination.

I marched up the hill, up my back stairs, and stepped, dripping, into the kitchen. Luke and Gwen sat at the kitchen table, steaming teacups in front of them. My mom stood at the counter, a wineglass in her hand. The kitchen was bright, and they looked warm and safe, like people in a gold-framed painting, not part of my reality.

They stared, wide-eyed, at my mud-covered face, the blood soaking through my clothes where the tree roots had cut.

"What the hell—" my mom began.

Luke rose to his feet as if to rush to me, but I spoke before he could. "Petra's dead."

Muddy water pooled on the tile floor.

"*What?*" My mom set her glass down so hard, I thought it might break.

I turned to her. "Petra's dead," I repeated. "Someone killed her. Nearly killed me too. A witch. Call her parents. Call the Mundane police to take her away."

My mother stood immobile with disbelief. Water dripped from my hair and down my cheeks, but tears did not fall. I left those warm, dry people in that bright room and went up the stairs, then up the next flight. I didn't stop until I'd pulled down the creaky ladder to the attic. I climbed it and fumbled for the light. A bare bulb illuminated the dusty furniture and carefully covered heirlooms.

In the corner, just as I recalled, was a short bookshelf as antique as the house itself. A leather-bound book decorated in intricate script sat on the bottom shelf: our coven's Book of Shadows. I sat in the dust and began to read.

CHAPTER NINE

VALERIA

After the night of Petra's death, I retreated to my bedroom, shut the thick velvet curtains, and closed the door. I emailed excuses to my teachers and silenced my phone. I'd decided I wouldn't face the world until I'd found some way to explain the mysteries that plagued our coven, and the gaping hole Petra had left at its core.

The Book of Shadows was as heavy as a brick and densely populated with inky, black script. Day blended into night and back again as I sat hunched over it by dim lamplight. I read like I was gripped by a strange fever that kept me fixed on those ancient pages, inspecting each one for any clue, any mention of malevolent magic. My eyes burned, but I welcomed the task. It allowed no time for grief. That would come later.

The first entries were written by Delfina Garcia herself: spells in neat, bold letters; rituals for health, for an abundant harvest, even spells to improve gold mining outcomes. All the original coven members had made entries too. Tobias Wiley, Jayden's ancestor, had listed the best spots in the forest to pick wild herbs. Levan Nichols had contributed his thoughts on astrological divination. I couldn't help but wonder about Levan. Had he been anything like Luke? I imagined a quiet man who gazed at the stars, his sharp, handsome features obscuring some private pain.

Even Elizabeth Foster had contributed an entry. My heart leapt when I discovered it, hoping it would hold some clue as to why she lost her magic or why Gwen's had returned. But it was about how to draw power and vitality from the new moon. The key, according to Elizabeth, was to sleep in the forest beneath its light—naked. A haunting image appeared in my mind: Elizabeth's pale shape moving between the trees at night, her hair wild, as the new moon shone above.

Many questions plagued me as I read in those feverish hours, but it had begun to look like, Elizabeth Foster's naked moonbathing was the most scandalous revelation the original coven had to offer. No dark secrets, no prophecies, and no malevolent magic.

My breakthrough didn't come until one dreary Tuesday evening, when I reached the entry of Delfina's granddaughter, Salud. There, in flowery cursive, were the words I'd been looking for.

The Principles of Malevolent Magic, 7 January 1899

We laid our founder, Delfina Garcia, to rest last Saturday. Though she will be sorely missed, I am now free to write about malevolent magic, a topic she forbade our coven even to speak of while she was alive. I will write what I know in hopes that my words might aid future generations of this coven I hold dear. I only wish I knew more.

At our core, witches are neither good nor evil. Inside each of us lies darkness and light. However, some witches possess the ability to use the darkness within for magical purposes. This is malevolent magic, a power so abhorrent and dangerous that those who practice it are shunned by other witches. Fortunately, malevolent magic is very rare. The power is passed through the generations in a small number of ill-fated bloodlines.

While elemental magic is part of the natural order of the universe, malevolent magic is not. Its very existence is at odds with nature, and she pushes back against it. Thus, malevolent witches can wield their power for only a short time before they are drained. Likewise, its rituals cannot be done without a sacrifice, usually the death of something vibrant and beautiful.

Some malevolent witches can control the Mundanes and make them obey their will. Others can summon a deadly spell against their fellow witches. Before my family left our native Mexico, we called it the Xholha, the Shadow Spell. It appears as a wave of shadow as opaque as night. If a witch is struck by the Shadow Spell, she will suffer great pain, and if she is not spared, she will soon die.

The hairs on the backs of my arms stood up. At last, I understood exactly what happened to Petra. She'd died suffering beneath a wave of shadow. A new grief washed over me, and tears blurred my vision as I read on.

I have heard whispers among the elders that a prophecy exists—the foretelling of an event that will tip the balance of the universe in favor of malevolent magic, leaving calamity and destruction in its wake. But alas, Delfina refused to speak of it. She would only assure me that this fate had been averted. My grandmother always had a weariness about her, but when I asked about this prophecy, she looked more sorrowful than I'd ever seen her. The burden of her secrets must have been great indeed. I wish I'd known what they were. Now they go with her to the grave.

The passage ended, and the last words Petra said to me repeated in my head. *It's happening again, like it did when Dorado was founded. There's this prophecy—*

Delfina had thought the danger was over, the secret buried forever. She'd been wrong. The image of Delfina that hung on our wall depicted someone proud and strong, nothing like the miserable woman her granddaughter described. What had changed her? I flipped back to the book's early entries, to Delfina's perfect penmanship. As I did, I noticed charred edges deep in the book's spine as if several pages had been burned away. The burn marks looked as ancient as the paper, as though Delfina had destroyed the words herself. Suddenly, I pictured my mother as she torched the bridge between Gwen's house and ours. The Garcia family, I thought, burning problems out of existence since 1860.

Something else was bothering me, too—another puzzle piece

that didn't fit. When the sunfire spell had turned on me in the forest, the witch who killed Petra had pulled the earth out from beneath my feet. It was the jolt I'd needed to shake myself free from my own spell. And though the dirt could have suffocated me, here I was, alive and breathing. I had the strange feeling that I'd been spared intentionally. Why would a killer let me live?

The grandfather clock downstairs struck six. It was almost time to begin the rites of death.

Reluctantly, I shut the book and dressed in the clothes I'd picked out, a beaded black dress and cropped satin jacket. No high priestess robes and dagger sheath tonight. We were going out in public. I hated the somber color of the clothes, but for this ritual, dark and dreary was the only way to go.

Fifteen minutes later, I'd parked my Mercedes in the cemetery lot. The ground was soft, and my shoes sank a little with each step as I headed to the historic section. I glanced warily at the grass, so short it resembled AstroTurf. I wondered why the Mundanes insisted on keeping the cemetery so neat and pretty. Death was neither.

A large old fountain bubbled on the broad cemetery path, its stone angels spitting never-ending streams of water. A general feeling of dampness permeated my surroundings as if the earth was still holding the rain from Gwen's downpour. It'd been a week since that horrible night. A part of me hadn't believed Petra was gone until the Mundanes came with their sirens and searchlights. I'd watched them carry her away on a muddy stretcher. All the while, the rain had poured.

I was sure the doctors had declared some medical explanation for her death—aneurysm, sudden heart failure. Magic would leave no trace they could discover. Only I had felt the deathly aura malevolent magic had left behind.

All the coven families had plots in the oldest section of the cemetery. Somewhere nearby was Delfina Garcia's final resting place, her secrets lost forever beneath the trimmed cemetery grass. A light fog floated among the headstones, and a tall, white monolith in the distance declared SARICH in aggressive block letters: Petra's family plot. There, above a freshly laid patch of sod, was Petra's grave.

I approached it, weaving through the other stones, observing the etchings on each. 1902–1956. 1879–1934. 1825–1880. The lives of witches of the past, reduced to a name and two dates. Now Petra's existence would be summed up the same way.

I stared at the cruelly short life etched into cold marble before me. Petra's life. The life I hadn't saved. In a strange way, I felt as if I'd died the day she did. The old Valeria was buried among the trees in the barren forest. Whoever I was now did not feel like her. There was a pain in my heart that allowed no room for the selfish things I used to harbor there. I was freshly turned earth now, waiting for something to grow beneath the soil. I didn't know what would emerge.

I thought of Gwen's tear-streaked face after I'd given her that stupid necklace. *Try not being a dick.* That was the last piece of advice Petra had given me. But I hadn't taken it. I hadn't even considered it. I would try now, I vowed. If I didn't, then what was I still doing here? Why was I alive when Petra, brave, and genuine, and kind, was gone?

"Hey, am I too early?"

I turned to see Gwen standing behind me, her figure covering the setting sun. The funeral had been miserable. We'd watched Petra's body lowered into the ground as her parents stood still and tearful over the descending casket, but the coven seemed to have an endless series of depressing rituals surrounding death. We'd arrived for round two.

"Yes—I mean, no. I mean, wanna help me set up?"

It amazed me that Gwen was even speaking to me after how I'd treated her the last few…years. Trying to be kind was like using a new, unpracticed muscle. For the first time, I found myself unsure of how to talk to her, as if I could somehow communicate my guilt and regret with a few words of small talk.

If she noticed my weirdness, she didn't acknowledge it. She knelt beside me, and together we removed the candles from my bag. I showed her how to place them around the fresh grave, like a protective circle. Gwen paused as if transfixed by the tombstone, one thin white candle in her hand.

"'Come! let the burial rite be read—the funeral song be sung!—An anthem for the queenliest dead that ever died so young.'"

"What was that?" I said, the rhyme still ringing in my head.

"Poe," she replied. "He's my favorite. I've spent a lot of time escaping into books when things got hard. Guess it's a habit now, to search for some kind of comfort in familiar words."

"It was beautiful."

"I'm sorry she's gone," Gwen said, setting down the candle and igniting it with a gentle silver flame.

I couldn't name all the things I was sorry for. We sat back on our heels, admiring the array of candles surrounding the tombstone. Gold flames danced on the ones I'd lit, silver on Gwen's, both casting an eerie glow in the darkening night.

"They're all going to think I did this somehow," she said. "I'm the newcomer. I'm the one with the unexplained powers."

"Gwen, when this whole thing began, I wasn't sure I could trust you. But Petra's death proved you're not behind this. I know you, and you're not a killer."

She turned to me with a weak smile. "So you don't think I'm a murderer? That might be the first compliment you've ever given me, and I've gotta say, it's a pretty crappy one."

"Well," I said tentatively, "maybe the next one will be better."

"How stupid." She wiped at her damp eyes. "A girl is dead, and I'm worrying about my own problems."

Guilt overwhelmed me. Guilt over the girl I'd failed to save, the coven I couldn't protect, the magic I had no clue how to fight. The sting of tears threatened to overtake me, and I feared if I began to cry, I would never stop.

An old, familiar impulse hit me. I could hide my pain with hurtful words, some remark that would make Gwen feel the same self-doubt I did. I pushed the idea back down into the dark recesses of my heart. I wasn't going to do that anymore. How dare I, as I knelt on Petra's grave?

Besides, I understood now. Those words wouldn't make me any

more capable of solving my problems. And those words wouldn't make Petra any less dead. Instead, I opened my mouth and told her the truth.

"I failed," I said. "I failed Petra, the coven—I'm supposed to be high priestess. But maybe I'm not. Maybe I'm just a kid playing in her mother's clothes."

Saying the words out loud was like bearing my heart to a knife's blade. But instead of cutting me down, Gwen sat there, serenely absorbing my ugliest truths.

"I try to outshine everyone around me because I'm afraid if I don't, they'll see how weak I really am," I went on. "I know I've treated you terribly. I can't tell you how ashamed I am of that."

Gwen didn't speak for a long time.

"You *should* be ashamed," she said at last. "Being on your bad side has really sucked. And you weren't exactly nice to me before that."

I braced myself against her coming tirade. This was what I deserved.

"You're petty. You're self-centered. You're quick to jealousy—"

"I know," I said, my eyes stinging with tears.

She put a hand on my shoulder, her expression serious. "But you're not weak. You never have been."

I let her last words resonate. They seemed to warm me as the night air grew colder.

"Now that's a compliment," I said. I turned to her, a million apologies on my lips. "Oh, Gwen, I'm sor—"

Footsteps sounded behind us. The others had arrived. We whirled around to face them, our moment abruptly over.

Jayden stood at the foot of the grave. His expression was stoic, his eyes dry, but there was something broken in him. I could see it on his face, despite the rose oil and concealer. Petra had been his closest friend, perhaps his only true friend. He was devastated. Behind him stood Luke, tall and solitary in the cemetery fog. Celeste's pale blue eyes darted around as if she believed whoever killed Petra might jump out at her at any moment. Max held a protective arm around his sister. He was the only one not ashamed to cry. And he was ugly-crying, eyes red and nose running as if he was determined to release not only his grief but the rest of ours too.

A strange feeling came over me as I looked at these people I'd known for so long. The night Petra died, Luke and Gwen had been with my mom in the kitchen, safe and dry. But I found myself wondering about the others. What had they been doing that night?

Without being told, they each took a place around Petra's grave. The rites of death didn't require it, but it was as if we each inherently understood that our coven existed in a circle, eternal and unbroken, like the circle carved above our hearts. They were quiet, waiting for me to give some grand proclamation. But I had no wisdom that would make it all make sense. All I had were scant pieces of knowledge. Crumbs, as Petra would have said.

"Before we honor Petra, I want to tell you some things."

I sensed them tense up as I began to tell them what I'd read in the Book of Shadows.

"But who the hell was it?" Max said, wiping angrily at a tear.

"I don't know. The book says very few witches can practice malevolent magic. It's one of those lineage things—you're either born with it, or you're not."

"And none of us were, right?" Celeste asked.

I hated the way they glanced uneasily at each other. The way they seemed to stiffen and grow apart from one another at the thought.

"Whoever did this didn't want Petra to tell you what she'd discovered," Jayden said.

"Maybe it was Gwen—" Celeste began.

"Let's not go down that road," I interrupted, to everyone's surprise. "We've been there before. Until we find out more, I want us united. That means *all* of us."

"Agreed," Luke said, giving Gwen's hand a squeeze.

"But how exactly do we find out more?" Celeste protested. "Petra's gone. We'll never know what she knew."

"Maybe not," I said. "But I'm searching every page of the Book of Shadows for…anything useful."

Guilt burned inside me, but I'd already decided: I would not tell them about the prophecy. Petra had asked me to meet her alone. Just like Delfina, she'd wanted to keep her knowledge a secret. It was a secret she died for. The less the others knew, the better. I just wasn't sure if I was protecting them or myself.

Perfect. I was a high priestess who didn't trust her own coven.

"All right," I said, changing the subject. "Enough business. We're gathered here to remember Petra."

Like the funeral, the rites of death would be a miserable affair, all mournful chants and tearful remembrances. I felt us all brace for the weight of it.

I sighed, searching for strength. "Today we honor Petra Sarich, our departed sister. She was—"

My words were cut short by a muffled *pop*.

We all turned to Jayden, who held a freshly opened bottle of champagne, a few bubbles trailing down its glassy surface.

"Champagne?" I said. "You brought champagne to the rites of death?"

Jayden's devilish smile seemed to hide his pain, if only briefly. "Why yes, it seems I did."

"You can't be serious."

"That's just it, Val. I think we've all been entirely *too* serious," he replied. "Our girl Petra dies, and we hold some stuffy grief ceremony? Does that sound even a little bit like something she would have wanted?"

"She would hate this," Celeste agreed, "All the tears and, like, feelings."

"Exactly!" Jayden waved the champagne bottle in her direction with a flourish. "If we're gonna honor her, let's do it right. We owe her that."

He had a point. Petra would have never approved of this sobfest. And as I looked at the tense, weary faces of my coven, it was painfully clear that what they needed more than anything was a morale boost.

I shot him a quick, appreciative smile, and though my heart was far from in it, I said, "You know what? You're right. Besides, we're *witches*. What's the point of all this power if we can't have any fun?"

"Then we party for Petra," Jayden declared, raising the champagne bottle above his head.

The night unraveled as the sun set. It was supposed to be just us, our coven celebrating the life of a sister. Our mistake was believing Celeste could keep a secret. One text to her latest crush and the Mundanes began to trickle in like the cemetery was the hottest new nightspot. Mundane guys arrived in search of Celeste, and girls followed not far behind. The Mundane girls came in packs of swinging ponytails, the chemical scent of their perfume hanging in the air. Jayden and I herded the crowd away from the grave site. They followed us happily and began to congregate around the stone fountain that divided the cemetery's broad main road. Someone fired up portable speakers and music pulsed through the night air.

"At least we won't be dancing on Petra's grave," I said to him.

"She'd probably love it if we did."

Jayden may have come to party, but he'd dressed for mourning. He wore a long black jacket, the collar turned up as if against a chill wind. A delicate cluster of white flowers was pinned to his lapel.

"Elderflower," I said aloud, suddenly remembering the day he'd shown up at Petra's house with a thermos of elderflower tea.

"It's a healing herb, you know," he said, the mirth draining from his face. "All those mornings Petra and I spent drinking that tea, we were just hanging out, but it felt therapeutic somehow, like the tea and the company were good for my soul. I didn't really think about it at the time. Now it keeps me awake at night."

"What do you mean?" I said, worried by the way his eyes grew distant.

He lowered his gaze. "I'm a strong witch, skilled in potions. I've perfected more beauty remedies and love tonics than I can count. But I've never practiced healing magic. I never bothered to learn the one thing that might actually help the people I—" His voice broke. "Maybe I could have saved her if I'd known the right formula. If I'd gotten to her in time. Maybe she'd still be here."

"Jayden," I said softly. "You couldn't have known. Don't be so hard on yourself."

"Listen to me, Val," he said, his expression steely. "It's too late for her. But next time, I'll be ready. I promise you that."

I'd never heard him speak so seriously. "All right," I replied. "And Jayden, if you want to talk more—"

"I can't. Not tonight. Maybe not ever." He took a long swig from the champagne bottle. "Besides, I thought we were celebrating."

I grabbed his jacket sleeve. There was something I had to do. Something I'd been dreading.

"I'm gonna ask you a question. We'll get it out of the way, and then you're gonna go enjoy the party, okay?"

"Uh, okay."

"Where were you the night Petra died?"

"Alone," he replied. "Sorry, no airtight alibi. Does that make me a person of interest? I mean, I am pretty interesting."

I shook my head. "Thanks, Jayden."

Tipping the champagne bottle at me with unconvincing revelry, he disappeared into the throng of partiers. The pop song on the speaker was replaced by an edgy techno beat. Mundanes passed around six-packs of beer swiped from their parents' refrigerators. People started to form a makeshift dance floor around the paved surface of the fountain.

I approached Max next with the same unpleasant question.

"It's cool. I get why you have to ask." His voice was warm and easy, but the muscles in his neck held an uncharacteristic tension. "I wasn't up to much. Celeste and I saw a some dumb rom-com at the multiplex."

Contrived romance and buttered popcorn definitely fit Max's MO. But a moment later, I found Celeste, and doubt began to spring like weeds in my mind.

"I was shopping on Main Street." She sat on the fountain's edge, her ankles crossed, her eyes on a group of boys in the distance.

"Alone?"

"Uh-huh."

"All night?" I asked. "You didn't do *anything* else?"

"No." She sighed as if bored with my questions. "I'm a slow shopper. I can be pretty hard to size. I have a long torso." One of the guys she'd been watching motioned for her to join them, and she stood up to leave. "Can I go now? I thought tonight was supposed to be fun."

Without waiting for a reply, she walked away, her shiny black heels digging into the gravel path. The ring of admiring boys closed around her, and I found myself outside of it, my heart racing like the feverish beat of the music. Celeste hadn't mentioned Max or the multiplex. Had she forgotten what she was doing the night her friend died?

Or was one of them lying?

The weight of an arm around my shoulder tore me from my thoughts. Thomas Fitzgerald smelled of cheap beer and cheaper cologne. He stood closer than I would have liked.

"Lis-s-ten, Valeria," he slurred. "I wanted to give you my condolences. You let me know if there's anything I can do."

"You can start by backing up like three feet," I replied, shrugging his large arm away.

He didn't move. Something cruel lit up in his red-rimmed eyes. "Yeah," he said. "I was really sorry to hear about Petra. A young life cut short like that. Think of all the things she never got to do. I mean, she was a solid eight. I totally would've banged her. Now she'll never have that opportunity. It's tragic."

Revulsion rose in me. I longed to strike him, to topple him into the grass. Sunfire pounded in my chest. Suddenly, Luke was stepping between us, Gwen behind him, her dark eyes wide and alert.

"Fitzgerald," Luke said in a low voice. "Move along."

Thomas raised an eyebrow. "You gonna make me?"

This is what he wanted, I realized. A fight. A win.

"I don't pick fights with"—Luke stopped, and I could see the word *Mundanes* on his lips—"people like you."

"You just don't wanna get your ass kicked in front of your new girl." Thomas's gaze drifted to Gwen.

Her eyes seemed to deepen with fear. Something bad was about to happen. The certainty of it gripped me tight, making my heart quicken. Thomas drained his beer bottle as he looked her up and down.

"You know, Gwen, I like the new look. You're actually kinda hot now. I mean, if you squint hard enough." He leaned into her conspiratorially, his lips on her ear. "How about a dance? Let's make Nichols jealous."

He tugged her toward him, and she staggered forward under his strength, but she regained her footing quickly and wrenched herself away. Something clicked inside her, and the look of fear on Gwen's face was replaced with anger. The change was immediate and barely perceptible.

"Don't touch me," she said.

It was not a plea. It was a warning. But Thomas couldn't tell the difference.

"Come on." He laughed. "Don't be such a prude."

Around us, people had stopped dancing. They stood, watching the scene unfold as if staring at an accident on the side of the highway. Thomas reached for her, and then he was on the ground.

Luke stood over him, one fist raised, ready to hit him again. But Thomas shot up faster than expected. He was bigger than Luke, heavier, and he struck Luke with the full force of his weight. Luke staggered backward, a red gash above one eye. Thomas raised the beer bottle in his other hand, ready to bring it down on Luke's face.

Gwen's eyes went wide, not with panic but with surprise as she understood what she was about to do.

"Stop." As soon as Gwen said the word, Thomas froze, the bottle still raised above his head.

Everything seemed to go quiet, the music the bubbling fountain momentarily drowned out by the magnitude of what was happening. Gwen stood in the center of a motionless throng as Thomas Fitzgerald submitted to her command.

"Put the bottle down," she told him, and he obeyed. "You like to make other people feel afraid, don't you, Thomas?"

His eyes were large, glassy pools. He nodded slowly.

"Now I'm going to make you afraid." She cocked her head to one side, considering. "Think about all the times you hurt people— the times you messed with someone smaller and weaker than you just because you could. Can you do that for me?"

He nodded again, and his face crumpled into an expression of pain as if he'd just relived a string of horrible memories all at once.

"Imagine what those people must have felt. Try to feel their hurt, their panic."

A low moan escaped his lips. His shoulders trembled.

"Hey, Fitzgerald, get a hold of yourself!" somebody cried in protest. A few kids giggled, but there was a nervous edge to their laughter. Thomas ignored them all. His eyes were lost in the blackness of Gwen's.

"Are you afraid now?" she asked.

"Yes," he replied, his voice barely above a whisper.

"Good." Gwen pointed at the ground. "Now kneel."

Her voice was even, but her chest rose and fell rapidly. Her outstretched finger quivered. Thomas's face flushed. His blank eyes filled with tears, yet he still obeyed, his knees digging into the rocky ground.

My skin crawled as the words from the Book of Shadows flashed in my mind. *Some can control the Mundanes and make them obey their will.* This was malevolent magic.

"Say you're sorry."

"I'm sorry—I'm so sorry—please—" Thomas wept out his apology.

"No tears, Thomas. You should smile," Gwen said, her voice flat. "You'd be a lot prettier if you smiled."

Thomas's lips stretched slowly upward, the terror in his eyes in sick contrast with the grin he now wore.

My mind reeled. If Gwen could do this, what else was she capable of? What else had she done? Her eyes met mine over Thomas's whimpering form, and I knew she saw the fragile trust between us crumble beneath the weight of this new revelation. She shook her head in a silent plea for understanding, but she was still holding Thomas under her spell. I was afraid she wasn't through with him. Afraid of what she would say next.

I took a breath, shut my eyes, and thought of rain.

The drops began to fall immediately. They weren't torrential like Gwen's storm, but they were enough. She began to tremble, her concentration wavering. Then Luke was behind her, rainwater mixing with the blood on his temple. He put his arms around her, whispering gentle words. Her grip on Thomas's mind broke, and she collapsed into Luke's arms as her obsidian eyes rolled back.

Thomas blinked and rubbed his face with shaky hands. Gwen's head lay heavily on Luke's shoulder. Around them, the party dispersed beneath a shower of rain.

CHAPTER TEN

GWEN

The river bubbled cheerfully along Main Street. It was Monday and I didn't have a shift after school, so Luke and I strolled hand-in-hand, perusing shop windows, warmed by the afternoon sun. The scene was so wholesome, it tempted me to forget the seriously messed up magic I'd done in the cemetery two nights ago. But I couldn't. Images of Thomas's terrified face had tormented me since that night. Luke had been casual with me—gentle, even. I knew he was waiting for me to bring up the subject of malevolent magic on my own terms, and it was driving me crazy.

Finally, as we passed the artisanal dog treat shop, I blurted, "Are we gonna talk about what I did to Thomas Fitzgerald or what?"

"Okay," he replied. "I'll start by saying thanks. You saved me from getting my face smashed in. You're my hero."

"And?" I was expecting—*hoping*—for some sort of reckoning.

"And maybe the next time he wants to harass a girl for fun, he'll think twice. If you ask me, you did the world a favor."

I thought of all the skeezy things Thomas had done over the years, wondering if Luke had a point. I didn't think Thomas or any of the Mundanes fully understood what had happened to him. But today at school, when he spied me across the quad, he booked it in the other direction. I had to admit that it felt good. Unfortunately, Valeria and the rest of the coven kept their distance when they saw me, too, their eyes narrow with mistrust.

"Okay, maybe Thomas deserved a good scare. But still, I discovered I have *malevolent* magic. Malevolent, as in evil." I paused, afraid to voice my next thought aloud. "It makes me wonder if there's something wrong with me."

Valeria had said malevolent magic came from anger, hatred. She was right. I'd felt it in my core. It had drained me to pull all that negativity into the world, as if the universe itself had pushed back against it. After I'd controlled Thomas, I'd been exhausted, barely able to drag myself into bed. All night, I could feel the magic still humming in my veins, haunting my dreams. If malevolent magic ran in families, Elizabeth Foster must have had this power too. Was that why the coven had revoked her magic?

Luke stopped suddenly, pulling me to a halt. "If you're waiting for me to tell you you're a horrible person because you have this power, keep on waiting. It's never gonna happen."

"But the Book of Shadows says—"

"The book says that inside every witch, there is good and evil. We *all* have darkness within us. You just happen to have the ability to use your darkness in a powerful way. That doesn't make you some kind of villain."

"I'm not sure Valeria would agree," I said bitterly.

Could I blame her? Malevolent magic had killed Petra. The moment I controlled Thomas, everything had changed between us. Any amends we'd made were broken now; her suspicion hovered over us like a dark cloud. I'd seen her face that night—she'd actually been afraid of me. I was embarrassed by how much it hurt to see her look at me that way.

"Give Valeria time," Luke said. "She might come around. She said herself there are two types of malevolent magic—the one that controls the Mundanes, and the one that kills. You don't have the killing kind, you have the...persuasive kind."

"She's not making that distinction right now. Think about it. All the coven's problems began when I showed up. Now that she knows I have this power, how do I come back from that?"

Luke brushed a stray hair from my cheek. "Do you remember what I said to you when you were afraid to dance at homecoming?"

"Screw 'em."

"That's right. Maybe Valeria doesn't trust you, but I do."

"Despite my freaky mind-control magic?"

His expression grew serious. His fingers cupped my cheek, tilting my face toward his, our lips almost touching. "With my life."

Luke's eyes drew me in, holding me in some secret, safe place. As long as he looked at me like that, maybe everything really would be all right. Sunlight touched the sharp, exquisite angles of his face. I had the urge to tangle my fingers in his dark hair, to feel the stubble on his cheeks, the warmth of his skin. So I did.

"What are you doing?" he asked with unbothered curiosity.

"Just making sure you're real."

He laughed. "You're crazy, you know that?"

He pulled me to him, but as our lips met, a grim thought played in my mind.

Perhaps I'm crazier than you think.

We got coffees to go and continued down Main Street. With Luke's arm around me and the music of the river in my ears, it was easier to let the worry go. We passed the shops I used to kill time in when I wanted to be anywhere but home. As we approached Larkspur, I cringed as I recalled my failed attempt to buy a homecoming dress there. *Our fitting rooms are for paying customers only. I'm sure you understand.* I could still hear the condescension in the shop clerk's voice, feel her uneasy gaze travel over my dirty clothes and scuffed-up shoes. And, like a fool with five hundred dollars in my pocket, I had shuffled away without a contradictory word.

A dress in the window caught my eye, and before I realized it, I'd stopped in my tracks to take it in fully. The top was sheer, with delicate scallops adorning the deep neckline. When I looked closer at the intricate lace pattern, I could make out roses and vines and leaves and thorns spreading across the bodice. The skirt was full, made of layers of light, gauzy fabric. It was black from head to toe, a rich midnight color that seemed to take on new dimensions depending on the way the light hit it. Its beauty made my eyes water.

"See something you like?"

"Huh?" I replied.

"That dress." Luke pointed at the window. "You love it, don't you?"

"No," I lied. "I mean, sure, it's beautiful, but—"

"And it would be beautiful on you," he added.

I could tell by looking at it that it would fit like it had been made for me. Luke knew it too. I could sense him picturing it on me. The idea made my cheeks flush.

"When would I ever wear something like that?" I protested.

"Oh, I'm sure we can find an occasion." A sly grin tugged at one corner of his lips.

I took a breath as dread gathered in the pit of my stomach. I knew where this was going.

"Don't buy it for me," I pleaded. "*Please* don't buy it for me."

He took my hand, and before I knew it, he was pulling me into the shop. The little bell above the door tinkled with artificial cheer. Great. I had already been treated like a leper in this establishment; now I was about to become a charity case here too. I was still putting most of my Diggin's salary toward any bills my dad couldn't pay, and the rest I was saving for college, or whatever the future held beyond this town. There was nothing leftover for raven-colored formalwear.

The woman behind the counter looked as austere as the last time I'd seen her, her hair pulled into an identically tight bun. She glanced up when we entered and grinned at Luke, but when she saw me, recognition passed over her face and her smile faded. I watched her small brown eyes dart over my new clothes, my hand in Luke's. For just a second, she let her surprise show, then her expression quickly rearranged itself into placid congeniality.

"Welcome in," she chirped.

Luke pointed to the dress. "How much is that one?"

She looked at us with a straight face and said, "Ten-fifty."

It took me a moment to realize she meant one thousand and fifty whole dollars. I tugged on Luke's hand. "Forget it," I whispered, hoping she couldn't hear. "Let's go."

"It's okay to let someone do something nice for you for a change," he said. "You deserve it."

I sighed, feeling myself waver. One moment of hesitation was all he needed. Before I could speak, he called to the clerk, a mischievous spark in his eyes.

"I'll take it!"

She arched an eyebrow. Luke didn't seem to notice, but I understood immediately. She wasn't questioning his ability to pay for the gown—she was wondering why he would buy such an extravagant thing for *me*. My cheeks burning with humiliation, I watched her zip the dress into a garment bag. Luke pulled a credit card from his wallet and handed it to her. She took it smugly, but as she was about to run it through the card reader, something inside me boiled over.

I wouldn't let him give this sniveling woman any money on my behalf. Why should I? After she'd treated me like some cheap, tarnished thing that didn't belong in her presence?

I knew I shouldn't use my magic. But the power was stirring inside me, rising with every beat of my heart.

"Wait," I commanded. I let the spell spread toward her like a spider's web, wrapping itself around her silly little mind.

She stopped what she was doing, her hand suspended over the cash register, her air of superiority evaporating.

"He's not going to pay for that dress." I told her. "Because you're going to give it to me. Now."

Her fingers began to tremble. Luke's card fell from her loosened grip and tumbled onto the counter, but she didn't seem to notice. Her eyes stared into mine, the pupils wide. She slid the garment bag toward me, her breathing rapid like a nervous animal, but she didn't struggle. In a few moments, it would all be over, and she'd rub her temples and wonder what had come over her. I smiled a cool, hospitable smile.

"Thanks," I said. "And the next time a lost soul wanders in here looking for a place to exist for a while, leave them be."

We left the shop, breathless but exhilarated. My body hummed with the thrill of what I'd just done. Luke felt it too. His wild laughter echoed down the street as we hurried away.

"You never cease to amaze me!" he exclaimed. "That was crazy, but I gotta say, it was pretty hot."

He spun me once before wrapping his arms around me. I could practically feel his heart pounding through his skin as he drew me close. We kissed in the middle of the sidewalk as the downtown shoppers passed around us. In one hand, I clutched the bag that contained the most beautiful dress I'd ever seen. It's mine, I thought. No one bought it for me. I took it because I wanted it. A headache was shooting its way through my temple and my knees were weak, but I didn't care.

"I used to think I'd be the one to get you into trouble, Gwen Foster," he said. "But now it looks like you just might lead *me* down the path to ruin."

He said it with a smile, but I felt the disturbing truth to his words. A voice in my head told me to worry, to retreat to my room and guilt-trip myself into never using this magic again. But I didn't want to do any of that. I wanted to shout, to run down the street with my arms open wide. For once in my life, to take what I desired. I wanted this power forever. I wanted Luke forever. Why should I deny myself now? I'd had a lifetime of denial.

I was suddenly consumed by the urge to go fast. To fly down this street and keep moving for as long as I could. I clutched the bag to my chest and started walking.

"Where are you going?" Luke called, rushing after me.

"I don't know," I replied, quickening my pace. "Down the path to ruin. Wanna come?"

He took my hand, but I stayed a few steps ahead of him as we made our way up Main Street. The magic coursed through my veins, hot and restless. My hurried steps pounded on the pavement. As we crossed 15th Street, a well-dressed man was getting out of a shiny new convertible. I could sense the power contained in its engine. I thought of Luke's car parked up the street. I could ask him to take me anywhere—to the ocean, the redwoods. But that wasn't good enough. I wanted to be in the driver's seat.

"Hey!" I called to the man, the harsh sound of my own voice startling me.

The man was middle-aged with a graying comb-over. He looked at me in surprise.

"I need your car," I told him. Even as my headache grew sharper, I felt the same unmistakable thrill I'd felt with the shop clerk. I was about to take control.

"Wh-what?" the man stammered.

"Gimme the keys."

It was easy to hold his mind in mine, practically automatic. He fished them from his pocket with a trembling hand and gave them to me.

"That's all," I told him. "You can go now."

And he did. The point between my eyebrows seemed to sing with pain, but the pain made a pretty halo in my vision. I couldn't stop now. I wanted the wind in my hair.

"Can't say I pictured you as a car thief," Luke said as I slid into the leather seat.

I heard his words, but it didn't feel like stealing. Right now, everything in the world felt like it was mine. I threw the garment bag in the back and turned the key in the ignition. The engine hummed to life. I grinned at Luke, the halo of pain framing his face. He was gorgeous.

"Get in," I said wryly. "I'm driving."

He shook his head at me in disbelief, but there was more than a hint of a smile on his lips.

"You might be the death of me, baby," he replied, "but what a way to go."

He got in beside me and I pressed on the gas. The car jolted forward, and I didn't let up. Soon, we were doing sixty down Main Street as people on the sidewalks stared. Let them, I thought. I pressed harder on the accelerator as the buildings thinned, giving way to open land. I didn't know where I was taking us; I just let the noise of the wind fill my ears, silencing my doubts. I felt the weight of the magic like something too heavy in my hands. I knew I couldn't hold it much longer. But for now, the air smelled of flowers and green things. The top was down, and the sun was warm.

About twenty miles out of town, I pulled over, exhausted. My temples throbbed as if gripped by some cruel hand. Luke drove us back to town as I slept on his shoulder. We left the car where we'd found it with the keys in the glove box, then he took me home. He kissed me gently in the driveway before pulling away.

All I could think of was sleep. I squinted hard against the light.

I entered my living room, clutching the black garment bag that held my dress. My dad sat at the coffee table, counting a few crumpled dollar bills.

"You're back early today—" I must have looked bad because he stood up, forgetting the money on the table. "Gwen, what's wrong? You were out with that boy, weren't you? That rich kid from Cascabel Road. I've seen him drop you off here a dozen times now. Did he do something to you?" The worry in his voice surprised me.

"No—I mean, yes, I was out with Luke. But he didn't do anything. I just—" I sighed. "I got a headache. He took me home."

My knees trembled, and I steadied myself against the doorframe.

"Well, come on, then," he said.

He draped one of my arms over his shoulder and walked me to my bedroom. As I collapsed on the bed, he shut the curtains. I couldn't remember the last time my dad had taken care of me and not the other way around. I was vaguely aware of the strangeness of it. My vision blurred and my eyelids sagged, but I thought I saw a dark spot under one of his eyes. A bruise nearly healed.

Guilt piled on top of the pain I already felt. Between the coven and Luke, I hadn't been around as much lately. I came home late at night to find him shivering on the couch, asleep with the window open wide. I slipped out early in the mornings, leaving him to wake in an empty house, no smell of breakfast waiting in the kitchen.

"Dad, are you okay?" I mumbled sleepily.

"What's that?" He pulled a blanket up to my chin.

"Your eye."

"Oh. I owe a guy, but it's nothing you need to worry about. Just rest now, okay?"

"Maybe we don't have to worry about that anymore."

"No," he said quickly. "Don't you offer me the money you're saving. I won't use it, I swear on my life."

"That's not what I meant."

I knew what my power could do now, the control I could hold over the Mundanes. Maybe it was time something in the universe yielded to me instead of the other way around. The thought lingered in the darkness behind my closed eyelids. Then I slept.

CHAPTER ELEVEN

GWEN

The gates of Valeria Garcia's house seemed to stare me down like some heavy iron foe. I hadn't spoken to her since the night I controlled Thomas—or, more accurately, Valeria hadn't spoken to me. I'd tried a dozen times to catch her eye at school, but she breezed past me, her lips pulled into a tight line of worry. There had been no announcement, no official decree, but the rest of the coven seemed to be in agreement: I couldn't be trusted.

Luke had become an outsider by association, hiding away with me in some secluded hallway while the others ate lunch in their usual spot beneath the Palms. I didn't want to care about what Valeria thought of me, and yet here I was, walking up to her house, unable to deny that I did.

I didn't know exactly what I was going to say to her. I just wanted her to listen, and maybe when I was done, she'd stop looking at me with that wary expression on her face, like I was some kind of evil creature and not the other way around. With a sigh, I swung the gate open and climbed the old wooden stairs. The house was imposing in the dimming light, its color more blood red than strawberry. I rapped twice with the heavy golden door knocker.

After a long moment, Valeria opened the door, and I almost

gasped aloud. I'd never seen her looking so exhausted, so human. Her hair was pulled into a messy bun that had nothing to do with fashion and everything to do with utility. Dark circles ringed her eyes. She clasped the Book of Shadows under one arm.

"Gwen," she said. "What are you doing here?"

I fumbled for a casual reply, something about how I hadn't seen her around school, how I'd been meaning to drop in. But a tidal wave of awkward self-expression rose in my throat.

"We haven't been speaking," I said. "Things have been weird ever since you found out I have malevolent magic. And I totally get that, believe me, but I'm not the person you think I am. I'm still a member of this coven. We can work together."

"Thank you for sharing," Valeria replied. "You done?" There was no bold challenge in her expression—no sly mockery either. Her face was a mask of weariness, of heartache.

"Yeah. That was it."

There was an uncomfortable silence. My eyes traveled to the Book of Shadows under Valeria's arm.

"Any luck?" I said.

"What?"

"The Book of Shadows. Did you find anything? You know, about what Petra knew…or why my powers are back?"

"Not yet." She sighed. "But if you need a spell to make your chickens lay more eggs, I'm your girl."

"Who would've thought the Book of Shadows would be so PG?" Examining Valeria, I got the impression she'd been holed up with that book every night since Petra died. "Let me help you," I said suddenly. "I mean, what am I good for, if not copious amounts of reading?"

"Grand theft auto?"

I felt my muscles tense.

"Celeste hits the shops on Main Street practically every day after school. She saw you take that Mundane's car. Said he gave you the keys like they were yours."

I scrambled for an excuse, for some casual words that would make it seem okay. But it was a doomed effort. How could I explain the pull of malevolent magic to someone who'd never experienced it? I felt the divide between us grow. The irony wasn't lost on me. I'd spent years terrified of Valeria; now she was acting like *I* was the one to fear.

But of course I wasn't. She'd known me longer than anyone. She had to understand.

"I know how this must look to you, but I came here to tell you you can trust me." An unwelcome desperation crept into my voice. "Please. Trust me."

"I can't. Not while you're using malevolent magic," she said, grimacing as if it hurt her to say the words. This wasn't the bully I'd grown accustomed to. Standing in the doorway, Valeria looked more like the little girl I used to know. A pretty girl with sad eyes. "I gotta get back to work," she said, stepping back into the house. "I'm sorry, Gwen."

The door closed, leaving me alone on the other side.

One dejected step after another, I descended the front stairs. Instead of heading home, I turned in the direction of Luke's house. I could have taken the road, but I went through the forest as if pulled by some desire for the peace that place used to bring.

I weaved between trunks and under bare branches. Past the clearing, the fallen tree lay dappled in shadow. The opening of the hollow gaped like a yawning mouth. I let myself mourn the days when problems could be solved and friendships forged with a carefully placed butterfly wing. Things would never be that simple again. If this was what it meant to grow up, I wasn't sure I wanted it. But I supposed none of us got a choice.

And if Valeria believed I was guilty of some awful crime, I didn't really have a choice about that either. I passed the hollow, resisting the familiar urge to glance inside. One thing was certain: she wouldn't be leaving me any secret offerings anytime soon.

A bitter feeling settled in my stomach. She's jealous, I told myself. Jealous of me and Luke. Jealous of my power. That was the only logical explanation for her behavior. When had Valeria Garcia ever cared about anyone but herself?

I marched on until Luke's house came into view. I felt a little silly emerging from the forest and walking up to his back door, but I didn't care. I wanted to see him, wanted him to hold me. Wanted that simple peace I used to find beneath the trees.

The back door opened into Luke's white-tiled kitchen. Mr. Nichols stood in the doorway, wearing a pair of bright red oven mitts. The scent of something sweet filled the house.

"Gwen! What a lovely surprise!"

"Hi, Mr. Nichols," I said shyly. "Is Luke home?"

"What's with the formalities? Please, call me Alexis. I can tell how happy you make my son. That makes you family in my book." He went to the oven and removed a tray of slightly charred blueberry muffins. "Oh dear, I'm afraid I lost track of time on these. Oh well, a little burnt crust never hurt anyone."

"Gwen? Is that you?"

Footsteps sounded on the stairs, then Luke stood in the kitchen, dressed in his usual wardrobe of denim and leather. I temporarily panicked, wondering if he'd be weirded out by my unannounced visit, but he looked at me as casually as if he'd been expecting me all along.

"Cool, you saved me a trip. I was about to go pick you up."

"You were?"

"Yeah. I have a surprise for you."

"What is it?"

He grinned. "You know how surprises work, right? Let's go. I'll show you."

"Leaving already?" his dad called as we headed for the door. "Take a muffin for the road!"

Luke shot me an exaggerated eye roll, but I turned back to the kitchen. "Thanks, Mr. Nichols—I mean, Alexis."

Heating up a frozen dinner every now and then was the extent of my dad's culinary skills. I wondered how different my life might have been if I'd grown up in a house like this, with a father who made blueberry muffins.

The faint light of the new moon did little to illuminate Cascabel Road as Luke and I sped into town. My talk with Valeria had left a pit of worry in my stomach. When I closed my eyes, I could see the dull, glassy expressions of the Mundanes I'd controlled. In my fingertips, I could still feel the magic coiled around their minds. I knew what I'd done was wrong. I just hadn't wanted to deal with it until now.

"I'm not going to use malevolent magic anymore," I announced to Luke as we turned onto Main Street.

Even as I said it, there was a tug of protest in my heart, a small part of me eager to hold onto the power I'd been given, to clutch it in my fists and never let go. After all, it was mine.

Luke turned to me. "All right," he said as casually as if I'd told him I was going to get bangs. "If that's what you want, that's what you should do."

He had a maddening way of making everything seem so simple. I smiled in spite of myself. I took his hand and let the shop windows fly by in my periphery. We drove another few blocks before he parked in front of the Hotel Dorado. It was an old brick building with white columns and giant palms in the lobby. At a whopping seven stories, it was the tallest building in town. On its rooftop was a huge, Las Vegas-style sign announcing its title in neon letters.

We stepped onto the street and I followed him inside, but instead of heading to the lobby, he made a quick right down a hallway of first-floor rooms. I almost asked, but we'd already had one conversation about surprises. I followed him into a stairwell at the end of the hall. Its stark gray banisters and concrete steps told me it was definitely not intended for guest access.

He put a finger to his lips with a playful smile and we climbed all seven flights, careful not to let our footsteps echo. When we reached the top, I was breathless but smiling.

Before us was a door marked STAFF ONLY. But when Luke pushed the handle, it turned easily.

"Did you just——" I began.

"Did I just do some magical lock picking to gain access to the best view in Dorado?" he replied. "No, I did that earlier."

He swung the door open to reveal a rooftop decorated with dozens of flickering candles. Beyond the low metal railing, the lights of the town glowed like hundreds of tiny flames. The river sparkled under the streetlights. Everything that seemed so ordinary on the street below was magical from up here.

The giant letters of the neon sign beamed at us, bathing the entire scene in a surreal glow. He took my hand and led me to the edge. As we drew closer, I saw there were vases of delicate white flowers set among the candles. Their pale petals seemed to shine in the surrounding dusk. I lifted one. Its scent was strong and intoxicatingly sweet.

"Epidendrum nocturnum. Night-scented orchid. I thought you'd like them."

"They're beautiful," I replied. "But you didn't have to do all this."

"I didn't have to, but you deserve it," he told me seriously. "In fact, you deserve much more than a few candles and a stolen view."

The sky was dark now, and the neon behind us painted it in hues of artificial yellow, like the backdrop to some strange play.

"Look," Luke said, pointing to a spot in the eastern sky. "See those five brighter stars? That's Cassiopeia."

I squinted. "It's hard to see with the light," I told him, gesturing at the neon letters behind us.

A wicked smile crossed his lips. I smiled back at him, though my nerves began to tingle. It was like that with Luke sometimes. There was magic between us; like the pull of the tide, it drew me to him, even as I sensed something crazy was about to happen.

"Then we'll shut it off," he said.

We turned to face the sign. Each letter was about a story high, illuminated by hundreds of bulbs. I couldn't imagine commanding them all to go dark. It made my head spin.

"I—I don't think we can. It's too big."

He took my hand. I felt the warmth of his skin on mine, magic dancing between us like electricity.

"Trust me," he said and closed his eyes.

I did trust him. More than I'd trusted anyone before. I couldn't explain it, but I was beginning to understand we belonged together. Just as surely as my magic was a part of me, so was he. All the years I'd wandered through life wishing for a place to belong, that place had been by his side. Those nights I'd spent gazing at the dark sky, the dull yearning in my heart had been for him.

I closed my eyes and willed the light away. I felt Luke's power beside me, felt the elements answer to us.

I squeezed his hand. Through my closed eyelids, I saw the yellow glow fade and disappear. I opened my eyes. The sign had gone dim.

"We did it!" I cried.

I whirled around to face the horizon again, only to see lights flickering out beneath us. Every light on the block below died. We watched in a hush as the next block went out, then the next. Traffic lights, shop windows, and the lanterns on the riverwalk disappeared one by one. Darkness spread through the town, the faint twinkle of the farmhouses blinking out across the river. For a second, I feared it would never end, that we'd envelop the whole world in darkness with our power.

We stood there in stunned silence until it finally stopped. When it was over, a curtain of black stretched several miles in all directions.

I knew what we'd done was only possible because we'd done it together. It wasn't a logical conclusion but a visceral knowledge that I trusted more than logic. We stared at the darkness at our feet like a king and queen surveying the realm under our command. Above us, the five stars of Cassiopeia shone clear and brilliant.

"I love you," Luke said, his voice carrying over the rooftops.

"I love you too." They were the truest words I'd ever spoken.

He kissed me. I thought I'd be used to it by now, the feeling of when his lips met mine. Instead, every time was more powerful than the last. Everything around us disappeared— the rooftop, the river. We were two heavenly bodies colliding in the night sky.

Luke pulled me closer, his touch like fire on my skin. Then I saw it in the blackness of my mind: the meteor.

Its heat made my eyes water. Its beauty overwhelmed me. At first I thought it was speeding toward me, but my body was weightless now. Perhaps I *was* that burning orb, hurtling through darkness, the solid earth growing ever closer below. Let it come, I thought, and kissed him harder.

Back in Luke's car, we were quiet as he drove me home through unlit streets. I wondered vaguely when the Mundanes would get the power back on, if they'd scratch their heads and declare it was the strangest thing.

As he pulled into my driveway, I noted with dismay a familiar car parked behind my dad's on the gravel strip. The house was as dark as the shop fronts on Main Street, but I made out two figures standing in front of my door. One was my dad. The other was a man I'd seen once before—the man who'd been at the house the night I'd discovered my dad bleeding on the living room floor.

An urgent fear gripped me. Without a word to Luke, I got out of the car and hurried up the driveway toward them. As I grew closer, I could make out the tension in my dad's voice, the cool anger in the other man's.

"What's going on?" I demanded.

Moonlight glittered in the stranger's eyes. "Hey there, Pop-Tart. You wouldn't happen to have the money your daddy owes me, would you?"

My gaze darted from him to my dad and back again.

"You leave her the hell alone!" My dad tried to sound intimidating, but his words were choked with fear. "I told you, I'll pay you. Just give me a little more time."

The man shook his head as if he'd heard a bad joke. "You've had enough time."

From his jacket he withdrew something dark and metallic. He pointed the gun at my father, one finger on the trigger.

Before I could think, before I could move, my dad pulled something from the waistband of his jeans.

No. When had he gotten this desperate? My dad had always kept a rifle in the house, an old rusty thing he used to take rabbit hunting in the forest. This gun was shiny, brand new. It trembled in his hand.

"Gwen, get out of here!" he cried, but I didn't move.

The night went still. The sound of the wind faded until all that was left was those two men and their silly, deadly toys. I didn't even need to speak this time. I waved a hand, and they both froze. With another glance, the stranger tossed his weapon into the damp grass.

I knew I should tell my dad to do the same, but magic coursed through my veins like adrenaline, unstoppable now. I steadied the gun in my father's hand, his finger firm on the trigger. I watched the fear of death rise in the other man's eyes, heard his gasping breaths. A strange giddiness swept over me. Even in this horrible moment, it felt good to hold this much power.

Then I saw my dad's eyes, wide and panicked. He didn't want this man dead, didn't want to see him suffer. The other Mundanes seemed unable to recognize what was happening to them when they were under my control, but I knew by my father's face that he did. Some long-forgotten memory of magic lingered in his blood, making him understand. He struggled against me, tried to lower the gun, to loosen his grip on the trigger.

"Please—let me go, Gwen." His eyes held mine in a desperate plea.

I wavered, but the magic inside me resisted. I turned to the other man, taking in the sweat that glistened on his brow, the way his mouth gaped in terror. Just a few moments ago, he would have killed us both. Why, I wondered, should I show him mercy now?

Luke was behind me, so close I smelled the leather of his jacket. He put a hand on my shoulder, his touch careful as if I were a bomb that might go off at any moment.

I felt my grip loosen at last, my knees trembling. I clung to the spell long enough to turn to the loan shark.

"You're going to get out of here and never trouble my dad again, do you understand?"

He glanced at me, then at the gun my dad still aimed in his direction.

"Y-yes," he coughed out the word. "Yes."

He disappeared down the driveway. I heard the turn of his engine, the sound of rubber on gravel, and he was gone.

With an exhale, I let the magic go. Pain shot into my temples, worse than anything I'd felt before. In my periphery, my dad fell to his knees, the gun skidding into the dirt.

I was aware of Luke helping me inside, the sound of our footsteps in the house's quiet interior. My bed seemed to rise to meet me, my cheek landing against the pillow. After that, I knew nothing but darkness for a long time.

THE SUN WAS high in the sky by the time I woke the next day. My head rang with the echoes of last night's pain. I walked through the house as if still dreaming.

The TV was missing from the living room. My dad's bed was stripped, his closet empty. On the fridge, a note read simply: YOU'LL BE ALL RIGHT WITHOUT ME. LOVE ALWAYS, DAD

For a long time, I sat at the kitchen table, exhausted and utterly alone. I called Luke.

In ten minutes, he was there to take me away from that house with its stale air and empty rooms. Back at his place, Luke led me upstairs. He closed his bedroom door behind us, and we sat together on his four-poster bed.

"Stay here with me," he said. "You're welcome to as long as you want."

"What?" I replied over the pounding of my temples. "You want me to stay...*here*?" I glanced warily at the expansive bed with its rich coverings. "I'm not ready—I mean, I've never—"

"That's not what I'm asking," he said quickly, removing his hand from my shoulder. "We have a guest room. It's all yours."

In my aching heart, I knew what I wanted. I longed to sink into the softness of his bed and sleep for a week, numb and safe by his side.

"I want to stay," I told him, my voice trembling. "In this room. With you. Please, will you just hold me?"

Wordlessly, he slid his arms around me. My head rested on his chest. Tears stung my eyes but didn't fall. I listened to the gentle beating of his heart. He didn't have to answer. I knew I was home.

CHAPTER TWELVE

VALERIA

Candlelight danced across my bedroom wall, throwing shadows on the dark floral wallpaper. My phone lit up abruptly on my nightstand, announcing it was charging. Finally, the power was back on. It had mysteriously cut out last night and stayed off all day, leaving my house drearier than usual and my cell battery dangerously low.

I reached for my phone and opened Instagram. For a second, I felt the familiar instinct to check my own page, to analyze my views and comments for some sort of quantitative measure of approval. But the notion seemed silly after the events of the past few weeks. Now I found myself using the app almost exclusively for its stalking capabilities.

I tapped on Celeste's latest story. In the photo, she modeled a new amethyst bracelet, two purple stones in the shape of a sun and a moon. ECLIPSE READY, the caption declared. The eclipse wasn't until Friday, but Celeste could never resist the urge to show off a new purchase, especially if a glittery filter was involved. I recognized her bedspread in the background; she was at home, or had been an hour ago. Max didn't post as much as his sister, but his content remained consistent: sweetly naive quotes about kindness inter-

spersed with photos of workout equipment with the caption PRAC-
TICE MAKES PERFECT.

In addition to scrutinizing their social media, I had literally
followed Max and Celeste on multiple occasions, hanging several
cars behind Celeste's SUV as she headed to the shops on Main
Street or trailing Max as he drove home from school. They went
about their usual routines, unaware of my watchful gaze. The only
thing out of the ordinary was that Max no longer smiled when
Jayden walked into a room. Maybe he had a new crush, or maybe it
had taken the introspection of tragedy for Max to finally realize
Jayden wasn't interested. Either way, nothing Max or Celeste did
seemed like the actions of a malevolent witch out to destroy our
coven.

Still, I couldn't ignore the conflicting stories they'd given me
about what they were doing the night Petra died. If Max had seen a
movie with his sister like he said, then why did she claim she'd been
shopping all night? I longed to just ask them, but Petra had been
killed because someone thought she knew too much. There was
safety in secrecy.

Of course, on my mental list of suspicious figures, the standout
was Gwen. When I'd faced the killer in the forest, Gwen had been
with my mom and Luke in the kitchen. No spell I'd ever heard of
would allow her to be in two places at once. But she'd controlled
Thomas, and her joyride in a stranger's car showed she didn't just
use malevolent magic in self-defense; she reveled in it.

Yesterday, I'd seen genuine emotion in her eyes when she
pleaded with me to trust her. As she stood in my doorway, a voice
inside me had screamed that this was *Gwen Foster*, the girl who used
to cry when she found a bird's egg toppled by the wind. Still, I
couldn't bet my coven's safety on the Gwen I used to know. A lot
had happened since those days. The strange part was, the harder
things got, the more I wished I had Gwen on my side.

I closed Instagram and turned back to the Book of Shadows. By
now, the mere sight of the book and the charred edges of its missing
pages was enough to make me want to take a hammer to something. Petra's last words rang in my head like some enigmatic poem.

It's happening again, like it did when Dorado was founded. There's this prophecy—

Whatever that prophecy entailed, someone had been willing to kill for it. And Delfina Garcia had gone to great lengths to conceal it from the coven's future generations. I was certain that prophecy had something to do with Elizabeth Foster and why she'd lost her magic, but I'd read the Book of Shadows from cover to musty cover and there was no mention of it.

Last night, I'd returned to the beginning of the book in desperation—the section in Delfina Garcia's prim penmanship. And there, in the orange glow of candlelight, I'd found a glimmer of hope: *A Spell for Those Who Seek Clarity.* At first, I'd brushed it off as some crunchy ritual for inner peace. But the more I thought about it, that didn't strike me as Delfina's style. Maybe she meant the type of clarity that could answer the questions keeping me up at night.

I'd asked Jayden to bring me the herbal ingredients without telling him what they were for. I didn't want to get his hopes up in case it was a dead end, I told myself. But perhaps my secrecy wasn't about protecting him. Maybe I just didn't want him to know I'd made a mistake.

I opened the Book of Shadows to the spell in question and withdrew the herbs from my desk drawer. The mingled scent of poppy and turmeric stung my nose.

Footsteps creaked in the ancient hallway and my parents appeared in the doorway, my dad in sweats and slippers, my mom in her silk robe. It was scary how accustomed I'd become to this new, unnatural version of my parents. Their features were technically the same—my mother's high cheekbones and thin, straight nose; my dad's salt-and-pepper hair, his brows dark and heavy like mine. But something was missing behind their eyes, that light that used to sparkle announcing they were alive, they were magical. It had been snuffed out the day they lost their power. I felt its absence every time I looked at them, and it made my heart ache.

"The electricity's back on, you know." My mom nodded at the candles on my desk.

"Can't a girl get back to her pre-Edison roots?" I replied.

My joke bounced off her like water off scotch-guarded satin. My dad took in the now-familiar scene: me hunched over the Book of Shadows in the dim light of my bedroom. He asked the question he'd asked every night for a week.

"Find anything, sweetie?"

My parents knew they should help, but without powers, they were short on options. Or perhaps it was their will that was lacking, gone with the light that was snuffed out inside them.

I smiled weakly. "Something worth a try."

"Don't stay up too late," he said.

There was no scolding in his tone, just worry over things he couldn't name. Things he couldn't change. I swallowed, turning to my mom. There was something I'd been meaning to ask her since the night Petra died.

"Mom?"

"Yes?" she replied, an edge of impatience in her tone.

"The night I faced Petra's killer in the woods, I was so scared. The sunfire turned on me."

"And how did you free yourself?"

"I didn't," I said, shame forcing me to lower my gaze. "The witch, whoever it was, knocked me to the ground. The blow kind of snapped me out of it."

As I said the words, I wondered again if this had been intentional. Why kill Petra then spare me?

"Then you were very lucky," she said.

I knew I would face the mystery witch again. Next time, I needed to be ready.

"How do I keep the sunfire under control?"

Her expression grew distant. "You can use an anchor."

"An anchor?"

"Something to ground you. A thought, a memory, anything that makes you feel connected to the universe…and the people in it."

It was hard to imagine my mother connecting to people, even in her own mind.

"Has—" I began, mustering courage. "Has the sunfire ever turned on you?"

"No." Her features hardened like mortar. "Make sure you blow those candles out before bed."

With that, she disappeared down the long hallway in the direction of her bedroom, leaving me with a familiar shrinking feeling, the knowledge that in the complicated equation that was our relationship, I was decidedly on the "less than" side. Of course the sunfire had never turned on her. When had my mom ever lost control of anything?

I expected my dad to follow her to the bedroom, but he lingered in the doorway.

"It happened to her once," he said in a conspiratorial whisper. "You were about ten. She and I had a fight over something stupid, and she went out to practice sunfire in the forest alone. When she came back, her face was pale, and there were scorch marks on the sleeve of her jacket where the spell had climbed up her arm."

I leaned forward like his words were drops of some life-giving elixir. So I wasn't the only screw-up?

"How did she get out of it?"

He snorted through his nose. "You think she told me?"

"She breezed past you without saying a word, didn't she?"

"Yup. Your mom doesn't like to let people know she isn't perfect."

I thought of the way I had avoided telling Jayden why I needed the herbs, just in case the clarity spell was a dud. The urge to hide any failure, real or potential, had to be a genetic trait in the Garcia family.

"She did tell me one thing, long ago," my dad added. "She thinks about you when she does the sunfire spell. You're her anchor."

He sighed as if the conversation had drained the last bit of his energy. With a nod, he shuffled off to bed.

I sat at my desk a moment, the Book of Shadows before me. I used to watch my mom in awe as she commanded the sunfire at coven gatherings, a roaring bonfire springing to life beneath her outstretched hands. All those times she'd wielded that immense power, there had been an image of me in her mind, grounding her and keeping her safe. The idea filled me with a warmth I didn't usually associate with my mom.

With renewed determination, I turned to the ingredients of my spell. The herbs sat on the table beside a kettle of river water. I placed them into the kettle and floated it over my outstretched hand. Beneath the kettle, I let sunfire ignite in my palm, the flames lapping at the bottom of the kettle.

As I did this, an image came to me: the first time I'd seen my mom use magic, me in loose braids and my mom's hair in curlers, both of us gazing out the living room window at the lush trees as her finger twirled over her favorite mug, the coffee and cream stirring within it, my little mind churning with the realization that she and I were powerful beings. The memory was so vivid, I could practically smell the caramel creamer. I smiled. If I was her anchor against unruly magic, she would be mine. I held onto the image until the kettle hissed with steam.

I poured the tea into a gold-rimmed teacup and held it close to my lips. Herbs floated on its surface, their pungent scent making my eyes water.

"World of spirits and shadows," I said. "Find me worthy. Let me see the unseen."

I took a generous sip. The second the warm liquid touched my lips, sleep descended, a heavy, velvet curtain over my eyes. My head drooped, and I didn't even feel my cheek hit the wooden desk before me.

In fact, my desk was gone. My bedroom was decorated with unfamiliar furniture, older even than the antiques my house normally contained. Shadows sloped on every ornate surface, candlelight danced in the hall. This was the house as it had been when the coven was newly formed, when Delfina Garcia lived here. Somewhere in the cavernous silence, I heard a faint sound, like the rustling of leaves.

With strange certainty, I followed the sound. In the hallway, mounted candelabras dripped wax onto the floor. The steps were silent beneath my feet as I descended the stairs. The rustling sounded again—not leaves but paper. Pages shuffled by a ghostly hand.

I stopped in the dining room. A fire roared in the fireplace, the room's only source of light. At the head of the long wooden table hung the portrait of Delfina Garcia, its paint still wet, her eyes like pools of honey.

The sound was coming from a corner of the room. I turned toward it. The grandfather clock stood sentry there as it still did in my time, the same intricate patterns etched into its wooden surface. The constellations that always reminded me of Luke spread across it like spiderwebs, surrounding a smiling sun. It gleamed with polish and smelled of fresh-cut wood. Inside its depths, I heard the whisper of paper again, pages brushing against the clock's walls. The sound unsettled me as if I were listening to the movement of some trapped creature.

I was suddenly struck with the knowledge that this wasn't just a dream. I was in the spirit world itself, or one iteration of it. I was not alone here. It felt as if at any moment, Delfina could appear, surprised at the unexpected visitor in her home. Petra was somewhere in this world too. If I stepped out into the forest, would I find her grinning at me beneath a mop of blue hair?

Footsteps echoed in the hall. My heart leapt into my throat as I jerked my head in the direction of the sound. The grand staircase was cloaked in shadows, but a figure stood at the bottom of the stairs, candle in hand, her white nightgown trailing the floor. I saw the proud, high cheekbones, the hair loose past her shoulders, just like the painting on the wall. But Delfina's eyes seemed to hold a lifetime of regret, of grief. The rustling sounded again from inside the clock.

The world around me was fading, the darkness giving way to sunlight from somewhere else, the light painting the inside of my eyelids crimson. I blinked. I was slumped over my desk. A pale morning ray peeked through my bedroom curtains. I'd slept all night.

I sat up slowly, as if my body wasn't sure what realm it now found itself in. The silence of that other world still echoed in my mind, followed by the faint whisper of turning pages.

The clock.

I rose, knocking over my chair, and hurried downstairs. It was Sunday and the house was empty, my parents off surveying some new real estate venture. I turned to the grandfather clock. Something was hidden inside, I understood—something I had to discover. My heart quickened as I thought of the letter Petra had seen in her mind's eye. The burning letter between lovers. Could it have been concealed in plain sight all along? Something important certainly was.

The sound had been coming from the clock's base. I examined its surface, tapping it like a safecracker in a movie. It sounded solid, but there had to be something I was missing. I tried to tug the clock away from the wall, but its legs caught the floor with a sharp screech.

I took a breath and concentrated on the air around its towering form, willing it to obey me. It was the heaviest object I'd ever tried to move with magic. Nothing happened. The clock shuddered as if in protest.

Then, with a crash, the whole thing toppled hideously to the floor. Glass broke, gears rolled across the hardwood. Oops. I hadn't meant to break it, but a tiny wave of satisfaction washed over me as I realized how much I'd hated that clock. Never again would its solemn sound echo through this house, counting out my loneliest hours, each chime a reminder of the legacy I was meant to uphold.

On the bottom of the clock was a hinged panel, so neatly placed into the grain that it looked like it might spring open at any moment to reveal whatever secret lay within. Delfina must have had a compartment built into the bottom. There was no keyhole, no dial with old brass numbers. Just a small wooden sun, its figure slightly raised above the panel's surface as if it were meant to be pressed. I pushed on it. It didn't give. I pressed again, harder this time. Nothing.

I tried vainly to hook my fingernails around its edge to pull at it, but it still didn't budge. Thirty minutes later, I'd tried every tool I could find in the garage, plus every use of elemental magic I could think of. Nothing worked. The wood didn't even chip. There had to be a spell protecting it, keeping out unwelcome visitors.

I thought about the sorrow in Delfina's eyes as she'd stood before me in the spirit world. She had taken great care to remove her secrets from the Book of Shadows, which meant she hadn't even trusted the members of her own coven. She wouldn't allow just anyone to access this hiding place. And yet—there it was. Why leave the panel visible at all, unless she wanted someone to get in? Perhaps it was meant for someone she deemed trustworthy. Who would Delfina Garcia trust? I gazed into the eyes of the smiling wooden sun, the symbol of our family's power.

Of course. Whatever was inside was only meant for a Garcia to find.

I extended a hand and summoned the sunfire. With flames lapping at my fingertips, I pressed again. The sun gave way beneath my finger, and I felt something click. Hinges creaked and the panel swung open, revealing a small, velvet-lined compartment. Inside lay a single leather-bound book emblazoned with the words THE DIARY OF DELFINA GARCIA.

My heart thumped in my chest. I took the book, inhaling the scent of must and leather. Turning the pages, I could see the entries were few and brief. There on the floor, amidst the ruins of the clock, I began to read.

July 14, 1860

I feel as if all my dreams are coming true at once. This fall, Levan Nichols and I will be wed. In the years I spent searching for others of witches' blood, I never imagined I would find a man like him, a gentle man who thinks more than he speaks, who cares more for the stars in the sky than he does for earthly power and glory. My love for him knows no bounds.

Today, the workers finished hammering the final nails into my house among the trees. The gold mines grow more profitable by the day, and I was able to spare no expense. Soon, Levan and I will share this home and all the joy within. The rest of the coven is also building extravagantly along Cascabel Road. Here in the seclusion of the redwoods, we are finally free to practice magic undisturbed. After years of wandering, our coven shall have a place to call our own at last. Our golden town. Our Dorado. Oh, what blessings the universe has bestowed upon us all!

August 4, 1860

A stranger came to Dorado today, a witch named Elizabeth Foster. Her eyes are black like obsidian, her skin as white as cream. She casts the moonfire spell, a perfect nocturnal counterpart to my sunfire. She told us she traveled a great distance to find others like herself, and truly, she must have wandered far, for she was bedraggled and nearly starving, without a penny to her name. I took pity on her immediately. No witch should be alone in this world. And what is Dorado if not a sanctuary for witches? Tomorrow, I will initiate her into the coven.

September 12, 1860

Everything changed after Elizabeth Foster joined us. How I underestimated her. Some weeks after her arrival, Levan grew distant from me. Now his dark blue eyes seem to look past me, searching for another. It is her he seeks, as if she holds some piece of his soul he'd been missing all his life. Never have I known heart-break like this. I've always possessed a leader's confidence, a certainty for what must be done. Now, for the first time in my life, I know not what to do. For the moment, I will cry.

October 17, 1860

It's worse than I could have imagined. Elizabeth has malevolent magic. She can control the Mundanes and command them to work her will. And now she has revealed to Levan that he, too, possesses malevolent magic. He has the ability to cast the Shadow Spell to torture and even kill another witch. Oh, my poor Levan! He was as surprised as I when she told him. He didn't believe her until she showed him how to cast it on her. When he did, she laughed like a madwoman through the pain.

Last night, I overheard her as she spoke to Levan in his quarters. She did not come to this coven in search of other witches as she'd claimed. She came only in search of him. Elizabeth and Levan hail from the same English village, though Levan's family left when he was but an infant. A clairvoyant witch in the village foretold a pair of soulmates, one from the Nichols family, one from the Fosters.

These two souls are destined to unite and, in doing so, gain limitless malevolent power, leaving nothing but death and devastation in their wake.

Levan's family were good-hearted people. They fled when they heard this prediction and vowed never to tell him of the prophecy or the malevolent magic in their blood. But Elizabeth sought him out, determined to fulfill their wicked destiny. As soon as she was old enough to leave home, she began her quest. At long last, she has found him here, in our little haven.

According to the prophecy, the moon will blot out the sun, meteors will rain, and on that day, a Foster and a Nichols will become one in malevolent magic. I knew immediately she spoke of the solar eclipse, which is to take place in two weeks' time.

On this day, they must perform a sort of dark nuptials, the details of which she did not explain. She only said that they must stand together in a circle of enchanted flames. Once the circle is closed, only malevolent magic can be cast within. She called the ritual the Meteoric Union, for when it is done, their capacity for destruction will be as unbridled as a meteor that rushes toward earth. The universe itself will yield to their power. Mundanes and witches alike will bow before them—or die.

I wish I could say Levan turned away from her when he heard her tale, that he told her to leave and never come back. Alas, he let her continue. She assured him that once the ritual is done, though they inhabit two bodies, their souls will be one, irrevocably bound by malevolent magic. My poor, foolish Levan—is he so in love with her that he is willing to forfeit his very soul? Is his thirst for power so great that he would lose his kindness, his humanity for the cold hatred of malevolent magic?

Now I know what I must do. I must find a way to bring Levan back from the brink—if not for me, then to protect our coven from the devastation that will follow if those two fulfill the prophecy. I hope for my sake that some part of him still cares for me. I leave now, and if I never write in this book again, it is because I have failed, and Elizabeth Foster has destroyed us all.

I breathed in sharply, suddenly realizing I'd been holding my breath. My thoughts raced with unanswered questions, too many to process. With trembling fingers, I turned the page to the final entry.

MAY 26, 1861

It is with a heavy heart that I return to this diary to write the events of the past months. I did confront Levan that night. I told him I knew everything. At first, I feared he would strike me with the Shadow Spell. Instead, his gentle nature overtook him, and he cried in shame. He confessed he had been tempted by the immense power Elizabeth offered, swayed by the pull of their shared fate. I couldn't hold back my compassion for him and we embraced there on the floor, our tears mingling as we wept. As we held one another, my heart rejoiced. I knew he had returned to me.

Oh, how I wish the story ended there, that Levan and I were wed and we live together now in peace. Alas, there was still the question of Elizabeth Foster. Levan and I stayed up talking by candlelight until dawn. We both knew the witch was too dangerous to leave alone. When she discovered he had turned his back on their union, we believed she would torture the Mundanes of the village to spite us. We are to blame for allowing her into Dorado. We dared not risk their lives because of our folly.

I know of one desperate spell that is said to drain the malevolent magic from a witch, but Elizabeth was too dangerous with any amount of magic. We had to remove all her power so even her children and her children's children will be unable to pursue the Meteoric Union.

Levan possessed the only solution. Elizabeth had told him how malevolent witches can revoke the magic fully from another witch, but the spell would collect a price—what or whom, we would not know until it was done. In foolish certitude, I decided as long as Levan and I were together, we could do no wrong. I helped him prepare the spell. He felled the tallest tree in the wood, and with our coven's dagger, he cut his palm and scrawled Elizabeth's name in blood on the fresh tree stump.

The next day, we awoke to discover all the crops in the village had turned a dismal gray. Leaves and stems crumbled into dust at the touch. The farmers stood in their fields, a look of ruin on their faces. In the village, Elizabeth Foster ran shrieking through the street. The spell had worked. She'd lost her power. In her eyes was a misery so deep it hurt to look at her. I knew then she was doomed to live as a cursed woman, with no place among the coven, yet a stranger in the Mundane world.

Winter descended upon us. With each day, our rations grew fewer, and the wheat lay dead in the fields. Our coven offered all we could, but we still came up wanting. Three Mundanes from the village starved. Would Elizabeth's wrath have claimed more lives than our foolish spell?

As we watched those Mundanes laid to rest, Levan and I knew we could never be together. Too many horrors had passed between us. In spring, he married another woman, a kind witch who will make a good wife. I, too, have wed, for we all must carry our coven into the next generation. But when I look at my new husband, I feel no joy. Sometimes, when our coven gathers, Levan and I exchange silent glances, our hearts heavy with the guilt we share. He has built his home next to mine. Perhaps this is the closest we can be to one another without the weight of grief.

Elizabeth Foster lives in a modest cabin on the other side of the river. A humble wood bridge grants her access to the forest, and sometimes, we hear her wandering through the trees, crying aloud. Malevolent witches hold the power to reverse their spells. Levan could return her magic, but he would never do so, no matter how much she begs him. She has become one more victim in this tragedy.

I will never know if what Levan and I did was right. What I know is that Elizabeth's pursuit of the Meteoric Union was at the root of all this evil. Future generations must never learn of the prophecy, for the power it promises is too great. Levan has sworn he will never tell his children they possess malevolent magic. The Nichols clan will be completely ignorant of their malevolent powers, just as Levan was before he met Elizabeth. For my part, I will banish all knowledge of malevolent magic from our Book of Shadows and forbid our coven to speak of it.

I close my book with this melancholy passage. I will forever be haunted by my mistakes. The only evidence of these terrible events will be this diary. I hide it away now so it can only be discovered by one with sunfire, by a Garcia. If one of my kin has sought this book, then peril must be upon our coven once again. I implore whoever reads this: if a Foster witch ever pursues a Nichols witch, keep them apart by any means necessary. If you fail, disaster will surely follow.

CHAPTER THIRTEEN

VALERIA

After the final entry, there was a passage written in a language I didn't recognize. Only blank pages followed. I shut the book hard. Anger welled inside me—fruitless, illogical anger toward a woman who'd been dead for over a hundred years. Delfina claimed she'd kept the prophecy a secret to protect the coven, and I was sure that was true. But I was all too familiar with the Garcia psyche; I was certain a part of her did it to hide her own mistakes. It was what my mother would have done in her situation.

And, I thought dismally, if I'd been in Delfina's shoes, perhaps I would have taken a flame to the Book of Shadows myself.

By erasing all evidence of the prophecy, she'd cast her coven into dangerous ignorance, though she'd solidified the legend I'd grown up believing: Delfina Garcia, the perfect leader, the standard I could aspire to but never achieve. In reality, the woman staring down at me from the painting in my dining room had been as flawed as me. She'd tried her best and come up short. It was now my turn as high priestess. I wondered if I would fare any better.

My thoughts turned to the prophecy, a union as dangerous and destructive as...*a meteor that rushes toward earth.* Why did that sound eerily familiar? Why did I associate those words with Gwen?

Her poem. I struggled to recall the verses I'd read aloud the day I humiliated her on the quad. *Oh, to be a meteor whose power lies not in light but in destruction.*

A sick feeling washed over me. Gwen had written about the prophecy before she even regained her powers. *Oh, to combust with you…* Those words had been about Luke. Had she known all along? It seemed impossible. But perhaps whether she realized it or not, her path had always led to the Meteoric Union. To him.

Luke.

My mind raced. Was he being pulled by destiny like a leaf in a current? Like Levan had been before him? *Keep them apart at all costs,* Delfina's diary warned. If the diary was correct, he had no knowledge of the prophecy or his malevolent power. Maybe I could talk to him, warn him of the horrible fate he and Gwen shared before it was too late. The eclipse was two days away. If I was going to act, it had to be now.

Before I knew what I was doing, I clutched the book in one hand and rushed out the door.

The now-familiar sight of dead trees greeted me as I raced over my front lawn toward Luke's. My heart pounding, I swung open the iron gate and hurried up the steps to his house. But I stopped before the heavy wooden door, my breaths coming quick and ragged. Why had I gone to Luke and not Gwen? I thought of the hurt I'd seen in Gwen's eyes the last time we spoke, when I told her I couldn't trust her. The wounds were too fresh; she wouldn't listen to me now, I told myself. Luke was the logical choice.

But in my mind was an image of Levan and Delfina wrapped in a tearful embrace, everything forgiven. Some desperate part of my heart ached for that—to hold him again, to feel his arms encircle me as we wept out the madness of these past weeks. I hesitated for just a moment, then I knocked.

Footsteps sounded in the foyer, and the door swung open with a creak. Alexis Nichols stood before me in a red-and-white checkered apron. The house smelled of dough and spices. The chandelier above our heads twinkled cheerily in the morning sun.

"Valeria," he said. "Always a pleasure. Come on in."

His dark hair fell around his eyes in messy waves. The center of his brow seemed drawn into a permanent frown, as if grief for his lost power was carved on his face.

"Thanks. Is Luke home?"

Doubt whirled in my mind. What if Luke didn't believe me? He was so into Gwen, perhaps he wouldn't *want* to believe. The book had to be my proof. I clutched it tighter.

"He's around here somewhere," Mr. Nichols told me. "I'll call him. Can I get you anything? I'm afraid the banana bread isn't quite ready yet."

"No," I said, trying to hide the nerves in my voice. "I just *really* need to talk to him."

Mr. Nichols didn't reply. His mouth was frozen in a pleasant smile, but his gaze had traveled to the book I held, THE DIARY OF DELFINA GARCIA engraved across the front. Silence settled over us for an uncomfortably long moment.

"I'll just see if he's in his room—" I blurted and took a step toward the staircase.

With a decisive movement, he grabbed my arm. I whirled toward him, at first more surprised than afraid.

"What are you doing?" I cried. "Let go!"

"Looks like you've been doing some reading." His tone was calm, almost casual, but his grip around my arm was viselike.

"I didn't know she kept a diary. What did you find in there, Valeria?"

My mind flooded with panic as his fingers tightened around my arm.

"You must have read about the prophecy by now. I assume that's why you're here to speak with Luke."

He knew.

I didn't have time to think. I didn't have time for anything now but escape. Adrenaline rushed to my limbs and I flailed, scratched, kicked at him. But he was stronger than me. He held me easily.

"I'll take that book now," he said. "Who knows what other nuggets of wisdom it holds."

He reached for it with his free hand. *Enough.* The word rang in my head like a gong. I didn't need to fight him with muscle and fists. Through my fear, I held an image of my mother, coffee cup in hand, and I let the sunfire rise, let the flames engulf my heart. An orange glow built in my open palm and, in a rush of heat, I launched it at him as hard as I could. He flew backward, releasing me and tumbling across the floor.

A little wave of pride washed over me. I'd controlled the sunfire, even as fear pounded in my chest. But there was no time to revel in what I'd done. This was my chance. I turned toward the door, but something made me hesitate. If I left now, I might never know the truth. I turned back to him, one arm extended, ready to hit him again.

"Okay, you better tell me what the hell is going on," I demanded. "And if you don't, I have plenty more fire where that came from."

He picked himself off the floor slowly, removing his apron in a little cloud of flour and dust. His dirty hair hung over his face. He brushed it aside with one white-powdered hand.

That was when I saw his eyes. There was power in them, a power I recognized. How could I have missed it before? The light that had gone out in my parents' eyes the day they lost their magic still shone in his.

"The overconfidence of youth," he mused. "My dear, the last time you faced me, I nearly put you in the ground."

Before I could speak, before I could move, he threw something at me—something dark, amorphous. A shadow.

It struck me and it felt like death on my skin, cold and devouring. It coiled itself around my body, a serpent the color of night, writhing and tightening its grip. I fell to my knees, the stench of death and misery filling my lungs. It was the same oppressive aura that had clung to the dead trees, to Petra's body.

The Shadow Spell. He was the witch from the forest.

"You!" I choked out the accusation through my pain. "*You* killed Petra! She found out about the prophecy. She was going to tell—so you killed her!"

"Yes, but don't worry, sweetheart, I won't kill you," he said, his voice like rotten honey. "Just give me the book, and everything will be all right."

A thick rope of black stretched from his extended arm, trapping me in its coils, draining the life from me. No. Through my panic, I knew one thing: I could not give up the book. If he wanted it, there had to be something important inside—something that threatened him.

I thought of the indecipherable words that followed Delfina's last passage and dug my nails into the ancient leather. From within me, I drew fire. I couldn't hit him as hard as the first time, not with the Shadow Spell writhing around me, but I narrowed my focus and shot an arrow of flames straight at the point between his dark blue eyes. As it struck him, his hands flew to his face. The inky mass suffocating me dissolved as he cried out in pain.

I sucked in air and struggled to my feet. He would recover quickly. I had to leave—*now*.

I turned toward the front door and froze. Luke and Gwen stood in the doorway. How long had they been there? My eyes darted between them.

"Mr. Nichols has gone crazy. We have to go."

I stepped toward the door, but they didn't move. My heart fluttered like a trapped bird, but I squared off in front of them, bracing for whatever came next.

"You knew about the prophecy," I said, though I wasn't sure now to which of them I spoke.

The words hung in the air like dust waiting to settle.

Luke replied, "My family has always known. You can't bury a secret as powerful as that. Delfina Garcia was a fool for trying."

A plume of darkness curled in his palm.

"Get out of my way, Luke," I said. "I'm warning you."

I summoned the sunfire once more, but it was Gwen who hit me first. Her moonfire flashed across the air between us, sending me sprawling on the floor. The two of them stared down at me, Luke's brow raised in cocky defiance, Gwen's gaze as cold as night air.

"Gwen—you're a part of this?" I cried.

"Don't act so shocked," she replied. "You said yourself I couldn't be trusted. Guess you were right."

I had spent so long doubting her. Why was I surprised to learn my suspicions were correct? And yet the betrayal stung like the spot between my ribs where her spell had struck. I pushed myself to my feet, powered by the sheer will to escape.

I sent a wave of fire flying at the figures in the doorway. They staggered back, but they were up faster than I expected. The moonfire crackled at Gwen's fingertips. A black serpent coiled at Luke's wrist, ready to strike. Beads of sweat glistened at his temples as he held control of the spell. Malevolent magic drained him, I understood, just like it did Gwen. No wonder the promise of unlimited power was so enticing to him.

"You really think you can defeat all three of us? That's the Garcia narcissism I know and love," Luke sneered.

Mr. Nichols still lurked behind me. Luke and Gwen barred my path. He was right. There was no way I could take them all. But as I watched the sunlight dance off the crystal chandelier, a plan coalesced in my mind.

"I thought Delfina and Levan destroyed all the evidence of the prophecy," I said, taking a tiny step backward.

A sly smile crossed Luke's lips.

"It's true, Levan never told his children about malevolent magic or the prophecy in our blood. He swore to rid himself of all memories of that *terrible temptation*," he said, his voice dripping with sarcasm. "But Levan's health failed in his old age. On the day he died, he burned a letter here in our hearth. His son was overcome with curiosity, and stole the letter from the fire without his father noticing. It was from a woman, written very long ago. She told of her undying love for him, how she ached for him every day. But she also wrote about the malevolent magic they shared. She begged him to return her power, even told him how to do it. And she wrote about the prophecy, the ritual that would unite them, the eclipse, the meteor shower," He closed his eyes as if recalling the words. "'*Our bloodlines are forever bound. If the prophecy does not come to pass in this generation, my darling, then it will in another. Fate cannot be denied.*'"

"A love letter," I murmured. A love letter engulfed in flames. Petra had gotten it right again.

"Exactly." Luke cocked his head curiously at me. "It contained some pretty dangerous information. So why would Levan keep a letter like that for all those years? It wasn't for the parts about malevolent magic—he already knew that stuff. I'll tell you my theory. He held onto it for Elizabeth's words of affection, the promise that she thought of him every day." Luke now spoke as if these revelations were nails he meant to drive into my skin. "You see, in the end, he never loved Delfina. He only loved *her*."

The words did hurt, but I held his gaze furiously.

"Why now? If your family had the spell to restore magic, why didn't they give the Fosters their power back generations ago?"

"The thing was"—Luke sighed as if suddenly bored with my questions—"when Levan's son rescued that letter from the fire, the flames had already begun to consume it. The signature was burned away. All my family knew was that we were destined to unite with one whose magic had been revoked, a witch forced to live as a Mundane. Each generation of my family watched the sky for clues to the bloodline that was bound to ours, clues to when the Meteoric Union would take place. But there was no sign from the heavens, and no eclipse came. We began to wonder if it was just a myth, the ramblings of a madwoman long ago.

"We concealed our malevolent magic for almost two centuries. Even the strongest witch needs a coven, and we knew we'd be cast out if we revealed our true power. My own mother didn't know until I was thirteen. I was angry at her for some stupid, childish thing, and this dark force just flowed out of me. I was as surprised as she was when it knocked her down in pain. She told me it was bad magic, something I should never use. But it was too late—I was already in love with it. My dad understood, though. He told me about the prophecy that very day, and we swore I would be the one to fulfill it. The eclipse had already been predicted, and even then, we could hear the whisper of meteors in the distant sky. Of course, my mom didn't understand. How could she? My parents fought about it. She said as long as we chose malevolent magic, she couldn't be a part of our lives."

I remembered Luke as a lonely boy, hiding away in a ghost town, weeping the loss of his mother. Now I knew why she left. The day I fell in love with him, he already loved malevolent magic.

"I was devastated," Luke went on. "If my own mother abandoned me because of my power, who would ever love me? I decided I'd be alone forever. The eclipse was only a few years away, and I had no way of finding the witch who shared my destiny. A part of me held out hope, but hope can be a frightening thing. So I buried it so deep inside I almost forgot it was there at all." He fixed his eyes on me now, but I looked away, dreading his next words. "And in the depths of that despair, I started dating you, Valeria."

Tears filled my eyes. "Why?"

"Because sometimes it's easier to be alone with someone else."

So that was it. He'd never loved me. I'd just been something for him to cling to as he fell. My eyes met his, and it was as if all the light had disappeared from the room. The blue in their center was like the night sky, a freezing place where you can't breathe. The boy I knew was gone. In fact, in one hideous instant, I realized he'd always been the cold, hostile person I now saw before me. I didn't know there was more inside me left to break, but looking at him now, I felt the last piece of my heart shatter.

"After our dates, I'd come home and stare at that letter, reading and rereading the promise that there was someone out there who shared everything with me, even malevolent magic."

I inched backward again and they stepped toward me, instinctively closing the distance. The chandelier cast tiny rainbows across the floor between us.

Just a little further.

"How did you find out it was Gwen?" I asked.

"Malevolent energy had been building in the air for months as the eclipse grew nearer. The stars hum with it. One night, they showed me the way. As I gazed at the constellations, Gwen's face appeared to me, and I knew." He smiled as if recalling some precious memory. "All those years of despair were for nothing. Fate was always going to reveal my path. Gwen and I are destined for this. Nothing can change it." He shot me a meaningful look. "Nothing can stop it."

"So you gave her her power back."

"Yes, the very next day. It was a beautiful spell, probably the gentlest thing you can do with malevolent magic. All restoration, no sacrifice."

"And then you took our parents' magic." I stepped back again, letting them close in.

Mr. Nichols spoke from behind me, his voice thick with condescension. "We didn't want your mother and the others interfering with our plans. Now they never will. Of course, I had to act like I'd lost my magic too. I suppose I played my role well, but I must admit it feels good to get everything out in the open. I've spent far too many years hiding the superiority of my family's power. When my son achieves the Meteoric Union, we'll never have to hide again."

How could I have been so stupid? I'd seen Mr. Nichols, talked to him several times since this began, but whenever I was in this house, I'd always been too focused on Luke to pay him much attention.

"We let the younger generation keep their magic," Luke cut in. "Like I said, even the strongest witch needs a coven. Now Gwen and I will rule yours. Our love will be eternal, and our malevolent magic will be limitless."

"You weren't worried *I'd* ruin your plans?"

"You foolish, self-important girl," Mr. Nichols said. "You were never a threat to us. You're not the powerhouse your mother was. We figured you'd be too busy fixing your lipstick to notice what was really going on. By the time you looked up from the mirror, it would be too late. And we were right."

It was like he'd reached into my heart, extracted the worst beliefs I held about myself, and put them on display. I stole a glance upward, my limbs trembling with rage and humiliation. I had them where I wanted them. It was now or never.

"Stop messing around and get the book, Luke," Mr. Nichols commanded.

The dark coils in Luke's palm writhed. I knew I should make my move, but I hesitated, turning to Gwen despite myself. If I didn't speak to her now, I might not get another chance.

"All right, I'll give up the book," I lied. "But first I want to hear from Gwen."

"What do you need to know?" she asked with flat indifference.

"Have you always known? Even back…in the old days. Did you know?" My voice wavered with unexpected emotion.

She shook her head. "I didn't know. But all my life, I've had this sense that I was destined for catastrophe. I'd either be crushed beneath it, or I'd be the one doing the crushing."

"And then Luke asked you to complete the ritual with him and you decided to dole out the devastation?"

"It was very romantic," Luke interrupted with a crooked grin. "I popped the question and she said yes."

He smiled at her, warmth returning to his chilly blue eyes. A strange understanding hit me. He really loved Gwen. Being with her wasn't just another step in his plan. He looked at her like a man who'd found something he'd always been searching for, something that felt like home. In some insane way, they really *were* soulmates.

"I had two paths before me," Gwen said to me. "Miserable loner or dark queen with limitless power. Which one did you expect me to choose?"

"Once I would have expected you to choose the kinder path. But that was the Gwen I knew a long time ago."

At this, a bitter laugh escaped her throat. "You're right. That *was* the Gwen you knew, and you treated her like shit. Did you know I used to run the other way when I saw you in the halls at school? You used to be the scariest thing in the world to me, Valeria. You could crush me with a word, with a flash of your brilliant smile. You held a metaphorical knife to my heart for years, and you cut me whenever it pleased you. So don't blame me if I don't want to be *that* Gwen ever again. Blame yourself."

With a flash of white light, her moonfire struck me, this time in the shoulder, sending a jolt of cold lightning through my veins. I hit the ground. I felt as if her words, not her magic, had knocked all the air from my lungs. As I knelt before her, I couldn't come up with a single reason why she should show me mercy now.

When I finally spoke, I spoke to her unselfishly for the first time in a very long time.

"You're right, Gwen," I said. "But please believe me when I say you will not come back from this. The night of the Meteoric Union, you will lose your soul. Are you prepared for that?"

She didn't respond, but her pale features remained fixed in an expression of cool arrogance.

"Enough talk, kids." Mr. Nichols clapped his hands, the sound reverberating through the vast house. "The book!"

The scent of burnt bread drifted from the kitchen. The chandelier's fine glass pieces sparkled above. It was strange, I thought, how something of such delicate beauty could hang in such a dangerous house.

"No," I told him.

The serpent at Luke's wrist struck, and my fire rose to meet it. The shadow broke against my flames, dissipating like smoke. But in the wake of the first Shadow Spell, the next came quickly from behind. Mr. Nichols hit me in the throat, making my eyes burn with the stench of death.

Through the fog of agony, my gaze fell on Gwen. She looked young, I thought hazily, the sad little girl I'd turned my back on, loneliness hanging off her like moss from a tree. Luke hit me again, his shadow tightening around my chest. The weight of both spells was worse than I could have imagined. I had no fire left within me. I felt my heartbeat slow.

Mr. Nichols's footsteps approached from behind me. My vision blurred, but I held the chandelier in my gaze, concentrating on the chain that suspended it. With the last of my strength, I pulled. It began to sway, hundreds of crystal pieces shimmering above Luke and Gwen. In a shower of glass and metal, it came down upon them both.

The second it fell, the shadows that wrapped around my body dissolved as Luke crumpled to the floor and Alexis ran to him. Gasping for air, I scrambled to my feet. Luke and Gwen lay dazed beneath the chandelier's twisted gold frame, their blood mixing with crystal on the floor.

I staggered past them, glass scattering beneath my feet. Still gripping the book, I left them in the midst of that ruin, slammed the door behind me, and ran.

CHAPTER FOURTEEN

GWEN

Luke told me everything the day my dad left. As I rested my head on his chest, absorbing the shock of loss, he began to speak. His voice was even, his words deliberate, as if he'd been rehearsing what he had to say for a long time.

"There are secrets I've kept from the coven. Sometimes, those secrets feel so heavy, I think I'll collapse if I have to hold onto them one more second," he said. "But I don't want to keep secrets from you, Gwen. Not anymore."

I was numb and exhausted from the malevolent magic I'd used the night before, the magic that had driven my father away. In that melancholy daze, his words didn't shock me. The closer I got to Luke, the more he felt like a part of me. I could sense there was something he'd been holding back. Now, more than ever, I didn't want missing pieces. I wanted all of him.

As I lay there, listening to the beating of his heart, I said, "It's all right. You can tell me anything."

Before my eyes a black shape began to pool in his palm, liquid and weightless as if unbound by the laws of physics. He told me about the Shadow Spell, how he and his father had been forced to hide it all their lives. As I watched the spell wrap itself around his fingers, I feared its power, yet I found myself lost in the beauty of its dark movement, unable to look away. An unexpected wave of relief washed over me. He had malevolent magic too. I wasn't alone. I never had been.

He told me everything he and his father had done—how they'd returned the magic that was rightfully mine, taken power from the elder coven members so no one could keep us apart. Luke swore Petra's death had been an accident. A horrible tragedy, not a murder. Alexis had been keeping an eye on her movements as she grew closer to discovering the prophecy. He had only meant to scare her, to keep her from talking. But things could sometimes get out of hand when malevolent magic was involved.

"You know how that is, don't you?" Luke said.

I thought of my father's finger trembling on the trigger of that shiny new pistol. Of course I did. Luke had an explanation for everything, and as I took in the angles of his beautiful face and watched the power he commanded at his fingertips, it was easy to believe him. Or perhaps it was easy to convince myself I did.

Then he told me about the Meteoric Union.

"Remember that night on the rooftop of Hotel Dorado?" he asked, his voice low, like thunder before a storm. "We looked down as darkness fell over this town. That night, we experienced just a fraction of what we're capable of. You felt like a queen that night, didn't you?"

I couldn't deny it. I had practically felt the cool metal of a crown digging into my temples.

"That's because you *are* a queen, Gwen. You and I are the rightful rulers of everything before us."

He painted our future in beautiful strokes until it sparkled like the sky on a starry night. We were destined for one another. The ritual would unite us forever. We would know nothing but glory and each other's love.

The strange part was that it all made sense. Luke and I *were* bound by fate; I'd felt it on a molecular level for a long time.

Hearing his words only confirmed what my heart already knew: we were meant to burn together, a brilliant meteor in the night sky. I'd seen it in my dreams before we'd even kissed. The power was ours. All we had to do now, he said, was take it.

"Others will never understand us," he told me. "We scare them too much. Our magic will drive them away, one by one, until there is no one left but me and you."

I thought of the way the rest of the coven had looked at me after they'd discovered what I was, of how Valeria had shut the door in my face when I'd pleaded with her to trust me. And I thought of my dad's terse goodbye letter. Luke was right. They had already abandoned me.

It was all too much. I sat up with a start, shock and fear and something like exhilaration mingling in the blood that rushed through my veins.

"Wait!" Luke cried. "Please don't leave."

"I wasn't going to," I replied seriously.

He sighed in relief, letting the Shadow Spell fall away and gripping both my hands in his. He spoke very clearly.

"Please understand—I want the power, but more than anything, I want *you*. When I learned you were my destiny, it was like I'd come alive for the first time. This world is a lonely place and you, Gwen, are my only salvation. All your life, people have treated you like something ugly, disposable, so you hid yourself away, thinking if no one could see you, no one could hurt you. But you don't have to hide from me. When I look at you, I see splendor and beauty. I see magic." His eyes bored into mine, daring me to doubt him. "So tell me, Gwen Foster: Are you ready to take the power that's rightfully ours and make those fools bow down before us?"

I wondered now what made me say it. Perhaps it was the malevolent magic still buzzing through my veins, or the fact that my dad was probably halfway to Vegas by then. I felt reckless, desperate for something I couldn't name. Was it this power he spoke of? I wasn't sure. I just knew I longed for anything that would guarantee the rest of my life would be entirely different from the first eighteen years—

that *I* would be entirely different. All I had to say was one word to make it so.

I took a breath and answered, "Yes."

He pulled me to him, kissing my face, my hair. His arms pressed so tightly around my body I couldn't breathe, yet I squeezed him back just as hard. But even as he held me, a heavy feeling settled in the pit of my stomach. Perhaps it wasn't the promise of untold power that made me accept his proposal. Maybe the truth was harder to admit, even to myself.

Luke was offering me a place by his side, a place to belong forever. Maybe that was more valuable to me than all the power in the world.

———

THE SOUND of a butter knife scraping against china snapped me back to the present. Luke, Alexis, and I ate in their pristine white dining room, the ruins of the chandelier still scattered about the floor to our right. Alexis Nichols had dressed for dinner in an old-fashioned smoking jacket. He'd even taken the time to set out the fine china and silver, but he hadn't bothered to clean up the mound of twisted metal in the foyer. The shattered glass and shards of gold made our family dinner feel surreal, like the perfect table setting had been pasted into some apocalyptic scene.

My body still ached from the impact and Luke and I were covered in cuts and bruises, but we'd survived the wrath of the chandelier just fine. I supposed I should be thankful for that, though part of me longed for the simplicity of a good coma. The events of Valeria's unexpected visit this morning whirled through my mind, making it hard to breathe.

"How are you liking the potpie?" Alexis asked.

Without turning to look at him, I knew the question was directed at me.

"Um, it's great, thanks," I replied, gathering a tiny bite of the damp, salty crust on my fork.

"You've barely touched it. Are you not feeling well? After dinner, I'll make you a nice peppermint tea. Good for digestion."

His words were kind, but there was an edge to his tone, a dark undercurrent meant to threaten me away from any second thoughts that might creep into my head.

"No, that's all right, Mr. Ni—Alexis. I'm fine," I replied.

I poked at a clump of peas on my plate, avoiding his gaze. Silverware clinked; ice tinkled in glasses. The house was so large and quiet that any sound within it felt jarring. I took another bite, hearing my own dry swallow in my ears. As a kid wandering through the forest, I used to look up at this tall white house and wonder what kind of people lived there, imagining the mysterious luxury it must contain. Now I lived inside its ivy-covered walls, and I longed for the peace of the forest. The floor seemed to tilt beneath me. The beautiful image Luke had painted of the Meteoric Union didn't sparkle so brightly after our conversation with Valeria.

He'd mentioned nothing of the rage I felt when I used malevolent magic. Would completing the ritual mean I'd feel that way forever, my heart growing small and hard like the pit of a rotten fruit? I'd already done terrible things, even as my conscience cried out against them. I didn't like to think of what I might do if that little voice was gone. Valeria's words repeated in my head. *You will not come back from this.* I saw my life stretched out behind me like the muddy waters of a river—all the years I'd spent alone, hiding away in the discomfort of my own skin. Perhaps Valeria was right. Perhaps I would lose myself in binding my soul to Luke's. If so, I wondered bleakly, would that be so bad?

I fixed my eyes on my plate, hoping my thoughts didn't read on my face. I could feel Alexis watching me, his gaze sending a chill down my spine. He had murdered Petra, I was sure of that now. When I met Alexis Nichols, I was taken by how wholesome he'd seemed, how...*safe.* To me, a devoted father was a phenomenon as rare as the aurora borealis, and I'd been drawn to his light.

Now I saw his dedication to Luke with new eyes. He loved his son, but he also loved the power Luke could offer him, *we* could offer him. He wouldn't let anyone stand in the way of that power, no matter the consequences.

I couldn't help it. I stole a quick, longing glance at the front door. It was about thirty feet from where I sat. I imagined suddenly rising from my seat, leaping over the twisted chandelier, and dashing to it. What would they do to make me stay? They needed me; there'd be no ritual without me. I'd seen what they did to Valeria. I knew Alexis would strike me with the Shadow Spell at the first sign of trouble, but I was just as certain Luke would not. Even as I spiraled into doubt, I could feel our connection as strongly as ever. He would not harm me.

From my periphery, I felt Luke watching me. I turned away from the door, shifting my focus back to the cooling heaps of chicken potpie as if I'd been daydreaming about something completely inconsequential.

"So," I said, in a convincingly chipper tone, "any dessert tonight, Mr. Nichols? I know you make a great——"

Luke rose abruptly to his feet, his chair scraping the hardwood with an unsettling screech. Without saying a word, he walked to the front door and opened it wide.

"If you want to leave, Gwen, go ahead," he said, his voice echoing in the vast silence.

I tensed, not sure how to respond.

"I mean it. If you don't want to do this, walk out this door right now, and I won't try to stop you."

There was a sincerity in his eyes that I would have trusted only a day ago. Now I didn't know what to believe. This had to be some kind of trick. But what if it wasn't?

Tentatively, I stood and walked to the door. I felt Alexis's eyes on me, but he didn't stir from his seat at the head of the table. I walked right up to the doorway. Another step and I'd be outside. The sun shone on the grassy front lawn, a breeze tugged at the ends of my hair as if inviting me to freedom. Luke stood beside me, one arm bracing open the heavy wooden door. I was so close to him, I could feel the heat radiating off his body, smell the scent of pine and leather.

What if I left right now? My thoughts raced. Where would I go? My dad was gone, and something inside me knew I couldn't go back to that empty house. There was nothing waiting for me there but stale smoke and misery. Valeria was next door, but she'd never take me in now. Not after I'd struck her down with my magic and watched as Luke tortured her under the Shadow Spell. Even if I made it to one of the other coven members, I was sure Valeria had already told them I was a traitor. They'd turn me away, or perhaps they'd hand me over to Valeria for whatever kind of justice was due to a witch like me. To leave now would be to plunge back into utter loneliness.

I hesitated.

Luke nodded as if reading my mind. "I can see you're beginning to understand. People will always hate us, fear us. If you try to go back to them, it will only bring you more heartbreak. All we have in this world is each other."

I looked at him, tears blurring his face into a watercolor of olive skin and midnight blue.

"Don't you see?" he said, his voice beginning to break. "They never loved you, but I do. I always will."

Even now, even in the midst of all this turmoil, I knew he loved me. I could feel it as surely as I felt my own heart beating. He touched my cheek, and I raised my hand to clasp his. I didn't know what I was doing. I had nothing left inside—no more strength, no more will. I was amazed how so much emptiness could fit inside one human body. My knees buckled. Luke caught me and held me in his arms.

When I blinked my tears away, his eyes came into perfect focus. There was a desperation in them, a madness, but I wasn't afraid. It was a look I recognized, a madness I knew in myself.

"You can't leave me," he said, and the words were not a threat but a plea. "I need you, Gwen. I need you."

He was crying now, his shoulders rising and falling with his pain. The sight of him this way only made my heart ache more. I'd never belonged anywhere until now. As scary as it was, to belong with someone like this was still better than being alone. He held me close as the heavy door fell shut with an echoing *bang*. I let him embrace me as he wept. I was crying, too, sobs shaking my body. Luke brushed the wetness from my cheeks, and the tenderness in his expression told me he'd mistaken them for tears of joy.

That night, I lay awake in bed by Luke's side, listening to his slow, steady breathing. I stared into the darkness for a long time before sleep finally came to me. When it did, I dreamed I was hurtling through the night sky, my body weightless, my trajectory fixed, the hard earth growing ever nearer below.

CHAPTER FIFTEEN

VALERIA

The lunch bell rang, and kids flooded the quad. The old art building loomed behind me as I waited in our coven's usual spot beneath the Palms. Luke and Gwen hadn't shown up to school. They were twenty-four hours away from limitless malevolent power; I supposed they were no longer concerned with anything as Mundane as academics. Part of me was braced for impact, as if I expected them to leap out from behind a tree and attack at any moment, but intuition told me they were biding their time.

Tomorrow was the eclipse. Tomorrow would be their day.

The Palms towering overhead felt imposing, as if they were glaring down at me, as if the universe knew my failures. After all that had happened yesterday at Luke's, I had no defense to offer them. I'd been so infatuated with Luke, so clouded by my own stupid jealousy, I'd missed the threat right in front of me. Petra had been right: history was repeating itself. A Nichols and a Foster were dangerously close to achieving the Meteoric Union. Only this time around, a Nichols was leading the charge.

And then there was Gwen. The fact that she'd chosen to go along with Luke's plan hurt even more than his betrayal. Was the shy, compassionate girl I used to know gone forever? Her words echoed in my mind. *Don't blame me if I don't want to be that Gwen ever again. Blame yourself.* Of course, her decisions were her own, but I certainly hadn't made things easy for her. I'd pushed her away the moment I discovered she had malevolent magic, and I hadn't exactly been kind before that.

As I sat there, regretting my past, I felt the future stretch before me, dangerous and uncertain. I shifted uncomfortably on the hard ground, placing a protective hand over my bag. Beneath the designer logo bulged the outline of Delfina Garcia's diary. I'd messaged the rest of the coven with a synopsis of my visit to Luke's, but the prospect of facing them in person made my heart race. Today would be no ordinary coven meeting. Today, we were going to talk battle strategy.

Jayden was the first to arrive, his steps echoing beneath a pair of red suede boots. He wore a fashionably disjointed ensemble, the boots at odds with ripped jeans and a black hip-length shift. To me, the meaning behind the outfit was clear: Jayden's world was upside down.

"That two-faced snake in a leather jacket!" he declared, plopping down on the grass beside me. "I should have known."

"I thought I knew Luke better than anyone," I said. "And I fell for it too."

I expected him to hit me with a quick one-liner, something about how I'd also fallen for the tiny purse trend two seasons ago. Instead, he gazed across the quad as if searching for the right words.

"I don't blame you, Val. Love makes us crazy."

"And stupid," I replied bitterly. "For years, I thought if I could just get Luke Nichols to care for me the way I cared for him, everything would be okay. All that time swooning over him, and I never knew he was a monster."

"Even if he had been Prince Charming, I don't think it works like that."

I turned to him. "What do you mean?"

He picked at a patch of bark on a palm tree's broad trunk. "I mean, nobody is going to swoop into your life and make everything okay. You need to deal with your own crap first."

I let out an involuntary giggle. "You read that on a cross-stitched throw pillow or something?"

"Nope. Found out the hard way. Laugh all you want, but from one rich kid with issues to another, trust me."

There was an unfamiliar vulnerability in his dark brown eyes. He was serious, and to my surprise, I realized he was deeply sad.

"Well, thanks," I replied. "Maybe if I'd figured that out sooner, I would have seen Luke for what he really was. I can't believe I actually suspected Max and Celeste!"

"Valeria—"

I went on, swept up in a wave of guilt. I told him about their conflicting alibis—how I'd watched them and followed them home from school.

"Valeria!" Jayden said again, and the urgency in his voice made me go silent. "The night Petra died, Max was with me."

"What?" I blurted. It hit me. The way Max seemed to avoid Jayden lately, as if something had changed between them. "Wait, are you and Max—?"

"No—I don't know," he said, not looking at me. "Maybe we could have been if I hadn't ruined it. All my life, I've held people at a distance. The only person I trusted was Petra. I figured all you need is one good friend, right?"

His fingers closed around a small vial he wore around his neck, dried herbs floating within, the dainty white petals of elderflower.

"Oh, Jayden—" I began, but he was still speaking, words pouring out of him as if he couldn't hold them back any longer.

"But I always thought about Max. His kindness, his strength. In the back of my mind, I knew he and I might have a chance at something real. The thing is, *real* is scary. *Real* means you can get hurt." He turned to me suddenly, as if remembering something. "Did you know Max has a puppy wall calendar in his bedroom?"

"Um, no," I replied, not sure where he was going with this.

"Well, he does. You know why? Because he likes puppies. Wanna know what's on my bedroom wall? Posters of trendy bands I don't even listen to. That's the difference between him and me. He's not afraid to be who he is. I'm always afraid, Val. Afraid to care, afraid to let my guard down. Most of the time, I'd rather be cool than be myself. That's why it took me so long to admit what I really wanted."

"But you finally did?"

"Yup," he replied dully, as if the memory cast him into some dark, cynical place. "After our parents lost their magic, I started thinking. I decided I was through with pushing people away. One night, I drove to his house and told him I felt the same way he did. I always had. He kissed me right then and there. It felt great, like he and I were about to begin something amazing. Like I was waking up at last from a long, cold sleep."

"That's wonderful!" I exclaimed, but the look in his eyes told me my celebration was premature.

"That was the night Petra died. When I found out what happened to her, I freaked. Just like that, the only person I'd ever trusted was gone. I swore I'd never lose anyone I loved again. So I took it all back." He shut his eyes against tears. "I told Max I'd made a mistake. There was nothing between us and there never would be. I was so ashamed of myself, I even asked him to lie about where we were that night. And he did. For me. Because that's the kind of person he is." He let out a joyless laugh. "He hasn't spoken to me since."

I felt my heart break for them both. I wouldn't blame Max if he stayed angry at Jayden for the rest of his life. But I couldn't say that. Not after the courage it must have taken to tell me the truth. I searched for the right words, but anything that came to me sounded silly and trite.

"I think he's going to need some time," I said at last.

He twirled a blade of grass in his fingers, a distant expression on his face. "What if we don't *have* time? I can feel a fight coming. I could die before I get the chance to show Max how sorry I am."

My fingers tightened into fists. "I will not let that happen," I told him. "I haven't always been a good leader or a good friend. In fact, most of the time, I was terrible at both. But I promise I'll keep the rest of you alive if it's the last thing I do."

I felt my heart flutter in my chest, and I realized I meant it. I would die for them if I had to. He looked at me, surprised by how serious I'd become.

"Thank you." He touched the vial around his neck again.

"What's in there?"

"Something I've been working on ever since she died. Maybe it's my way of making amends with the universe…if that's even possible for a guy like me."

I thought of all the wrong I'd done. All the hurt I'd caused. And I thought of Gwen.

"Good people make mistakes," I said. "Sometimes one wrong turn can get you lost at sea with no road map home."

"Okay, are we in a car or boat in this metaphor?"

He laughed, and I squeezed his hand in mine. Being this honest with another person felt surprisingly good, like it was something my soul had been craving for a long time.

"I don't know! I'm just saying, if we're willing to try, maybe all us lost, imperfect people can get back home. Maybe we can even light one another's way."

The sound of footsteps on concrete announced the arrival of Max and Celeste. Jayden dabbed at his tears with his sleeve before turning to face them.

Celeste clung to her brother, her arm gripped tightly in his as if she might buckle under some invisible weight. Max's brow was furrowed, his jaw tense. He didn't look at Jayden as he approached. He kept his gaze down, the ground infinitely more appealing than the boy who'd broken his heart.

And that was all of us. I was struck by how small our coven had become. As they sat in a loose circle before me, I could practically feel the empty spaces left by Luke, Gwen, and Petra.

"Okay," I said to our meager group. "You all know why we're here. Luke and Gwen are about to gain some seriously dangerous power. This is the part where we decide how to stop them."

"And how do we do that exactly?" Max asked.

Hesitantly, I withdrew the leather-bound book from my purse. "There's a passage at the end of the diary," I said. "I think it's a spell."

"Great—" Jayden began, but I held up a hand to stop his excitement.

I turned to the diary's final page and showed them its contents. There was a liquid quality about the cursive letters. They seemed to wind into one another, none forming recognizable words. The longer I gazed at the writing, the harder it became to discipher.

"It's enchanted somehow," I told them. "She must not have wanted this spell to fall into the wrong hands."

"But we're not the wrong hands!" Celeste said indignantly, as if Delfina Garcia had personally offended her.

"I guess the book doesn't know that," I replied, setting it down on the grass, still open to the mysterious page.

A disappointed silence fell over the group.

"Maybe I could talk to Luke," Max said finally as he settled on the ground beside his sister. "I mean, we've known each other all our lives. We're supposed to be brothers. Maybe he'd listen."

I shook my head wearily. "He believes the Meteoric Union is his destiny. He's been waiting his whole life for this. Nothing's going to change his mind now. I'm sorry."

"What about Gwen?" said Jayden. "Is she like Patty Hearst with Stockholm syndrome, or has she gone full wicked witch?"

I thought of the last time I'd seen Gwen, the loneliness I'd felt from her, even as she stood by Luke's side.

"There's a desperation about her. I don't know what she's capable of," I replied. I hesitated before speaking my next words. "But we were friends once. Back when we were kids. She was kind then, much kinder than I ever was. I want to believe there's still good inside her."

They were quiet a moment, pondering a reality where Gwen Foster and I had been anything close to friends.

"But didn't she attack you at Luke's house?" Celeste said. "Didn't she let Luke torture you with the Shadow Spell?"

I sighed. I couldn't deny Gwen was dangerous. The dull pain in my shoulder where her moonfire had struck me was proof of that. "Yes, and if the time comes, I will deal with her. But for now, we make Luke our number-one target."

"Are you sure you can do that?" Max said, putting a hand on my shoulder.

"Yeah, I mean, he's your ex-lover!" Celeste added.

I resisted the urge to roll my eyes at Celeste's flair for the dramatic.

"I've seen who Luke really is, and it's ugly," I told them. "I'm not his fool anymore like Gwen is. I know he can't be saved, or maybe he's not worth saving. In a way, it sets me free. I'm ready to do whatever it takes to stop him."

As I spoke the words, I felt their truth in my soul. When it came to Luke, there was nothing left to do but take him down.

A flicker of movement caught my eye. The writing in the diary was rearranging itself, words appearing on the page as if the book had been waiting for that moment to reveal its secret.

The heading, in Delfina's proud script, read *A Spell to Vanquish Malevolent Magic.*

"Looks like we're trustworthy after all," Jayden mused.

We are now, I thought, marveling at the magic Delfina had cast on the page. I'd sworn aloud I was ready to defeat Luke, no matter what, and the book seemed to sense the sincerity of my words. So this was how she'd prevented the spell from falling into the hands of the enemy.

I grabbed the diary eagerly.

"'There is but one spell that will allow a coven to drain the malevolent magic from a foe,'" I read aloud, then I skimmed over the flowery prose. "It says we need to enchant a mirror using a drop of Luke's blood. Once the mirror is imbued, we can aim it at Luke to draw the malevolent magic out of him."

There was a stunned silence as they considered the enormity of our task. Jayden announced with forced enthusiasm, "Hey, look, we have a plan!"

I nodded in agreement. "We can use this spell to drain Luke's malevolent magic before he and Gwen can complete the ritual."

My voice rang with resolution, but my heart raced. We didn't have much time.

"If we enchant the mirror with Luke's blood, you think it'll work against Mr. Nichols too?" Jayden said. "After all, they share a bloodline. What's that saying? The apple doesn't fall far from the malevolent tree?"

"If he gets in our way, I guess we'll find out," I said somberly.

"This spell sounds dangerous," Max said.

"Duh," Celeste replied.

"I meant for Luke. Couldn't it…hurt him?"

I scanned further, searching Delfina's prim penmanship.

"'No harm will come to the malevolent witch, as long as he possesses the will to survive,'" I read aloud, then the next words caught my eye. Dismay tugged at the pit of my stomach. "'To achieve the spell's full power, it must be performed by the entire coven.'"

Another silence, longer this time.

"I hate to state the obvious, but two of our members are currently on the wrong side," Celeste said.

I touched my shirt above the spot where the sacred circle was carved into my chest. Luke and Gwen had circles over their hearts, too, and they certainly wouldn't be participating in the spell. I felt a cloud of doubt settle above our heads.

"I know," I said. "We'll have to settle for less than full power. Unless anyone can come up with a better plan."

"How about we run?" Celeste offered.

The rest of us eyed her with skepticism.

"Okay, hear me out. They want a coven to lead, right? What if we just skip town? Boom. Thwarted."

I looked down at the kids on the quad. From up here, they looked tiny, fragile, like any one of them could be crushed with a well-aimed fist. If Gwen and Luke achieved the Meteoric Union, none of them would be safe from their wrath. And what about our parents? How long before Luke got bored and used his Shadow Spell on one of them? I shook my head as the desperate reality hit me.

"I can't run away from this," I said. As I looked at my coven, taking in the new warmth in Jayden's eyes, the brave jut of Max's chin, and the innocence of Celeste's worried pout, I felt fiercely protective of each of them. "But I can't put you all at risk. I'll face them alone tomorrow. I'll stop them before they can do the ritual."

"Nice try," Jayden said. "*We'll* face them together."

"I'll be there," Max said, his voice low with conviction.

Celeste kept her gaze fixed on her toes. "No," she murmured. "We're dealing with witches who can kill us on a whim. I want to graduate. I want to study fashion at NYU. And someday, I want to go to Mykonos and stay in a suite with an infinity pool that looks out over the ocean. I am not dying at fifteen over some stupid prophecy."

"Celeste," Max began gently, "I know you're scared—"

"You're damn right I am," she shot back, a quiver of tears mixed with the anger in her voice. "If you were smart, you would be too."

She mumbled something that might have been an apology before rising and marching down the steps. I watched her silhouette disappear among the laughing students below.

"I'm sorry," Max said. "I'll talk to her." But the look in his eyes told me he wasn't sure he could bring his sister around.

"It's okay," said Jayden, his brows drawn. "Celeste is right. We all have plans, futures. But since the rest of us seem to be temporarily insane, tomorrow we fight."

"Thank you." I placed a grateful hand on each of their shoulders. "Meet in my garden tomorrow morning before the eclipse starts."

"What are you going to do tonight?" Max asked warily.

"We need blood, right?" I replied. "I'm going to Luke's."

AFTER NIGHTFALL, I stole through the woods between my house and Luke's. The birds hadn't returned to the forest since the trees died. The air was still, and no sound of living things rustled in the bare branches. Luke's house loomed like a giant tombstone in the distance, bone-colored and austere. It was strange how different the house looked to me now. The last time I'd climbed the ivy trellis to

Luke's window was the night we'd watched the aurora. I could still feel my feet on the shaky rungs, my body alive with the unnamable excitement that always used to take hold when I was about to see him.

Tonight, every window was dark. No one was waiting up for me.

I slid the back gate open and glanced at the western wall. In the dim moonlight, the ivy that crept up was black and amorphous. I made my way to the leafy mass and began to paw at it in the dark. Dewdrops chilled my fingers.

There. My freezing hands connected with something solid amidst the layers of vines. The ivy had grown over it, making it barely visible, but the trellis was still there. Luke had never thought to move it, even after everything he'd done had come to light. Perhaps it wasn't carelessness but cockiness; perhaps he simply didn't consider me a threat. I was reminded suddenly of a button Petra used to wear on her backpack: CARRY YOURSELF WITH THE CONFIDENCE OF A MEDIOCRE WHITE MAN.

I curled my fingers around the splintery wood and placed a foot on the lower rung. Here I come, lover.

Up I went, clawing for handholds among the vines. The handkerchief I would use to collect Luke's blood was folded in my back pocket. The ceremonial dagger, at home in its sheath, was pressed against my thigh. An invisible heat seemed to radiate from it as if it knew it would soon be put to use.

My fingers grazed the windowpane, and I hoisted myself up to peer inside. The room was dark, the white moon reflected back at me in the glass. Was he in there? With careful hands, I tried the window. I almost laughed when it slid up easily. Unlocked as usual. He wasn't even a little bit afraid of me. I hoped that was about to change.

I lowered my head and squeezed myself through, placed one foot gently down on the bedroom floor, then the other. I shivered. Somehow, it felt colder in here than it did outside.

After a moment, my eyes adjusted to the dim light. A square of moonlight filtered in from the window behind me, illuminating two sleeping faces. Luke was closer to me, his breaths deep and slow.

Gwen slept beside him, her hair spilling over the pillow in black rivers.

I knew Luke's bedroom floor creaked. All our floors did, as if the centuries-old wood was protesting generations of trodding feet. I took one long, careful step, then I stood frozen, looming over Luke. His left arm hung off the side of the bed.

All I needed was a drop of blood. The coven's sacred dagger was always sharpened as fine as a razor blade. If I floated it right, I could prick his fingertip no harder than an insect bite. He wouldn't even wake, and I'd be out the window before he knew what happened.

A chill tickled my neck. That was the plan, anyway.

With trembling fingers, I drew the dagger from its sheath and pulled the handkerchief from my pocket. I took a breath and let the dagger hover at Luke's open palm. My mind went blank until all I saw was the knife and its target. I touched the knife's point to Luke's finger, as light and brief as a chaste kiss.

In a second, a single red drop grew on his fingertip. He stirred, but his eyes remained closed. I caught the droplet in the air, held it with my mind like a precious ruby and closed the handkerchief around it with one hand. Done.

I pressed the handkerchief into my back pocket and called the dagger back to my hand.

I was about to step silently to the window when something flickered in my peripheral vision—the tiniest flash of light. I froze.

Gwen's eyes were open. The moon was reflected in them, a glint of silver in her black pupils. We stared at each other in the darkness. I realized both of us were holding our breath as if waiting for the other to exhale first. She'll call to him, I thought. Any second, she'll call to him.

But the seconds ticked on.

I looked at Gwen, her eyes wild with fear, her fingers clenching the covers, knuckles white. It was hard to believe this was the same girl who used to run barefoot with me through the trees. The girl who was free to answer to her own whims, to the raven's call. Now, as she sat frozen by Luke's side, she looked more like a captive than I'd ever seen her.

Before I knew what I was doing, I jerked my head toward the window in a silent gesture. *Escape with me.* Her eyes darted to the window, and I could tell she understood. She seemed to vacillate, her chest rising and falling with rapid breaths. But then her eyes landed on the knife that glinted in my hand, its sharp point poised dangerously near Luke's outstretched wrist.

"Luke!" she screeched, her voice high and edged with panic. "Luke!"

There was no time. A second later, he was lunging forward. His hands flew toward me, searching for something to tighten around, something to control. I retreated toward the window, but he caught the hem of my shirt. Even in the dark, I could see a black mass gathered in his other hand.

I cast a ball of sacred fire straight at his heart. It struck him in a phosphorescent burst, sending him tumbling over Gwen, his head hitting the floor with a dull thud. He lay there, momentarily dazed. I dove toward the window, still grasping the knife. Now I was ready to use it, ready to slash at whoever tried to stop me.

With my free hand, I gripped the windowsill and swung my legs over. My feet plunged into a mass of ivy. I kicked wildly for the rungs of the trellis. With a shock of pain, my toe hit something solid and I found my footing. The cool night air felt like freedom, like victory. But before I could lower myself to the next rung, a pair of hands tightened around my wrists.

I looked up, expecting to see Luke's cool, indifferent eyes. Instead, Gwen's pale face floated above me. She leaned her head and shoulders out the window, her grip so tight her nails dug into my skin. The look on her face was desperate, complex. Even as her fingers drew blood, I wondered if she was trying to stop me or if she just needed something to cling to.

Her eyes bore into mine. The loneliness I'd felt from her the last time we met seemed amplified now, bottomless. I'd missed a dozen chances to tell her before, but I knew this might be my last.

"I'm sorry," I called up to her.

"I'm sorry," she repeated back to me, her tone as lifeless as her eyes. I couldn't tell if she was apologizing for what she had done—or what she was yet to do.

The floor groaned as Luke stumbled to his feet. I wrenched myself from her grasp, leaving bloody streaks across my arms. Then he was at her side, his dark magic snaking toward me. I drew the sunfire up to meet it, but before I let it go, I looked at Gwen, holding her gaze with purpose.

"The birds don't care if you're pretty!" I cried.

I saw the look of confusion in Luke's eyes and the understanding in hers. I let the fire within me fly, sending them both tumbling backward.

As I scrambled down the trellis, I expected Luke to come after me, or Mr. Nichols to appear at the back door, Shadow Spell in hand. But when my feet touched down, I found myself alone. Why hadn't they followed? The question nagged at me, but I wasn't about to wait around for them. With a final backward glance, I darted toward the woods. I had a stop to make, and there was much to do before sunrise.

CHAPTER SIXTEEN

GWEN

I stood alone in Luke's bedroom as the sun climbed slowly in the pale sky. It shone, warm and brilliant, like it did every morning. But the heavens were moving on an unalterable path. In little more than an hour, the moon would overtake that glowing orb, casting it into black.

I turned to my reflection in the mirror. The dark folds of my skirt fell around my waist like a midnight waterfall, the lace at my breast as delicate as flower petals. The dress fit perfectly, just as I'd imagined when I spied it in that shop window downtown. That day, I'd asked Luke when I would ever wear such an extravagant thing. *I'm sure we'll find an occasion,* he'd replied.

This was the occasion. The Meteoric Union. He'd been dreaming of this moment even then.

"You're stunning." Luke said, appearing behind me. "I knew you would be."

His gaze met mine in the mirror. He was dressed impeccably in a black velvet suit. As he neared me, he smelled of clean linen and the gel he'd combed through his hair, but there was another scent beneath those Mundane chemicals, something coppery and wild. He circled his arms around my waist and kissed the bare skin of my neck. Despite my nerves, I felt myself lean into him, grateful for the warmth of his body.

"Look at yourself," he commanded. "What do you see?"

There was a strange glamour to the pale girl who stared back at me from the mirror, this girl wrapped in Luke's arms, her body draped in expensive fabrics. She looked grander and more formidable than me. And yet, as I watched her, I felt the invisible weight on her shoulders, saw the doubt in her dark eyes. I'd taken the dress from that miserable shop clerk because I'd wanted it, because I didn't care if I hurt her to get it. Was that the person I was destined to become? Someone who found power in cruelty?

The sun shone through the window. Soon its light would fade, and my time to decide would run out.

For lack of a better answer, I replied, "I see Gwen Foster."

"That's right," he said. "This is the last time you'll look in this mirror and see Gwen Foster. After today, the line where your soul ends and mine begins will be washed away in fire and magic. Forever after, when you look at yourself, you'll see *us*. Our union and the power that goes with it."

His anticipation was palpable, a live wire humming beneath his skin. The muscles beneath his temples flexed and released. "I didn't get the chance to thank you for stopping Valeria last night," he went on, one hand combing through my hair. "Who knows what she could have done if you hadn't woken up when you did. She might have killed me in my sleep like the coward she is."

I wasn't convinced Valeria had intended murder. I thought I'd seen a subtle movement of the knife near Luke's palm as my eyes had fluttered open, but in that bleary place between sleeping and waking, I couldn't be sure.

"I couldn't let her hurt you," I told him truthfully.

Luke and I were a part of one another, our fates entwined like the veins beneath my skin. When I saw the knife in Valeria's hand, some ancient instinct had taken over. All I could see was that blade against his wrist. I'd called out, not to Valeria but to him. Our love was destructive, I knew that. It would burn across the land, leaving nothing but embers in its wake. Yet here I was on the day of the Meteoric Union, in his arms again.

He turned me to face him, taking both my hands in his. I could feel the magic building between us, dark power gathering with each beat of our hearts. I hadn't done any malevolent magic since the night I used it on my dad, but I felt it inside me every day. The closer I was to Luke, the stronger it raged, scratching at my insides like a caged animal.

I took a breath and forced myself to ask the question I'd been pondering for days. "Do you know what the sacrifice will be? You know, for the ritual?"

Luke gazed out the window at the naked forest below. A faint smile tugged at his lips. "Yes," he replied. He went silent, and I realized he wasn't going to tell me. As if reading my mind, he added, "Trust me, it'll be easier if you don't know. Not until it's time."

A shiver ran up my spine. To complete a malevolent ritual of this magnitude, I doubted a few dead trees would suffice. This time, blood would be shed.

"Guilt is for Mundanes, Gwen. We're way beyond that now." He took me by the shoulders and leveled his gaze with mine. My malevolent magic seemed to sense his hands on me, as if it knew today was the day. A sickly heat rushed through me, stronger than ever. My fingers tingled with power, itching for a trigger to pull. Perhaps they'd find one soon enough. "This is your day, baby," he went on. "Every terrible thing you've ever felt—all the misery, all the loneliness—ends now. After this, there will be nothing but power and glory and our love."

They were such pretty words. I leaned into him and let myself believe it all. I let myself be at home in the dark, icy place that was his heart. I wondered if I could stay there forever. I'd have Luke, and all the power I'd ever dreamed of. No one would hurt me ever again. I would just have to get used to the cold.

He pulled away from me at last. Outside, a thin sliver of black clung to the sun. It had begun. As Luke watched the sky, I could practically see his heart pounding in his chest.

"Are you ready?" he said.

I wasn't. There was one more thing I had to do. I took a breath that caught in my rib cage.

"If these are my last moments as Gwen Foster, I think I want to…commemorate them somehow," I said.

He looked at me, confused but unbothered. "How?"

I gestured to the forest below us. "This forest has always been my favorite place in the world. I'd like to take one last walk through the trees. Alone."

I saw a glimmer of mistrust cross his face, but in a split second, it was gone.

"Of course," he replied.

Together, we descended the stairs and crossed the kitchen. Luke held the door wide, just as he had the day we stood in front of the ruined chandelier. That day, I'd decided I had nowhere to go, no home except by his side. If everyone besides Luke had given up on me, why shouldn't I turn to him and let my heart grow cold forever?

And yet, miraculously, perhaps someone still held out hope for me—even now. I thought of the words Valeria had called up to me as we grappled on the trellis. The words had echoed in my head all night.

Beyond the neatly kept garden, the tangled forest waited. I kissed Luke's cheek and stepped onto the back porch.

"What's this, son? Has your bride-to-be gotten cold feet?" A voice sounded from behind me.

I turned to see Alexis Nichols standing in the kitchen, his blue eyes cool with suspicion.

"No," I said quickly. "Just going for a walk."

Alexis didn't reply to me. Instead, he turned to Luke. "You would let her walk out the door this close to the ritual?"

"You know, I pity you," Luke said to his father. "You've never experienced a love like Gwen and I share. Of course you haven't— no one has. So you'll just have to take my word for it." His gaze pierced mine. "Gwen would never betray me."

Alexis looked from Luke to me and back again. At last, his features seemed to soften.

"Well, Gwen, who am I to question young love? Go ahead, but

first, please—let me officially welcome you to the family. The universe blessed me with a son, and now fate has blessed me with a daughter."

He strode toward me, arms wide. Before I knew what was happening, he'd pulled me in for a hug.

His embrace was just a little too tight, his arms like the coils of some predatory snake. "Don't go far," he said in a voice so low I doubted Luke could hear. "You know how important this day is. Today, everything will go as planned." He added, his whisper hot on the back of my neck, "I will make sure of it."

Alexis's arms loosened around my rib cage, and I sucked in air.

"Have a nice stroll, Gwen," he said, his tone bright again.

"I won't be long," I replied.

It was the truth. I was beyond running. I understood my destiny had to be faced, not escaped. As I descended the back stairs and made my way through the garden, I recalled a line from Poe. *I could not love except where Death was mingling his with Beauty's breath.* With those ominous words echoing in my mind, I crossed into the solitude of the trees.

CHAPTER SEVENTEEN

VALERIA

I squinted at the dark shape that had begun to consume the sun's rays. All over town, the Mundanes were gathering with their eclipse glasses and binoculars to view the celestial phenomenon, but outside my window, our woods were silent. Delfina's diary said the Meteoric Union had to take place within a circle of enchanted flames. The clearing was the only place in town Luke and Gwen could pull that off without being noticed. A battle would clash among those trees soon enough.

I dressed in the robe of the high priestess, its bright red fabric gathering like fire around me. Standing before my vanity mirror, I placed the gold crown on my head. Its gilded shine set off the color of my eyes, but today, I was more concerned with the power it symbolized.

Whatever happened today, Luke would not forget who I was: high priestess and rightful leader of our coven. If I died, I would die in this crown.

My hair fell straight around my shoulders. I hadn't thought to put on any makeup. My eyes were alive with the sunfire that pounded in my chest, my lips set resolutely. I'd examined myself in this mirror a thousand times, worrying over an emerging blemish or a stray hair. The reflection that gazed back at me today was different. I looked strong, ready for whatever danger awaited. It was a kind of beauty I'd never seen in myself before, and I liked it.

Suddenly, Mr. Nichols's taunting words rang in my ears. *We figured you'd be too busy fixing your lipstick to notice what was really going on.* I fished Reckless Red from my purse and brushed it over my parted lips. It shimmered, crimson and spiteful.

I smiled. I was ready now.

"Your mother and I are going with you," my father announced from the hallway.

He stood in the bedroom doorway, spinning his wedding ring, as he often did when he was nervous. One twist over, one twist under.

"Dad, you know you can't—" I began.

"It's the right thing to do," he said, his voice steady, decided.

"The hell it is!" I argued. "Without magic, you'll be defenseless."

"We can't let you face these traitors on your own. It's too much to ask of a bunch of kids."

There it was. My parents didn't think we could defeat Luke. They didn't think *I* could defeat him. When my dad looked at me, did he see the strong, capable person I'd just seen in the mirror? Or, to him, was I still the selfish child I used to be?

Today, the sun would fade like a waning moon. For better or worse, something new would follow. The girl I had been was waning, too, dissolving around me like shedding skin. I hoped whoever emerged would be stronger, but also kinder.

"Dad, you have to trust me—"

As I spoke, my mom joined us, her steps creaking down the ancient hallway. I got the sense she had been standing just out of sight for some time, listening. My dad opened his mouth to lecture me on all the things I didn't know, all the things I wasn't ready for. But my mom spoke first.

"She can do this," my mother said. "Let her go."

"What?" I stared at her, putting a hand on the vanity table in case I toppled over. A vote of confidence from my mom was more disorienting than I'd ever imagined.

"Lili, you can't be serious," my dad said.

"I'm perfectly serious." My mom turned to me, her features softening. "I've always pushed you to be strong, Valeria. But I thought strong had to mean hard. Now I'm realizing there is strength in compassion too. You went to Luke's alone last night. You risked yourself for your coven without a second thought. That's what a leader should be." She lowered her gaze in what almost looked like embarrassment. "I don't know if I would have been brave enough myself."

Peace settled over the three of us. A resolution. I studied my parents—the new patches of gray in their hair, the worry lines growing deeper across their faces.

"I won't let you down," I told them. "And I'll get your magic back. Maybe not today, but I'll do it. I promise you."

"I know you will," my mom replied.

There was a smile at the corner of her eyes. Was that what pride looked like? I wasn't sure, but it felt like the sun on a chilly day.

By the time I reached my back door, my bag slung over my shoulder, Jayden and Max were waiting for me at the edge of the forest. With dismay, I saw there was no sign of Celeste.

Above us, blackness had already devoured a quarter of the sun. A chill tickled my skin, and I wondered if Celeste had the right idea after all. The air had grown cold and a harsh wind had picked up as if nature understood something sinister was about to begin.

Jayden was dressed for battle in a vintage army jacket, his fingernails painted the dull silver of gunmetal. The vial of elderflower elixir hung from a chain around his neck. Beside him, Max wore his letterman jacket and a look of distinct unease.

Jayden shot me his best attempt at a wry smile. "How'd your looking glass turn out, Alice?"

From my bag I withdrew an old gold-framed mirror about the size of a dinner plate. "See for yourself."

I'd enchanted the mirror the night before, binding it with the handkerchief that held Luke's blood and burying them both in the garden. When I dug them up this morning, the handkerchief was clean. A red tinge covered the mirror's surface as if the blood lay trapped behind its glass.

"Curiouser and curiouser," he remarked.

I replaced the mirror and withdrew two lengths of rope.

"We're all clear on the plan, right?" I said. "Once the circle of flames closes around Luke and Gwen, no magic but the malevolent kind can be done within it, so we need to act fast. When we face Luke, I'll aim the mirror. You two back me up. On my cue, we'll recite the spell. Please tell me you practiced the incantation I sent you—"

"Valeria," Max cut in. "You're the strongest witch among us. You're the best chance we have. You shouldn't have your hands tied up holding a stupid mirror." Though his voice wavered, his jaw was set with determination. "Let me do it."

"No!" Jayden answered before I could.

"Whoever's holding that mirror will be Luke's biggest target," I told Max soberly.

I looked at Max, the boy who had hoped this could all be handled with a few well-chosen words. His arms were crossed, his shoulders sloped in a way that made him seem small, despite his broad frame.

"I'm not a fighter," he replied. "I never have been. I won't be any good against them. But this is something I can do. Let me do this for the coven—please."

As he spoke, it was clear how much the coven mattered to him, even after everything he'd believed about it had been shattered. Perhaps now that it was broken, it was more important than ever.

Despite Jayden's protests, we came to an uneasy agreement. Max would hold the mirror, and we would protect him at all costs.

"Then these are for me," Jayden said, taking the rope and looping it through his belt with shaky fingers.

As darkness closed in from above, I had the overwhelming sense that death awaited us. I just didn't know whose.

The sun was more than half-swallowed now. It was time to go.

The three of us seemed to draw a collective breath, holding it as we entered the woods. The army of bare trees shook in the wind as if readying themselves for battle. As we picked our way over roots and fallen branches, Jayden stepped closer to Max. I fell behind, trying to give them whatever privacy I could, but the cold wind carried their words to my ears.

"Max—" Jayden began.

"If you're trying to apologize just 'cause you think I'm gonna die today, don't bother," Max hissed. "It feels a little disingenuous, if you know what I mean."

"I was just going to say what a fine morning it is," Jayden replied, his voice as casual as he could make it. "You can decide whether or not you want my apology some other day. I know you're going to come out of this just fine."

"If you believe that, maybe you're stupider than I thought."

"Oh, I'm very stupid." Jayden put a tentative hand on Max's shoulder. "But I swore I'd never lose another good person if I could help it. And you…are the best person. So you have nothing to worry about."

Max glanced at him with what might have been a smile, but his gaze quickly returned to the dry brush under his feet. "Be careful out there today."

Jayden exhaled as if their conversation had been scarier than anything he was about to face. Above us, the last light was dying.

I made out the clearing ahead. Two dark figures were moving there. As we came to a stop, the eclipse reached totality.

Night didn't fall softly. It crashed around us, plunging us into darkness. In the sky, pale light ringed the black moon, which seemed to stare down like the pupil of some watchful eye. The stars emerged brighter and more plentiful than I'd ever seen them. Luke and Gwen stood before us, their figures barely visible in the darkness.

"Tenebris Ignis." The sound of Luke's voice made my skin crawl. My fingers curled into fists.

At his words, a half ring of tall black flames ignited behind them, its open mouth facing us. The fire raged atop the dead earth.

The glow it cast was stark and colorless, more like the absence of darkness than the presence of light.

Standing before those unnatural flames, Luke and Gwen were formidable and more than a little frightening. Black lace clung to Gwen's pale skin like it was a part of her. Her hair was a dark curtain around her face. Her expression was flat, but as I looked closer, a deep well of emotion seemed hidden behind her eyes. Luke's handsome features had taken on a wild quality, his smile a little too wide, his eyes sparkling. He looked like he was about to enjoy himself immensely.

Luke had littered the ground with white flowers—night-scented orchids. The sickly odor of burning petals hit me, stirring the uneasiness in my stomach. At first, none of us spoke. A snapped twig would've sounded like a thunderclap. I let the sunfire gather in my palm, preparing to strike.

Finally, Luke broke the silence.

"You showed up to your own massacre, Val," he said. "Wow. You really can't turn down an opportunity to be the center of attention."

"Says the man who's literally standing in the center of a magic ring of fire," I replied.

He grinned at me, the curve of his lips turning his expression cruel. "It's called the killing circle. And you'll join me inside soon enough."

I felt fear grip me as I began to understand. No.

No. How could I have been so stupid?

His laughter was ugly. "You're getting it now. Of course, the Meteoric Union requires a sacrifice. It demands the death of a high priestess. That's you, lover. You could have prevented this whole thing if you had just stayed away. But instead, you had to swoop in and save the day like the hero in whatever pathetic fairy tale you've told yourself."

Tears stung my eyes. I thought of how Mr. Nichols had stopped short of killing me the night Petra died. How no one had followed me yesterday after I escaped on the trellis. They hadn't wanted me dead.

Until now.

My heart pounded. The flames that curled at my fingertips flared like they'd been struck with gasoline.

My gaze shifted to Gwen. She hadn't moved, but her eyes were on Luke, her face frozen in an expression of genuine shock. He hadn't told her I was the sacrifice, I realized. I watched as the revelation washed over her, unknowable thoughts churning in her mind, clouding her features.

Luke kept his gaze trained on me. "I have to admit, it's quite an apt way for you to die," he went on. "Brought down by your own self-importance."

"We'll see who's dead before the night's over." I shivered against the wind as I said the words. They felt like an omen. Something was wrong. This night was too important; Mr. Nichols wouldn't miss seeing his special prince become a king. So where was he?

"Baby, before the night's over, you're going to step into this circle and ask me to kill you," Luke told me. "You'll be *begging* for it."

I was about to respond when something shot toward him from the darkness. A rock struck him in the temple, leaving a small red gash where it made contact. I didn't have to look at Jayden to know he'd been the one to fly it,—his way of saying *Enough talk, screw this guy.*

Luke winced and put a hand to his head to touch the trickle of blood that had appeared there. Then everything happened at once.

"Get back!" he shouted to Gwen, pushing her behind him.

With a movement of his hand, the circle of fire closed around her, protecting her, trapping her. She watched us from over the flames, her eyes wide, her magic useless. He raged at us, the Shadow Spell charging from his fingertips.

Max grabbed the mirror from my bag. On cue, we began to chant, our words echoing through the trees.

"Malevolent man, face yourself and see your wrongs."

Luke seemed to understand immediately that the mirror was a weapon. He took aim at Max and launched the Shadow Spell just as I threw my sunfire. The two spells—one dark, one blazing —met between us in a shower of sparks and a cloud of smoke. I held my mother's image in my mind, letting it anchor me to my power. This time, I could see the pride on her face.

My blood seemed to be made of fire, burning with everything I held dear, everything I would protect. My spell overtook Luke's, gaining on him and striking him in the chest. He stumbled backward. He met his own eyes in the mirror. For a split second, his cocky grin wavered.

"Malevolent man," we repeated, "your dominion hath run out."

Luke charged the Shadow Spell again, its black tendrils slithering toward me. Suddenly, his arm caught in midair. A cry of pain escaped his lips as he struggled against the rope that had wrapped itself around his wrist.

On my right, Jayden's expression was like stone, his concentration tangible as he held the rope in his mind. Slowly, he forced Luke's arm behind his back.

Immediately, the spell rose in Luke's other hand, but Jayden had already sent the second rope soaring at him. Again, Luke's wrist caught. Jayden's breath came hard as he pushed against Luke's strength. I joined my will with Jayden's. Together we bound him, beads of sweat glistening at our temples, and still we kept up our chant.

"Malevolent man, face yourself… "

Max's fingers trembled but he held the mirror steady, pointing right at Luke's writhing form. Even tethered like this, Luke sneered at us.

"This is your plan? Some rope and a…*magic mirror?*"

It sounded ridiculous when he said it. But as we chanted, a thin black plume began to rise from Luke's chest as if siphoned from the depths of his heart. The essence of Luke's malevolent magic. It was working.

Our coven wasn't complete, but we could still hurt him—still take some of the power he held dear. The dark shape wound its way toward the mirror and the smirk fell from Luke's face. He fought to free himself, thrashing against the ropes.

"Now!" he shouted.

At first, I thought he'd spoken to Gwen, but his gaze traveled past her into the dark forest beyond. A second later, the earth opened up beneath Jayden, just as it had for me the night Petra died. He fell backward into the dirt, roots winding around his legs, dragging him down. In a moment he was waist-deep, clawing at the ground around him. The ropes we controlled dropped uselessly to the ground. Our chant stopped abruptly. The slow plume that had extended from Luke's chest evaporated like ocean spray.

The only sound that followed was Jayden's gasping breaths. I saw the panic in Max's eyes, saw his fingers tighten around the mirror, his knuckles white.

Jayden struggled against the heavy dirt, but he didn't descend any further. Mr. Nichols was keeping him alive. Of course he'd been out there in the darkness all this time, ready to take us out at the first sign of trouble. I whirled around, trying to see him, but he was hidden somewhere in the trees, beneath the velvet blanket of the eclipse.

The Shadow Spell spread and curled from all ten of Luke's fingertips. I sent sunfire flying at him again, but this time, it wasn't enough. The hatred that fueled Luke's power was stronger than it had ever been. The darkness that covered the land had magic in it, the same magic that flowed through his veins. This was, after all, his day.

Luke's spell loomed closer, and as it did, I saw it wasn't reaching for me. Its target was the man holding the mirror.

It wrapped itself around Max's waist. He cried out as it coiled upward, but he held his grip on the mirror, tears sparkling in his eyes, knees shaking. In another moment, the darkness held Max around the throat. I knew what it felt like to be trapped in those coils. I knew the agony that shot through you like ice water in your veins.

But still he stood.

Desperately, I struck Luke across the eyes with a wave of flame, clawing at him with my power. Luke staggered back; the Shadow Spell evaporated around Max's neck. But a second later, a dead tree, tall as a house, came up from its roots and tumbled toward us, guided by Mr. Nichols's invisible hand. It landed in front of me with a devastating crunch of branches, knocking me off my feet. Stars danced behind my closed eyes.

"No!" Before I could see, I knew by Jayden's cry that Max was down.

I hauled myself to my feet, searching for him amidst the bare branches. Max lay in the dirt, eyes closed, his body pinned beneath the heavy trunk. A few feet away, the mirror lay in large, jagged pieces. It was beautiful in its ruin, the firelight dancing off its askew planes.

I took in the devastation around me. The broken mirror. Jayden half-buried, his face smeared with dirt and blood. Max, unconscious beneath tangled branches. I felt the gravity of defeat overtake me.

"You've lost, Valeria," Luke said, arrogance dripping from every syllable. There had to be another way. There had to be.

I extended my hand, summoning one more wave of sunfire.

"That won't help you now. Look at your coven. They're lying in their graves. I say the word, and my father buries one of them."

"No!" The wounded cry escaped my lips.

"You can save them," Luke went on. "Sacrifice yourself, and they live."

"You won't kill them," I bluffed. "You want to be high priest? You need a coven to lead."

"I think I can spare one," Luke replied. "I just have to decide which." He pointed a lazy finger at Jayden. "What about him? He's never been much of a follower. He could make trouble for us. Might be best to take him out now."

In an instant, the ground was closing in around Jayden, pulling him in deeper. He gasped for air and black earth poured into his mouth, choking him. Another second and he'd be gone, his light extinguished forever.

"Wait!" I cried.

Jayden's descent stopped immediately. He spat out dirt, his eyes defiant.

I took a breath. A strange peace seemed to settle over me. It was almost comforting in its finality. I'd spent so much of my life thinking of nothing but myself. In death, I would turn toward those

I loved. In the end—and this *was* the end—I would keep them alive.

I took a step toward Luke. I could almost make out Gwen's face across the wall of flames that held her. I thought I saw tears glint in her eyes.

"Val! Don't!" Jayden called. But the earth was already releasing its grip on him as if Mr. Nichols was anticipating the trade.

The flames that surrounded Gwen parted. Luke took my arm, and together we walked into the circle. I felt the heat at my back as the fire closed around the three of us. Movement drew my gaze upward. Above us, blazing shapes streaked the black sky. A meteor shower.

The magic disappeared from my fingertips and my hands fell uselessly at my sides. I heard Jayden's shouts grow distant. The crown pressed cold on my temples. I supposed it would belong to Gwen after I was gone. Now I was close enough to see her clearly. Her figure seemed to glow against the blaze of black flames. Her expression held more misery than I'd ever seen, as if in the last few moments, she'd resigned herself to some devastating loss.

"Do it, you bastard," I snarled at Luke.

He smiled, his eyes on me like I was a glittering prize he'd finally won. "I told you you'd be begging for it."

He didn't hesitate. He flung the Shadow Spell at me and it took hold, wrapping me in cold torment. The now-familiar stench of death filled my nostrils.

I fell to my knees, but I made sure to hold my chin high. I would keep the damn crown on my head. I looked Luke in the eyes and let my disdain for him boil. I wanted him to remember me like this. I wanted him to know that, even as he killed me, I saw him as a small, pathetic thing.

My surroundings grew dimmer. Beyond this world lay that other one, the land where I'd seen Delfina Garcia in my dream. I hoped she would be waiting for me there. I didn't want to be alone. At last, tears spilled down my cheeks. It wouldn't be long now.

A grim smile was plastered across Luke's face. He was enjoying my last seconds, the power he held over me. His blue eyes gleamed, so focused on my suffering they saw nothing else. Beside him, movement flickered in the corner of my fading vision. Gwen was reaching for something beneath her skirt. Then—

A flash of metal, a swift, silent movement. Luke didn't make a sound, but he tumbled forward.

The Shadow Spell dissolved around me, releasing its stranglehold. I crouched in the dirt, gasping for air. As the world shifted back into focus, Luke knelt before me, our coven's ceremonial dagger buried in his chest.

The reality of what Gwen had done washed over me. *The birds don't care if you're pretty.* I'd seen the confusion in Luke's eyes when he heard me call out to Gwen on the trellis; he hadn't questioned the meaning of those words. Why would he? He couldn't imagine a place where she and I existed without him, a time before either of us were his. But Gwen knew. She'd heard me loud and clear.

Last night, after I'd escaped from Luke's, I stopped to leave her one last gift in that secret place where only she knew to look. There, she had discovered not a butterfly wing or crow's feather but the dagger in its sheath, its blade sharpened to a deadly point. I didn't know how she'd managed to sneak away to the hollow, or whether she'd doubted what she had to do.

In the end, the result was the same. I was alive, and she was free.

Luke was like a macabre puppet, suspended in a position of shock and pain. His hands rose to the knife's wooden handle as if he didn't believe it was real. He clutched it and pulled it out, letting it tumble to his feet. Fresh blood soaked his shirt in an expanding circle.

I expected wrath. My body braced to fight off Luke's attack on me or Gwen. Instead, as the blood poured from his heart, the only emotion on his face was sorrow. His love had betrayed him. Somehow, after all he'd done, he hadn't expected that.

A sound escaped Gwen's lips. It wasn't a cry, and it wasn't joyful. It was the loss of air, as if she'd just been punched in the gut. After that, she didn't breathe for what seemed like a very long time.

Luke collapsed, landing faceup among the scattered flower petals. Gwen stood above him, as pale as I'd ever seen her. With what seemed like great effort, he reached for her. Even now, he reached for her.

For a moment, I saw the boy from the ghost town all those years ago. The boy who'd told me he was cursed to die alone.

As if by instinct, Gwen extended her hand toward him, but she stopped halfway, her white fingers hovering a foot from his. She shook her head, a slow left and right, as if deciding she would never reach for him again. Whatever she did from this day on, she would do without him.

Luke's uplifted arm fell to the dirt with a thud. His breaths slowed until they came no more. He lay silent, still as a doll, a beautiful thing now dirtied by earth and blood. His eyes were still open, gazing upward at the dark sky.

At last, Gwen fell to her knees as if her body had been waiting for this moment to release. A violent sob shook her. She leaned forward, her face brushing the earth, her shoulders heaving. The circle of fire died as Luke did, the flames growing weaker until a smoldering ring of ash encircled Gwen and me. With the fire's strange light gone, blackness surrounded us again.

Above us the meteors flashed along their trajectory. The world grew blurry, and I realized tears were filling my eyes too. I didn't notice the presence of a motionless figure standing among the trees beyond us. I didn't see the movement of the knife until it was too late.

From beyond the clearing, Alexis Nichols floated the dagger, wet with his son's blood. It moved silently, guided by rage, its shape barely visible in the starlight. With cold certainty, he raised it above Gwen's huddled body and plunged it into her back.

CHAPTER EIGHTEEN

GWEN

I knelt, shutting my eyes against the world. The air was heavy with pain and anger. I couldn't tell anymore what was mine and what was Luke's. He lay motionless a few feet away, his profile silhouetted by the light of a hundred falling stars. There was no more life in his blue eyes. Luke was gone.

The void he left seemed to howl around me, cold and bitter as the wind. And yet I felt the heat of triumph creep into my bones. He was gone and I was still here, goddamn it. Still me. Tears filled my eyes, joy, sorrow, loss, and relief distilled into a single shimmering substance.

The dagger struck. It hit me hard like an angry fist, but the searing pain deep between my ribs told me this was something crueler, more penetrating. Alexis.

Wetness trickled down my back, warm blood turning cold in the chill air. I felt the blade withdraw, ready to pierce me again. Through half-closed eyes, I saw him at the edge of the smoldering circle. My breath caught. In his gaze was a fire made of hate and rage and grief. I'd taken his son, his most precious possession. He would kill me now and delight in it. Metal flashed in the starlight. The knife floated inches from my throat.

"No!" Valeria's voice rang out.

The knife flew toward her, out of Alexis's control. Its handle landed safely in her open palm, and she tucked it into the belt of her robe. A second later, a wave of fire discharged from her other hand, bathing the clearing in its glow. It struck Alexis in the chest and he flew back, past the ring of ashes. He landed among the bordering trees and didn't stir.

Blood trickled down my ribs, sticking to the lace of my dress. *Drip, drip, drip.* Little puddles splattered the ground around my huddled form. The world spun and my body gave out beneath me. From where I lay, I could see Jayden struggling to haul himself out of the earth, Valeria rushing to help him. Their movement was blurred, their voices distant.

All the while, Luke gazed upward, unblinking, one arm outstretched towards me. We lay side-by-side in the dirt like lovers interred together. I, too, turned my eyes to the sky. How many times had I dreamed I was hurtling on a collision course through that endless night? As the cascade passed overhead, I felt the earth, cold and solid beneath me. I was no longer falling. For better or worse, I'd landed.

Part of me grieved the boy I'd just killed. It was like I'd cut a tumor from my heart without anesthesia; I was glad it was gone, but it still hurt like hell. Everything hurt. My ribs were on fire, my breaths weak. It was late, and I was so very tired. I felt my eyelids close, a heavy velvet curtain casting the world around me into sweet darkness.

A hand smacked me smartly across the cheek.

"Stay the hell awake!" Valeria said in her most authoritative tone. "If you die, I'll be so pissed at you."

Her presence was fresh air, cutting through the fog of sleep that surrounded me. I smiled faintly and gripped her outstretched hand in both of mine. She pulled me upward with surprising strength. Somehow, I stood, though the wound in my back burned with fresh pain, and my legs quivered. I didn't know how long I could stay on my feet, but my veins pulsed with adrenaline, the raw will to survive.

Branches crunched to my right. Jayden stood over Max's

motionless body, his brows drawn together in concentration, his arm outstretched toward the fallen tree trunk. The ancient tree shuddered but didn't lift from Max's sleeping form. Valeria took one of Jayden's hands. Together, they focused on the tree's impossible weight. I pushed, too, with what strength was left within me.

With a low wooden creak, the tree rose. It trembled in midair long enough for Jayden to grab Max by the shoulders and haul him from beneath the trunk, then it fell back to earth with an echoing thud. Jayden fumbled for something at his neck, a small glass vial, and held it to Max's lips.

I watched Max's eyes flutter open. Color returned to his face. In a moment, he sat up, dazed but grateful. A look passed between them, something only they understood.

"Told you," Jayden said to him with a wink.

Branches snapped abruptly at the edge of the clearing. Alexis stood among the trees. Even in the dim light, I could make out the tense lines of his muscles, his body ready to hurt, to kill. He fixed his gaze on me and summoned the Shadow Spell. But something glinted in the dark above his head, starlight on glass. For a second, I saw it clearly: a bottle filled with something red .

What the hell?

It shattered, showering him with broken glass as the liquid rained down. The elixir sizzled the second it touched his skin. He cried out as steam rose from his face and arms. The Shadow Spell at his fingertips dissolved as he clawed at his eyes.

Valeria laughed as if she'd just remembered some long-forgotten joke. "Looks like Celeste finally found a use for that toxic love potion."

Celeste stepped toward us from the opposite end of the clearing, looking terrified but also pretty pleased with herself.

"Turns out it works great on creeps," she said. "Sorry I'm so late, guys. I never should have left you hanging like that."

She hurried to her brother, stepping protectively in front of him. Though her hands trembled, she held them up like a boxer ready for a fight.

Alexis's skin stopped smoking, and he trained his eyes upon us again. He drew the Shadow Spell into both of his hands—one aimed at Valeria, the other at me, the traitor. I remembered how he had held me in the doorway of that creepy old house, how his embrace had felt like a python tightening its grip around its prey. I forced myself to face him now. Even as the life bled from my body, I would not let him swallow me.

As the Shadow Spell flew at us, we met it with our own magic: sunfire from Valeria's palm, moonfire from mine. It was the first time I'd used my power in unison with Valeria's instead of at odds with it.

The two spells lit the clearing in an eye-watering blaze of crimson and silver. He staggered backward, where we held him for one glorious moment. But he was stronger than us, his power fueled by the agony of a loss we did not feel, hatred we could not equal. I could practically see it radiating off him in toxic waves. Revenge was all he wanted now.

His spell gained on us, striking Valeria first, making her cry out. An icy tendril wrapped around me, cold death forcing itself into every empty space within me. We landed together on the hard ground. The mirror lay in pieces between us, reflecting the Shadow Spell against the black sky.

My eyes met Valeria's, a moment of silent desperation passed between us. Her gaze traveled to the fragmented mirror.

I don't know which of us reached for a piece first. We seemed to move simultaneously, guided by the determination that all would not be lost.

I took the cold glass in my hand, felt it bite into my palm. Together, we aimed our broken pieces at Alexis and resumed the chant.

"Malevolent man, face yourself and see your wrongs—" we choked out the words.

Beside me, Jayden rushed to grab another shard, followed by Celeste.

"Malevolent man, your dominion hath ended." The words were louder now, a chorus of angry voices.

Alexis held the Shadow Spell on us both. Though pain

enveloped me, I kept going, kept forcing the words out, each breath a battle won.

In my periphery, Max dragged himself toward us and the mirror. With slow, determined movements, he reached my side and took the final piece. As he joined the chant, our voices became one, neither male nor female, neither old nor young, our words an echo of every struggle against evil. The spell had needed all of us to really work; I could feel it as our voices blended.

With Luke gone, our coven was complete again, every heart emblazoned with the sacred circle, every member working against a common foe.

The mirror had been meant for Luke, but the same malevolent magic ran through Alexis's veins. As I held it, I felt it thirst for his power. A plume of smoke began to rise from his chest. It coiled outward, dividing again and again until it was five black rivers, each flowing toward a different piece of the mirror, the churning darkness emptying itself into the cool silver. The Shadow Spell around our throats loosened, then released. Valeria scrambled to her feet, but I couldn't. With every ounce of strength I had, I held the mirror up to the man before me.

Alexis's face was contorted into a mask of rage and fear. The Shadow Spell gathered at his fingertips, but it was weaker now, diluted like ink mixed with water. His eyes darted wildly over each of us as if he didn't know which one of us to attack first. We held him from all sides, our chant ringing through the trees.

He set his gaze on me, gathered the last of his power, and sent it flying straight at my heart. But the tendrils of his spell were as light and insubstantial as a spider web now. They dissolved harmlessly into the wind. And still the dark stream of magic flowed from his chest, thicker than before, until the last of it emptied out of him into our mirror. When it was done, the shards were stained a sickly black.

Alexis hit the ground like a felled tree, landing near Luke in the bloody dirt. His face was pale, his expression blank. He'd become an empty vessel, a shell. His son was dead. His power was lost. There was nothing left for him now. No revenge, no dominance, no Meteoric Union. I stared at him, unashamedly transfixed by his ruin. His eyes were like Luke's, only so much older. He glared at me, blinked once, and those blue eyes closed forever.

The last drop of adrenaline seemed to drain out of me. Blood still poured from my wound. I hadn't felt it until now—its warmth running down my ribs, my heartbeat growing weaker with each spilled drop. My grip on the mirror released, and I collapsed.

Luke was gone. Alexis was gone. And soon, I would be too. The pain that seared between my ribs grew fainter. Tears blurred my vision. I had just taken that first, terrifying step into a world where I answered to no one, clung to no one—I had been ready for that. But it was over now.

Above me, a few weak rays of sunlight began to emerge from behind the darkened moon. I heard the shouts of the others, their quick footsteps on the ground. They were alive. Valeria was alive. Everything else was just a drop in that ocean of sky.

Jayden's voice sounded in my ear. He was saying something, urging me to do something.

"Drink," he said again.

Cold glass touched my lips, and I tasted bitter herbs. My body warmed as the liquid trickled down my throat. I hadn't realized how cold I'd been until the moment I wasn't. My breaths grew deeper, easier. All the hurt I held inside seemed to empty into the gaping sky. At last, I slept.

CHAPTER NINETEEN

GWEN

The sky was pink and darkening to crimson as I picked my way over fallen logs and mounds of pine. It had been two weeks since the eclipse, but as I walked, a dull ache still throbbed between my ribs. I'd grown accustomed to the feeling, a reminder of the violence of that day. I wondered if I was crazy for venturing back into the forest. Had anything good ever happened to me there? Still, I made my way with determination. Tonight wasn't about me.

In the distance, I could see a dozen figures mingling between the branches. They weren't gathered at the clearing where the charred traces of the killing circle still remained. This time, we'd have a new but no less disturbing meeting place.

Though my ribs cried out a little with each step I took, I was getting better. I still couldn't shake the feeling that I had never been meant to survive that day—that if I did not become an object of destruction, I was destined to die in destruction's path. I'd sensed it when I lay in the dirt, the life spilling out of me, but Valeria had kept me awake and Jayden's potion had kept me alive. I'd awoken the next morning in a hospital bed, tangled in IV tubes, the sun glaring through my closed eyelids. The doctor who spoke to me used the word *miracle* to describe my condition. I had to agree. It was miraculous in its own way, the divine intervention of the witches I'd betrayed.

Jayden had been there in the hospital at some point during those hazy hours of pain meds and lime Jell-O. I'd opened my eyes from a nap and he was staring down at me, his figure silhouetted against the fluorescent lights.

"Just wanted to make sure you weren't dead," he said casually.

"I'm not," I managed to reply. "Thanks to you."

He shrugged. "No more good people were gonna die on my watch."

"Good," I said, my eyes on the white tile floor. "I don't think that term applies to me anymore."

"Don't be so sure. You were lost at sea, but maybe you can still find the road home."

"Wait," I replied foggily. "Am I in a car or a boat?"

"Ask Valeria. It's her metaphor."

I pondered that a while. "Thanks," I said at last. "For being here."

"Don't go canonizing me or anything." He shrugged. "Max is down the hall. I've been with him all night."

The image flashed before me—Max's lifeless form sprawled beneath the fallen tree. Max had a fractured rib and a concussion, Jayden reported, but he was already healing up nicely, one more miracle for the doctors to puzzle over. I'd seen Jayden give him the same healing potion he'd given me. It was probably the only reason Max had been able to do the spell with us that night. The only reason we'd united as one voice.

After a while, Jayden ducked out with a curt nod, and as the hours passed, no more visitors came. The doomed black gown I'd worn to the ritual had been cut off me in the ER, and it would remain somewhere inside that labyrinth of sterile halls, ripped and bloodstained. I left the hospital the next day in a set of too-big nurse's scrubs and stepped out the door into a world of absolute uncertainty.

I breathed in deeply and began to walk, not toward the vast white house in the woods but to the tiny cement one on the river's edge. When I opened the rusty metal door, it didn't feel like home, but it felt easier than that other place ever had. There was no sign that my dad had been back—no takeout wrappers in the trash, no empty bottles on the kitchen counter. That was fine by me. I wasn't ready to see him yet. Still, a small, vulnerable part of me imagined a day when I'd walk up that gravel driveway and find him there, working on an old car or mending the hole in the screen door. Perhaps he'd nod hello. And then? I wasn't sure what would happen after that, or what I wanted to happen. The wounds were still too fresh on both sides.

I suspected my father knew a little about magic after all. Or perhaps he merely understood self-destruction, how it tugs at you like a current from within, stronger than your will. He and I had that in common now.

My new clothes were still at Luke's. Silk dresses and Tahitian pearls, gold rings and shiny satin, all the beautiful things he'd bought for me—I couldn't bring myself to step back inside that house for any of them. There was something sadly final about abandoning the glittering treasures he'd given me; it was like acknowledging he was really gone. I knew I'd never love anyone else the way I'd loved him. And that was okay. Our love had been a brilliant, deadly thing. It would have consumed everything around us until we ourselves were ashes.

I'd spent the last two weeks going through the motions of the life I used to lead: I picked up extra shifts at Diggin's and checked my bank account every time I made a purchase at the Bargain Mart. I sat alone at lunch. I even dressed in my old clothes, pulling on whatever remnants still hung in my bedroom closet as if squeezing myself back into a shell I'd long outgrown.

I was as alone as I had been before I met Luke, only now I owned my solitude. Being me was no longer the painful experience it had once been. Waking up every day as Gwen Foster was a gift. I'd bled for it, killed for it. And when I walked into school each morning, I took up space. I met the gaze of every person who crossed my path without fear.

Everyone except Valeria.

Both generations of the coven stood crowded among the trees before me, the parents bending their heads to speak closely to one another. I could hear their voices floating toward me. Their conversations were casual enough, but their words were edged with nervous energy.

They were circled around the stump of a recently felled redwood, its trunk cleanly severed by human machinery. This was the tree Valeria had discovered the day the forest died, the tree Luke and Alexis had cut down in the spell that had robbed the parents of their power. We were standing in the place where all this madness had begun. Luke and his father had tried to wipe it away, but I could still make out a faint streak of red on the stump where they'd written each adult coven member's name in blood to seal the spell.

The voices hushed as I approached, and I felt every pair of eyes settle on me. Valeria and Ms. Garcia stood at the front of the crowd, Valeria in a brilliant yellow sundress, her long hair straight, her feet in sandals. It was her mother who wore the high priestess robes and crown of gold on her head. *Guess they really believe I can pull this off,* I thought warily.

Max was beside Jayden, one arm comfortably around Jayden's waist. There was something unfamiliar about Jayden, a new ease in the way he stood, as if he'd finally let go of some immense weight. I nodded at them. Jayden met my gaze with a hesitant smile, but Max beamed back at me. He even gave me an encouraging thumbs-up. The gesture was so silly, so contradictory to the circumstances we found ourselves in, I grinned back in spite of my nerves.

Just as she had on the night of my initiation, Valeria led me into the circle. We stepped right up to the edge of that enormous stump.

"You sure you know what you're doing?" she whispered.

I fixed my eyes on the forest floor and mumbled a few less than reassuring words.

I had found myself unable to face her since the eclipse. *Sorry* felt painfully insufficient, but the word had repeated in my mind ever since that day, its echo keeping me awake as I stared into the darkness of my bedroom. I was sorry I'd let my anger fester like a wound inside me. I was sorry I'd fallen for a boy who cared as much for power as he did for me. And I was sorry I let that boy hurt her. But all those apologies sounded empty and selfish when I rehearsed them in my head, so I kept my head down each time we passed in the halls at school, just like I used to back when Valeria Garcia was the scariest thing in the world to me. Those times felt distant, inconsequential. Now I understood there were far worse things to fear.

One day, she'd walked up to me during lunch as I sat reading in the quad. After seeing her fight for her life in a blaze of fire, she looked out of place in such a Mundane locale as the high school's grassy knoll. The other kids passed around her, blissfully unaware of the events we'd lived through, how close we'd all come to destruction. She didn't seem to feel out of place, though. In fact, there was a new serenity about her. Valeria had always walked around school like she was posing for the paparazzi; she didn't just greet people in the halls, she gave them her good side. Today, she looked just as beautiful as ever, but she moved as if she didn't care who was watching. She casually placed an ancient, slightly charred piece of paper on top of the book I'd been reading.

"This is more important than your latest Gothic romance," she said.

"Believe me, I'm off those for the foreseeable future," I replied, closing my copy of *The Yellow Wallpaper* before turning my attention to the page in front of me.

I held Elizabeth Foster's letter in my hands, the one the Nichols family had passed down through their generations. The single piece of paper that had kept them waiting, all these years, for their destiny.

"Luke said something interesting the day I dropped the chandelier on you guys," she told me matter-of-factly. "He said in her letter, Elizabeth begged Levan to restore her power. She even told him how to do it." Valeria twirled a lock of shiny brown hair. "I figured if that spell could restore her power, it could probably restore power to *any* witch."

I understood immediately. She meant her parents.

"It has to be done by a witch with malevolent magic. You jerks are the only ones who can reverse your spells," she said, a little grin on her lips.

"Where did you get this?"

"Where do you think?" she replied, her smile vanishing. "This is the result of one supermorbid visit to the Nichols' house."

The house had stood empty since the eclipse, cobwebs gathering on its front porch. She'd found the letter in Alexis's study, tucked away in his roll top desk as if he'd planned to come back to it that night.

Now, as I held the paper's charred edges, I wondered how different things might have been if it had burned to ash all those years ago. On the page before me were the words *For the Restoration of Magic.* My heart quickened and I read on.

Unlike other malevolent rituals, the restoration of magic does not claim a sacrifice. All it requires is an offering.

I inhaled the letter's musty scent, thinking of the witch who wrote it. Elizabeth Foster had been tempted by malevolent magic, just as I had. But in the end, it was Levan who'd turned his back on it forever. I hadn't told anyone yet, but I'd vowed to do the same the minute I awoke in that hospital bed. I would never use my power to control the Mundanes again.

Now I stood before the coven, a traitor here to make my offering. I took a breath and began the spell as Elizabeth had described it.

From my pocket I withdrew eight hyacinth seeds. I held each seed to my lips and whispered each of the parents' names. I felt the heat of malevolent magic stirring in my blood with every name I spoke, but the now-familiar anger didn't come. Instead, peace settled over me, like I was no longer fighting against a current but moving with it.

I knelt at the foot of the stump. The ground seemed to hum with anticipation as I covered each seed with dirt. Heat radiated against my skin, but whether it came from me or from the earth itself, I couldn't tell.

Valeria handed me the ceremonial dagger. How strange it looked now, its blade clean and shiny. I would forever imagine it covered in rust-colored stains, Luke's blood mixed with my own. I took its simple wooden handle and drove the knife into my palm. As I did, I felt power pour out of me. It didn't bubble and fester inside like a poison—this power felt more like letting go.

I watched the blood pool in my open palm, then I let it drip over each seed's hiding place, its deep red color blending with the deep red of the soil.

"'Earth, give back what was stolen,'" I said, quoting the incantation in Elizabeth's letter. "'Earth, restore what was lost.'"

It was as if everyone present held their breath at once. The forest seemed to hold its breath, too, the wind silent in the branches. Everything hung in suspense as we watched my blood seep into the tiny mounds where the seeds were planted.

The slightest movement caught my eye. A green stem emerged from the dirt. Leaves unfolded around it as it rose until, at last, a tiny red flower exploded from its center. I'd witnessed magic on a larger scale before, but these fledgling blooms were purer magic than I'd ever seen. Before I could speak, another mound erupted into a blood-red hyacinth, then two more followed. Soon, all eight had sprouted around the stump's gnarled roots. The petals were brilliant amidst the pale shades of dead things.

As I stared at the vibrance I'd created, cries erupted behind me. I didn't need to see the faces of the parents to know that magic had bloomed inside them too. I'd done it.

When I did turn around, my eyes met Ms. Garcia's first. She nodded at me with unspoken gratitude before her expression gave way to one of pure joy. Valeria rushed to her, and the two queens clung to one another in victory while Valeria's dad wrapped them both in his arms. Jayden's mom nearly fell to her knees, doubled over with laughter and tears. Celeste and Max ran to their parents, colliding in a group hug. Max's dad broke out in an impromptu victory dance, and Max joined in as if we'd all just won the Super Bowl.

The only ones who didn't move were Petra's parents. They stood together on the edge of the circle, hand in hand. Slowly, a smile spread across their weary faces. Though they didn't jump or shout for joy, there was something different about them. I could see it in all the parents. It was like a flame had ignited within them, and if you looked closely, you could see its light just behind their eyes. They were alive again.

Jayden approached me first, pulling me into a hug.

"You did it, you crazy witch," he whispered. "Thank you."

Max piled on after him, squeezing us both in his strong arms.

"That was pretty cool of you," Celeste said, planting an air kiss on both my cheeks.

Max hit me with an unpredictable barrage of high fives and fist bumps.

But as Valeria rejoiced with the others, she seemed to avoid my gaze, the way I'd been avoiding hers the past two weeks. Disappointed tears stung my eyes. Suddenly, I was embarrassed. What had I expected? For her to walk up to me and tell me all was forgiven? Luke had almost made her his sacrifice. She didn't owe me anything.

I watched as a party materialized before my eyes. Music floated out of portable speakers as Celeste and Max squabbled happily over the playlist. Jayden's parents produced jugs of ceremonial wine from a wicker picnic basket, and Valeria strung lanterns from branches and ignited them in a burst of orange fire. Their flames glowed cheerfully in the dimming light. The coven celebrated like people who had come out the other end of a long, dark tunnel and were seeing light for the first time in months. They shouted and danced in giddy, silly happiness.

The giant stump lay before me, its rings expanding in uneven circles, too many to count. I thought of the other felled tree, the one with moss that hung like a curtain over its child-sized hollow. The solitary hyacinth that had appeared at its stump the day the trees died was mine, the flower that grew when Luke restored my magic. It was the best gift Luke ever gave me. In spite of everything, I was grateful to him for that.

I gazed through the trees toward the distant silhouette of the Nichols' house. It had only been vacant for two weeks, but the ivy seemed to have grown thicker than that brief time would have allowed, overtaking its walls as if the wilderness would claim the house as payment for what the Nichols men did.

The Mundanes, of course, had demanded a story to account for one dead boy and a girl with a stab wound in her back. Alexis had been an easy scapegoat. The coven told the authorities that Alexis had snapped on the day of the eclipse. He'd attacked me and killed Luke before taking off into the darkness. He was officially considered a fugitive. The police put out wanted posters, APBs, all the usual stuff. They could search all they wanted, but they wouldn't find him. Valeria's parents, along with Petra's, had stolen Alexis's body away that night and burned it, then they'd gone to the spot where the forest met the river and tossed his ashes into the rushing water.

Jayden had told me all this in the hospital with the wide-eyed zeal of someone relaying a juicy piece of gossip. He claimed when they burned Alexis's body, Mrs. Sarich had roasted marshmallows over the open flame. I was pretty sure that part was his own embellishment. But I believed him when he told me the river seemed to flow faster after they dumped the ashes, as if the forest were purging itself of the thing that had harmed it.

Now I looked around at the trees, tall as buildings around us. Maybe the forest had magic of its own. Or perhaps Delfina's spirit had hurried the waters along, ridding her coven of evil as she'd tried to do in life.

Luke was buried in the family plot, his grave not far from Levan's. The coven didn't hold a funeral. I wouldn't have attended if they did. There was nothing more I needed from Luke, living or dead.

I stood apart from the revelry, my arms crossed against the subtle chill in the air. I should leave, I decided. This joy was theirs, not mine. A familiar loneliness crept into my bones. Suddenly, I wanted to retreat, to hide under the covers of my lumpy old bed and sleep for a week.

"Got a minute?" Valeria stepped away from the celebration to join me on the periphery.

I couldn't help but laugh at the absurdity of the question. "Not a lot of pressing social engagements on my schedule right now," I replied.

We stood there a moment in uncomfortable silence. I longed to speak, but all my words felt inappropriate for the magnitude of what we'd been through together.

"Valeria—" I began.

"I get it," she interrupted. "I've been thinking a long time about what I want to say to you, and I want you to know I get it."

"What?"

"I get what you did. I mean, what you almost did." She sighed. "If I'd been offered limitless power and the eternal love of Luke Nichols, there was a time when I would have wanted nothing more."

"I appreciate the sentiment," I replied. "But you never would have gone along with the Meteoric Union. You're better than that."

"And so are you. I knew you'd realize it in the end." She shifted her eyes to the ground, her sandaled feet tracing lines in the dirt. "So...how have you been? You know, since... "

"A little lost," I answered honestly. "I walked away from my destiny, so I guess I'm not really sure what to do now."

"You could start by talking to your friends."

I forced myself to ask the question at the center of this strange moment. "Are we...friends?"

"I don't know." She looked at me now, her brown eyes serious. "But I think we're supposed to be. Maybe *that's* your destiny, the fate you and I have always shared."

The light was fading overhead. It was that rare time of evening when the sun and moon occupied the same sky, sharing the brilliant, darkening heavens in equal beauty.

"Maybe." The air didn't feel so chilly anymore.

Ms. Garcia approached us, the flames of the lanterns dancing off the golden crown on her head.

"Well?" she said to Valeria. "Did you ask her?"

"I was getting to it!" Valeria said, clearly annoyed that her mom had interrupted.

"We want you to come live with us," Ms. Garcia said bluntly.

"Excuse me?" I searched her honey eyes for mockery, for a hint of that old Garcia-brand cruelty, but I found none. She was sincere.

"I'll never forget the day I found you playing with Valeria in the forest," she said. "I didn't see the magic in you then. I turned you away, burned the bridge, and banished you from this place." She paused as if lost in the memory. "I regret that to this day."

I felt my face flush. My fists closed, grasping for what little dignity I had left.

"If this is some kind of charity thing—" I began.

"It's not," she insisted. "Please let me finish. This is a story you need to hear. A few years after I burned the bridge, I was here in the forest, practicing the sunfire spell. I'd had some stupid fight with Valeria's dad. I wasn't focused. The spell got out of control. It began to cling to me, burning me. I was deep in the woods and alone. It could have killed me. It would have, but suddenly, your father was there. He had a hunting rifle on his shoulder and a dead rabbit slung at his hip. He knew he was trespassing, but he still came to my aid."

I stared at her, speechless.

"He called to me and shook me by the shoulders, as if by some miraculous instinct he knew how to pull me out of the spell's grip. He saved my life. When it was over, I tried to convince him he'd seen some light show, some trick of the eye, but it was too late. The strange thing was, he didn't seem afraid of what had happened. He said his grandmother used to tell him stories about witches in Cascabel Woods, about the power his own family had possessed long ago. He'd never believed them until he saw what I could do.

"I was stunned. The man had no magic of his own, and yet he knew more about magic than any Mundane should. Neither of us could explain it. All I knew for sure was I owed him my life. He'd discovered our secret, so I offered to make a pact with him. He would never tell anyone about what he'd seen, and in exchange, I'd use my power to give him something he wanted. I'm embarrassed to admit I thought he'd ask for money or maybe luck at the blackjack table, but he didn't even consider those things." She held my gaze in hers as if willing me to listen to what she was about to say. "He asked me to look out for you, Gwen. If the time ever came when he could no longer take care of you, he wanted me to make sure you always had a place to call home."

The air left my lungs, her words striking me in the chest. I thought of the note my dad had written me the day he drove off and understood it for the first time. *You'll be all right without me.* I pictured my dad, the weathered lines around his eyes, the quiet sadness he always seemed to carry. Even after I'd hurt him, even as he left, he believed I'd be taken care of.

"I did a sacred ritual swearing to honor his wishes," Ms. Garcia went on. "All I needed was a lock of that beautiful black hair of yours."

My hands traveled to my hair instinctively, recalling that hazy dream from years ago—a man and a woman at the river's edge, a lock of hair changing hands in the orange glow of a cigarette lighter. It had been real. It had always been real.

"I wish he'd told me," I said.

"He had to keep our magic a secret. Those were the terms. He couldn't tell anyone, not even you." She hesitated. "I just wish I'd done a better job with my end of the bargain."

"You mean, besides offering her snacks and sparkling water like an overzealous flight attendant?" Valeria said.

I laughed, but I was still reeling from everything I'd learned.

"And all this time, no one else knew about your pact?" I asked Ms. Garcia.

She sighed, and I got the distinct feeling she was embarrassed again. "When I lost my magic and yours returned, I didn't want to tell the rest of the coven about the deal I made with your dad. If they thought I'd had any reason to believe you had witches' blood and I'd kept that knowledge a secret...I worried it would look bad. Like I'd ignored some kind of threat."

"The Garcias are really into hiding their mistakes," Valeria interrupted. "It's something we need to work on."

"I'm sorry, Gwen," Ms. Garcia went on. "At first, when I heard you'd moved in with Luke, I was glad. I thought maybe he was the home your dad had wanted for you. By the time we found out what Luke really was, I feared you were already lost."

"I was," I replied, turning away. "I would have stayed lost if it wasn't for Valeria. She kind of saved me."

"She hid the dagger for you."

"I think she saved me before that," I said thoughtfully. "Luke had me convinced I was alone. That he was the only person who would ever care about me. But when she shouted up to me on the trellis and I heard those words only she and I understood, I knew Luke was wrong."

"He certainly was," Ms. Garcia replied. "So, Gwen, what do you say?"

"In case you haven't noticed, our house is huge. And empty on, like, a metaphorical level," Valeria said. "It would be a lot more fun with you around."

A hundred excuses raced through my mind, all the reasons to stay hidden in my loneliness. But I didn't say any of them aloud. I was already nodding, already accepting their offer. And then Valeria was hugging me, and Ms. Garcia was taking my hand in hers.

"We won't treat you like a charity case," Ms. Garcia said. "But be damn certain we are going to treat you like a member of this coven, because that's what you are."

I felt my heart leap in my chest. I looked to Valeria. Was I still part of the coven?

She nodded, understanding before I'd asked.

"Yup, we're one big dysfunctional family," she said. "The coven is a lifetime gig. I mean, I hope it is. Now that you restored our parents' power, they'll stay right here, keeping the magic alive in Dorado. And our generation gets to spread our wings. When school's over, you'll go into the world and do amazing things. We all will. But me and Jayden and Max and Celeste will be back here someday to carry on the coven's legacy. I hope when that day comes, you'll be with us. It's where you belong."

"Belong," I repeated, smiling. "That doesn't sound so bad."

She smiled back, and it was like ice beginning to break over frozen water. My eyes traveled to a scar on her palm. I recognized it immediately. It was the place where the mirror shard had cut as she aimed it at Alexis. I bore a matching one on my own hand.

"Jayden could probably come up with something to get rid of that," I said, pointing at the mark.

She shrugged. "I think I'll hold onto it a little longer." She held a finger to the uneven surface of her palm. "I feel like I've earned it."

I understood. None of us had come out of this unscathed. The scars on my skin weren't the only ones. More covered my heart, the tender part of me that had loved for the first time. And I'd earned those scars too.

Above us a sparrow sang, its voice high and clear in the evening air. It was the first bird I'd heard in the forest since the trees died. How strange it sounded to me, that pure, hopeful song. Before long, it would be spring.

ABOUT THE AUTHOR

Ava Caldwell currently resides in Northern California with her cat, dog, husband, and baby. She loves spooky stories and mysteries, both real and fictional. She is fascinated by the Victorian era. She enjoys getting herself little treats every time she leaves the house. The Birds Don't Care If You're Pretty is her first full length novel, but she has published short works of fiction and humor. Ava is a proud native of Chicago, a fact which comprises a large part of her personality.